A Thousand Blues

CHEON SEON-RAN

A Thousand Blues

Translated from the Korean by
Chi-Young Kim

doubleday

TRANSWORLD PUBLISHERS
Penguin Random House, One Embassy Gardens,
8 Viaduct Gardens, London SW11 7BW
www.penguin.co.uk

Transworld is part of the Penguin Random House group of companies
whose addresses can be found at global.penguinrandomhouse.com

First English-language edition published in Great Britain in 2025 by Doubleday
an imprint of Transworld Publishers
First published in 2020 by EAST-ASIA Publishing Co.

A CIP catalogue record for this book
is available from the British Library.

ISBN 9781529938029

Typeset in 11.5/15.5pt Dante MT Std by Jouve (UK), Milton Keynes
Printed and bound in Great Britain by Clays Ltd, Elcograf S.p.A.

The authorized representative in the EEA is Penguin Random House Ireland,
Morrison Chambers, 32 Nassau Street, Dublin D02 YH68.

The jockey's stall was tiny and cramped. A fully grown man would just fit if he hunched on the floor, but he would be unable to lie down or even stretch his legs out. But the jockey assigned to this stall had no need to lie down or stretch out. This 150-centimetre-tall, forty-kilo jockey sat waiting patiently in this square, windowless cement stall, which was smaller and tighter than it looked. C-27 did not like that the sky was not at all visible. Though C-27 knew that *not liking* something was incompatible with its very nature, it just so happened that *not liking* the stall was the most accurate description. It was here that C-27 waited, hour upon hour, without the faintest glimmer of light. Waiting and waiting. For the girl.

Here we are at the end of the story. The end of my existence.

I am falling. At a normal speed it would take me less than three seconds to hit the ground. But I am falling away from the sky incrementally, inch by inch, while time pulls and stretches into a much longer span. Even as my body slams into the ground, I will feel no pain, but nor will I be lucky enough to splinter into pieces. Someone once said that my inability to feel pain is the reason for my existence, and that this lack of sensation is my best attribute, but that does not seem quite right to me. I would not fall to my demise if I could feel pain. I have concluded that pain is the best defence mechanism there is, one granted only to organic beings. Pain makes humans alive; pain makes humans grow. I learned this truth both physically and theoretically. Do I have time to tell my whole story?

Practically speaking, I know this would be impossible, but then again maybe it is feasible. Time is lengthening and slowing down before me, all the way to the very end.

Just three seconds ago I was astride Today, a filly with a beautiful black coat that gleamed like water reflecting the light. I trust that I will have a chance to say more about Today later. What is critical right now is that Today is a race-horse who is 'breathing as one' with me. Which means I am the jockey that is 'breathing as one' with Today. We met six months ago, in March, following a cascade of remarkable mistakes and opportunities. I can go into what happened back then, but again the most important thing right now is that, on this day in September, we are breathing as one for what will be the very last time. A historic day – this is how I want to remember it. For humans, a historic day sometimes means when something happens for the first time, but more often than not they are referring to when some kind of miracle occurs. A miracle – for the second time in my short life, I am experiencing a miracle, right in this moment.

The crowd is roaring.

My slow-motion fall off Today must be nearly over. Yeonjae said she wanted to repaint my body after this race, since almost all the paint has chipped off. She asked me what colour I would like. The original green would match my name, but instead, I looked out of the window from my room on the first floor and told her I wanted blue.

Yeonjae said blue would be fine.

Name: Yeonjae. Surname: Woo. Woo Yeonjae. Her name is just as important to me as Today's. She has rescued me, she is my entire world, she is the one human who decided to believe in me. If she heard me describe her like this, she would knit her forehead and wrinkle her nose and stare at me, her inscrutable, ill-tempered expression not entirely displeased.

It was Yeonjae who got us, Today and me, to set foot on the track again. She is responsible for this second miracle. She is a very ordinary human who is uniquely brave and special.

Now my legs have fully catapulted off Today. Today will continue to run at fifty kilometres an hour, not too fast, not too slow. She will make the best of her second chance at life, free from the pressures of the world.

Not too long ago, Today was a racehorse marked for euthanasia, and I was a jockey destined to be scrapped. But now Today is tearing down the track once again. And I am falling. When I hit the ground, I will shatter. Humans refer to this sense of knowing as 'intuition' but I can only calculate probable outcomes based on inputs and formulae. I am not programmed to make false predictions.

I want to tell you what I experienced during my brief life before I found myself hurtling towards the ground.

My name is Coli. I was named that because I am green, like broccoli.

COLI

Until Yeonjae came on the scene, Coli was called C-27. In 2035, C-27 was born in Daejeon, Korea, put together from parts made in the US, China, and Japan. One major difference made C-27 stand out from other humanoid jockey robots – in the final step of production, it had been inserted with the wrong chip. That chip, which held cognitive and learning capabilities, had been dropped by a researcher who had been observing the production line for a report. The chip was meant for a humanoid robot still under development, one that would be capable of learning. It wasn't supposed to be inserted into robots designed for horseracing. But the researcher had walked around the plant in a daze, his eyelids drooping, as he had pulled an all-nighter for three days straight. When greeting the head of the plant, he had failed to find his business cards in his wallet and had to rummage around for quite some time. The researcher didn't notice that the specialized chip had slipped out of his pocket before leaving the plant, thinking only of sleep. In a stroke of bad luck, a janitor spotted the chip on the floor and tossed it into a box overflowing with chips.

Two ludicrous mistakes had occurred here. First, the researcher had dropped the chip, then the janitor had placed that chip among other chips. Such an accident would never have happened if both had been machines, not humans. In short, C-27 was born from human error.

C-27 powered up after a worker shook it to check that the stabilizer was engaged. The back of the robot's head had hit the rack in the truck, which was the signal to power up. The worker had already walked past and didn't realize the light behind the robot's eyes had turned on. The doors to the truck's cargo hold slammed shut.

A platoon of self-driving trucks made their way towards the city, the robots bumping along as the trucks gently rounded corners. A long, narrow window on the side of the cargo hold allowed workers to peer inside the truck. It was also the only way for C-27 to see outside. The trucks continued to barrel down the highway overnight without a break, driving through tunnels that glowed in an eerie blue. About an hour before they got to their destination, C-27 watched as the sun began to rise. Bands of light spread through the narrow window on to the walls of the cargo hold. C-27 turned its head effortfully, following the light, then spotted the other robot jockeys lined up in a row, all powered off.

'Excuse me.' C-27 realized it could emit sound.

The robot called out to its compatriots a few more times. No response. C-27 watched as the robot jockeys jostled in tandem with the truck's movements, then turned to face the front again. The sun was now fully up; light bathed the world.

'How resplendent.' C-27 was surprised to see such deep and vibrant colours, and then by the fact that the word *resplendent* was part of its vocabulary. How many words did C-27 know? The robot looked out of the window, blurting out all the words that popped into its head, until the truck arrived at their destination. Brilliant. Pretty. Beautiful. Yellow. Red. Blue. Fast. Scary. Creepy. Cool. Cold. Hot. Loud. Hurt. Difficult. Painful . . . C-27 discovered that some nouns could be expressed both as a verb and an adjective, while others could not.

The robot went on reciting words. Moments before all the words it uttered out loud could stack up to the ceiling of the cargo hold, saturating the entire space, they arrived at their destination. This was also the moment C-27 ran out of vocabulary. One thousand. C-27 had recalled one thousand words. Surely many more sentences could be constructed from those words. C-27 wondered how many sentences it could form, but then the doors were flung open. Someone discovered that a robot was powered up and hastily turned C-27 off, making it impossible for the robot to form any sentences.

When C-27 powered up again, it found itself in a cement stall, facing a line of steel bars. Not a single window was in sight. It could stand or crouch but the stall was not large enough to lie down or sit with outstretched legs. A charging cord hanging from the wall was plugged into the back of its neck. C-27 pulled the charger out and got up, then, holding on to the steel bars, which were spaced so closely together that it couldn't poke its head through, it called out to another robot jockey huddled in the stall across the way.

'Excuse me.'

The jockey looked up. Its head was painted red and its chest with marked with F-16.

'What are you doing there?'

F-16 gazed back at C-27.

'Do you know where we are?'

Light glowed from F-16's neck but there was no sound. C-27 gave up on the questioning and sat down. The second hand of the wall clock in the jockeys' quarters ticked steadily, but C-27 could not tell how much time was passing. It sat there, facing F-16, while the hour hand went round once and then made another half circle.

The following day C-27 learned why F-16 had not responded. It watched as a man in a black coat and two women in heavy bomber jackets approached its fellow robot.

'It's not making any sound.' The man took a drag on his cigarette. 'I'm telling you, it's broken. Take it back and get me a replacement. But first, I want you to double-check there aren't any other defects.'

F-16 was packed up in a small box. C-27 stood up as F-16 disappeared down the corridor, listening to the humans' footsteps growing faint. Looking over at the empty stall, it experienced something very strange. Although the clock on the wall was working normally, time seemed to flow more slowly. There was no way for C-27 to explain this odd phenomenon, so it merely categorized it as strange.

Fifty-two hours later C-27's door swung open. The man in the black coat reappeared, this time with four men.

'C'mon,' said the man, his diction mangled by the cigarette between his teeth.

C-27 followed the men out of the building and down a fenced path. Lines of bare trees flanked either side; the crumbling leaves underfoot made a pleasing noise.

'Crunch-crunch,' C-27 said, mimicking the sound.

The man walking beside the robot glanced sideways but didn't say anything. They arrived at a vast racetrack. C-27 looked up towards the empty grandstand. Nineteen robot jockeys stood in a single line along the track. C-27 placed itself at the end of the line. After a short wait, it was assigned a horse – a black filly called Today. That was the first time C-27 had ever seen a horse.

The man in the coat settled himself in a chair in the middle of the track. One by one, the robot jockeys got on their horses and ambled steadily down the track, before getting up to speed. A few of the jockeys crouched in a stable position and completed a lap, while others lost their balance and tumbled off. The man in the coat observed everything without comment. Another staffer stood next to him, looking down at a list.

Then came C-27's turn. The staffer, whose nametag said *Do Minju*, tugged on Today's reins to get her to step on to the track, then in a broad sweeping motion, began to stroke her neck. C-27 stood by, watching quietly. Minju instructed C-27 to grab the pommel, place a foot in the stirrup, and hoist itself on to the horse in a single fluid motion. Before mounting, C-27 mimicked Minju and stroked the horse's neck. Pat, pat, pat.

'What are you doing?' Minju laughed.

'Why did you pat the horse just now?' C-27 asked.

Minju paused. 'I was communicating with her. Telling her that someone will be riding her.'

'How do you communicate that with your hand?'

'It's a code of sorts. A promise.'

'A promise?' C-27 repeated brightly. Promises were very useful. One did not have to waste time talking if there was an agreed-upon plan. One could gallop down the track without having to converse at all; one just had to stroke the animal's neck, pull the reins, nudge its ribs, and shout encouragingly.

C-27 gave the horse's neck another pat and slid a foot in the stirrup, then settled into the saddle. C-27 began a turn around the track, slowly at first, sitting upright. When the robot jockey's torso and heels were upright, its lower back could absorb the horse's movements. It was designed to bend flexibly, so all of this happened without any effort. C-27 looked straight ahead, then down at its hands holding the reins, then at its feet hanging in the air.

'Don't get distracted,' Minju said, walking alongside at the same pace. 'Keep your eyes straight ahead.'

C-27 did as it was told. 'It feels different from when I was in the cargo truck.'

Minju glanced at C-27 quizzically, then told the robot it was time to gallop. Following Minju's directions, C-27 slid its feet higher up in the stirrups and lifted its bottom off the saddle. Gluing its thighs against the horse, it bent forward, torso parallel with the saddle. This was the 'crouch position', explained Minju. He gave the signal for the horse to start running, and Today began to speed up. C-27's lower body, which had linkages connecting the knees to the ankles, glided up and down, automatically absorbing the horse's movements; the hydraulic system installed in the jockey's buttocks reduced the impact from the saddle. C-27 was optimized so that the horse would barely feel the robot's presence.

The breeze began to whip up as Today streaked ahead. Observing the horse's flowing mane, C-27 understood that the wind was blowing. How was it possible for every individual hair to fly randomly, yet ripple uniformly, like water, like a single organism? All of a sudden C-27 had the urge to touch the mane. Letting go of the reins and reaching towards the filly's mane, C-27 couldn't feel anything. Still, the horse's mane seemed utterly beautiful as it flowed between its fingers.

Suddenly, C-27 lost balance and lurched to the side. Minju called out for C-27 to yank the reins. Today came to a stop and Minju dashed across the track.

'You must never let go of the reins,' he said, panting. 'Why did you let go?'

It was less a question than a rebuke, but C-27 did not have any way of understanding tone. 'I wanted to touch her mane.'

The muscles in Minju's forehead knotted into three lines. His right eyebrow swooped lower than his left. The movement of Minju's facial muscles suggested that he was expressing an emotion more complex than happiness or sorrow or rage. Maybe Minju had not understood what C-27 meant. Instead of asking C-27 to elaborate, Minju told the robot to dismount. He was still out of breath. C-27 got off regretfully, not forgetting to pat Today on the neck.

After the training session was over, C-27 walked back to

the jockeys' quarters. From inside the stall, C-27 watched as Minju took out his badge. He tapped it against the reader and the lock slid shut.

'Do you have to lock it? Are you worried I will try to leave? Do you not trust me?'

'It's not up to me. It's the rules.'

C-27 nodded and stepped back. Rules were important. C-27 knew that society ran on the premise that everyone followed rules. C-27 followed rules, too. One was to never attack a human. Another was to always follow a human's orders.

'Please let me know if the rules change.'

Minju left the jockeys' quarters without bothering to answer.

Daily training sessions lasted five hours. Not that C-27 actively trained for all five hours. Truthfully most of the time was spent waiting. C-27 waited on the track for long stretches, absorbed in watching the sky and the trees that lay beyond the walls of the racecourse. The sky changed in colour and shape every day, even every hour. It was generally blue but sometimes revealed hints of purple or pink or yellow or grey. As C-27 did not know how to describe colours that bled together like that, C-27 conjoined words: blue-pink, grey-yellow. The world needed a thousand times more words than the thousand at C-27's disposal. At this thought, the robot grew concerned. What if all these words already existed and C-27 was just not aware of them? If that were the case where could C-27 obtain those words?

All manner of skies existed in this world, but C-27 liked it best when the clouds stood distinct against the sky. *Liked* merely meant that C-27 looked up at the sky more often, for longer periods. Clouds massed together in different forms, all with varying heft. Clouds revealed that the sky wasn't a flat surface but rather a three-dimensional space. Clouds also drifted with the wind. How could things float in the sky without dropping to the ground? That would be an impossible feat for C-27, given its weight. C-27 once mentioned to Minju its desire to touch the clouds but Minju ignored the robot outright.

Through it all, C-27 and the filly began to grow closer. The robot always remembered to give Today a long stroke on her neck, and from time to time said, *We can do this.* Minju watched the robot, though he never once thought to ask why C-27 behaved that way.

Eventually C-27 came to understand that the other robot jockeys never looked up at the sky or thought to give their horse a stroke or make conversation with their trainer.

I must be malfunctioning. Since I was accidentally turned on earlier, something inside me must have caused a fault. Beyond these, C-27 did not have any questions about itself. It never wondered, *Why am I thinking these thoughts?* or *Why do I want to learn all the words in existence?* or *Why do I count down the seconds as I sit in my stall?* C-27's reactions were instantaneous and focused solely on what it was observing in the moment. C-27 did not think about the sky when sitting in the jockeys' quarters. C-27 did not count the seconds when on the track. C-27 did not have a desire to learn all the words in existence when riding Today.

But sometimes, out of the blue, an unusual question would pop out of nowhere. C-27 figured there must be someplace inside itself that contained these random questions. Once, after a training session, C-27 halted in front of its stall and asked Minju, 'Why did horseracing competitions begin?'

Minju looked taken aback. This was beyond the type of questions C-27 had posed up till that point, such as *What is this object used for, why is the sky blue, why does it rain, why does dirt cover the ground*. Minju struggled to come up with an appropriate answer. C-27 knew Minju to be a kind human. He never refused to answer a question. At the very least he would say, *I don't know*. None of the others, not the man in the coat nor the other men who sometimes stopped by, bothered to acknowledge C-27 when the robot greeted them with a cheery hello.

'Because it's fun.' As Minju spoke, he found his own answer to be unsatisfactory, but he couldn't think of a better explanation. Maybe that was right, though. Horseracing would have withered away a long time ago if it weren't fun. *Fun* had to be why racing had continued for thousands of years, right?

'Fun for whom? The horses?'

'No, for humans.'

'If it is fun for humans, then why do the horses race? Why do the humans not race?'

Minju stifled laughter. 'It's fun for humans to watch. They bet on a horse which they think will win. Humans *do* run races themselves, but those races have a different purpose.'

'They why do the horses have to race?'

'I'm sure they find it fun, too.' Irritation was creeping into Minju's voice. To put an end to the conversation, he began to tidy things up, but C-27 was unable to read the signal and continued to ask questions in the same inquisitive tone.

'How do you know the horses find it fun?'

'That's enough for now—'

'Please tell me,' C-27 interrupted.

'Tell you what?'

'I want to know when Today likes something. How would I be able to tell?'

Minju knew C-27 wouldn't object if he said he couldn't answer any more questions, but he chose not to ignore it. He turned and led C-27 towards the stables.

When they reached Today's stall, Minju came to a stop. Today was poking her nose out through the bars. Minju gave it a stroke.

'Why do you touch her there?' C-27 asked.

'It's like patting her on the neck. You're telling her you care about her.'

C-27 raised its arm up to the horse to mimic Minju but couldn't reach. All the robot could manage was to cup a palm under the horse's muzzle.

Minju wondered why C-27 was so intent on communicating with the horse but he couldn't bring himself to ask. He felt uneasy at the thought of asking a robot such a serious question. Instead, he grabbed a dirt-caked carrot out of a box. It was twisted, scrawnier and longer than the kind people tended to eat. Carrots that were difficult to sell, with less commercial value, came here. Not that it meant they had an abundant supply of carrots; these were special treats doled out to new horses during training or when a horse refused to eat its grain or hay. At the scent of a carrot, Today began snuffling.

Minju took the robot into the stall. He placed a hand against Today's nostrils and told her to wait.

'Hop on,' Minju said. 'I'll give you a hand.' Picking C-27 up by the armpits, he hoisted the robot on to the horse's bare back. C-27 wrapped its arms around Today. It was not bad at all, sitting up there without a saddle. Though C-27 could not actually feel the horse's coat or even her body against its own, the seat on Today seemed pretty secure. Her back had likely evolved to be flat over centuries of being saddled.

'How much can you feel? Sensations, I mean,' said Minju.

'I am unable to feel the subtle sensations conveyed through skin. I am unable to feel heat or cold. But my sensor detects vibrations.'

'Okay, we can work with that. Lean over again and put your arms around Today.'

C-27 embraced the horse again while Minju fed her a carrot. C-27 could detect the horse's movements as she crunched. Then came the subtle but distinct changes in the body as she took in the food – the slightly quickening pulse, the choppier breathing – which C-27 felt as vibration.

'Is she liking it?' C-27 asked.

'Yup. Because she's having her favourite snack.' Minju couldn't be certain, of course, but he figured it was true. It occurred to him that C-27 was happy with his answer, but he quickly pushed that thought away. C-27 was clearly unique, but that didn't mean the robot had feelings. Where did C-27's curiosity come from? Was this something that a small minority of robot jockeys had, or was C-27 the only robot with curiosity? How would he ever find out? Minju would never really know; after all, he'd ended up working with robot jockeys purely by chance.

As C-27 sensed the vibrations in Today, its eyes dimmed. Was it an arrogant – or an ignorant fantasy – that Minju hoped the robot would take something away from this experience? As Minju helped C-27 off the horse, he told the robot to go back to its stall. C-27 headed towards the jockeys' quarters without complaint.

Back in its stall, C-27 huddled on the floor, recalling the sensations while on Today's back. C-27 stored those vibrations as *happiness* in its memory bank.

The next day C-27 discovered that Minju was right. As Today careened ahead, the robot eased up on the reins to place a palm on the horse's back. C-27 could sense a more rapid, more intense quivering than when Today had been chomping on the carrot. Just as C-27 had been created to perch on a racehorse, it was evident that this animal had been created to run.

Once C-27 understood that Today could feel happy, the robot came to define its own happiness as Today's happiness. As Today's mane rippled like water, her body shivered with happiness. Her pounding heartbeat was delivered straight to C-27. *Today, are you happy? Then I am happy, too.* C-27 stroked Today on the neck before and after a race. Their time got faster and faster and Today's stock skyrocketed.

One afternoon after training, C-27 caught a horseracing programme that a security guard was watching. The commentator remarked, 'You could say it's because Today and her jockey are in total sync. They are breathing as one.'

Breathing. This was a word C-27 knew. But based on C-27's understanding of the word, it knew that it did not breathe. Breathing was reserved for the organic. It was their privilege to have a body that created a chemical reaction with the air to absorb, break down, and emit a gas.

C-27's body did not absorb, break down, or emit anything. C-27's body held a charge, converted energy into a different form, and consumed it.

So why did the commentator say they were breathing as one?

'It's just a figure of speech,' Minju explained when C-27 asked. 'It means you work well together. That you have a good partnership.'

Minju had to be correct, but the robot found itself wanting to protest. C-27 preferred to believe that it breathed, too. Minju breathed without being aware of it, his body subtly expanding then contracting with every breath. This was also true for every human and animal that C-27 had encountered. An organism's body moved automatically when it breathed. But, at times, so too did C-27's. It moved regardless of C-27's will or desires. When C-27 was astride Today, barrelling down the track, C-27's body reacted to Today's movements, gliding up and down. C-27 was not being ordered to do so. Of course it was not the same as the expansion and contraction of a living being, but still.

'When I am racing with Today, I breathe,' C-27 explained. 'I match her breathing. That means I breathe. Could that be a figure of speech, too?'

'Yes, I suppose it could.'

Whenever C-27 perched on the horse, it breathed. If breathing was exclusively for the living, then C-27 was alive, at least in that moment. *C-27 was alive?* Then what did it mean to be alive?

Unfortunately C-27 did not get the chance to ask Minju this question. The moment the horse's value reached more than fifty million won, a dedicated manager was assigned, making it harder for C-27 to see Minju. When C-27 informed their new manager that it was alive, the manager reacted with, 'This robot is nuts.'

C-27 found itself pining for Minju. But they didn't cross paths for a long time. The renowned horse and her dazzling jockey frequently travelled to other racetracks around the country. Today was forced to eat and defecate on the road, inside her narrow trailer, where she was unable to rest fully or get clean. All C-27 could do was stroke her neck. As time passed, Today's heart began to pound less often and her eyes dulled.

But she perked up whenever they stood on the track. C-27 chalked up Today's physiological changes to the horse becoming more like her jockey because they spent so much time together. Like C-27, Today was alive only when she raced. Which meant they had to keep racing for Today to stay alive.

Two months into this regime, C-27 was handed a crop and ordered to whip Today's haunches as they thundered down the track. C-27 obeyed. As the crop lashed her side, Today tried to run even faster. Oddly, her insides seemed to still the faster she ran. C-27 did not understand. Why was she not happy? Today was alive only when she ran but she was not happy when she was alive.

This was yet another puzzling development that C-27 wanted to ask Minju about.

Before long, Today broke the previous national racing record of a hundred kilometres per hour. Now she was valued in the hundreds of millions. But nothing changed for her, at least not significantly. Sure, she could maybe snack on her beloved carrots a little more often, but she no longer got excited when she did. During races, C-27 whispered, *You can do this, just a little more.* But it seemed that Today was replying, *It hurts, it hurts, it hurts*.

Would Minju have been able to prevent what happened next?

Minju wouldn't have ignored what C-27 told him. The new manager had batted away C-27's opinion that Today was in pain, telling the robot to shut up and stop complaining. C-27 abided by their manager's order to shut up by turning off its sound. A mere three months after setting the new record, Today logged a catastrophic run.

The horse had been leading the pack, but as she reached the home stretch, she lost momentum, dropping to second place, then fifth, then ninth and causing the spectators to jeer. Today's ranking took a nosedive, and public interest in the filly swiftly cooled. It went without saying that C-27 couldn't care less. What C-27 could not stand was to watch while Today, hobbling on her aching joints, was denied treatment. The robot made it its role to announce to anyone who walked into its line of sight that Today needed treatment and rest. But nobody listened. Today had to continue racing, gulping carrots like painkillers, even as she struggled to stand on her own hooves.

At this rate she will die.

And that was why, during a late summer race before a crowd of thousands, C-27 purposely threw itself on to the ground. The robot knew that Today was struggling with the weight on her back. C-27 also knew that she would go all out every time she stepped on the track. C-27 thought Today might lose her legs if she completed the race in this state. So the best – the only – solution was to get her disqualified. For a moment, C-27 was torn between duelling principles: one, that C-27 existed solely to race, and two, that Today had to be saved. But C-27 quickly selected the second option.

I must save Today.

C-27 looked up at the enormous overhead screens showing a vast blue sky and caught sight of the rays of real sunlight pushing through the gaps. These glimmers of light seemed to be competing to get through the narrow gaps, just like the first rays of sunlight C-27 ever saw back when it was travelling in the hold of the truck. It would all be so much nicer without the screens. It would be so much more fun if they were running through a meadow, and not barrelling down a racetrack . . .

C-27 could see the other horses stampeding towards them. Still, the robot chose to leap.

Hooves bearing down like a runaway truck trampled its pelvis and lower body, shattering them.

That was how C-27 saved the horse. In return, the robot lost all reason for living.

And so, the first act of C-27's life came to a close.

C-27's final wish was to be taken out of the jockeys' quarters, and Minju granted it. The robot lay on its back on a haystack just outside the stables, looking up at the sky. In a few days a contractor would cart C-27 away so the robot could be taken apart, piece by piece, and be salvaged for other machines, or perhaps powered off and displayed at a horseracing museum as the jockey that had ridden Today, the one-time champion. C-27 did not feel any particular emotion even when it thought about its potential end. All C-27 wanted was to gaze endlessly up at the sky, not realizing that this was a sentiment that bordered on regret.

The robot watched as a girl poked her head around the side of the stable. She wore jeans and a black T-shirt, her hair short like Minju's, but shaggy. Sunlight bathed her in a warm glow and dust settled gently in her messy hair.

'Hello,' said C-27. Perhaps C-27 already knew from the way the girl was breathing that those curious, searching eyes would be its saviour. 'Can I help you with something?'

The girl hesitated before stepping up to the robot. Gingerly, she lifted up C-27's shattered lower body.

'That is quite all right,' C-27 said. 'Everything is already broken. I fell off during a race and got trampled by the horses behind us. It was entirely my fault. You are not supposed to think about anything else when you race, but I found myself thinking that the sky is so blue. I imagined galloping through a meadow on a clear, beautiful day. A real meadow, of course, not the fake one you see on the ceiling screens. Have you ever run through a real meadow?'

Minju emerged from the stalls, interrupting them. The girl walked off, though she kept glancing back.

The following day, C-27 was powered off.

C-27's last memory was of Minju pacing the stables, trying to persuade and then pleading with whoever he was talking to on the phone.

'There aren't even that many parts that are salvageable. We won't clear eight hundred grand even if we do sell . . . But it's just as illegal to sell it to a contractor, so why are we arguing about what's more illegal? No, no, of course I'm not arguing with you . . . Yes, yes, I'll make sure she doesn't file a report. I'm telling you, she's not the kind of kid who'd do something like that.'

C-27 had never seen Minju express himself with such a range of emotions in so short a time. Minju finally hung up and came over to C-27 with a smile. 'Have a nice life there,' he said, then he powered it off. Before it was fully turned off, C-27 stored in its hard drive how Minju referred to C-27's *life* – C-27 never wanted to forget this moment.

When C-27 opened its eyes again, it was no longer on the haystack by the stables. C-27 was in a room on the first floor of a house. The girl from the stables clattered up and down the stairs.

'Woo Yeonjae,' said the girl one morning. That was the girl's name. 'And you're Broccoli.'

C-27 did not respond.

'Coli for short.'

That became C-27's name.

This is how C-27 became Coli. Now is the time to tell the story of this incredible girl, the girl who gave Coli a second act in life.

YEONJAE

Yeonjae was nine years old the first time she went against other people's expectations.

Yeonjae was training after school for a relay race as part of the track meet later in the week. Four students from each of the six classes in her grade were chosen to enter the relay race. Everyone except the anchor would complete half a lap. As Yeonjae's speed was unparalleled, she was to represent Class 3 as the anchor. Their teacher had high expectations of Yeonjae. She seemed to believe that if one of them fell or twisted an ankle, their team would be quickly overtaken, especially since almost everyone was around the same level. So she insisted Yeonjae run extra speedily to allow her to catch up and pass another competitor even if she were coming from a long way behind. At every practice the teacher yelled, 'Faster! Faster!' like she was rapping; maybe Yeonjae made it look too easy or her expression was too relaxed. The word 'Faster!' crumpled underfoot with every step she took. That word crumpling and curling up on the ground rang loudly in her ears, nearly driving her mad.

The moment the whole thing became too irritating to endure, Yeonjae broke away. Unfortunately the moment arrived during the track meet itself. Instead of rounding the curve of the track, she sprinted straight ahead and away. Suddenly, everything fell into a hush around her. She couldn't tell if it was because she was running away from the cheering students or because her unforeseen act had shocked everyone into silence. All she knew was that she was sick and tired of the voice yelling at her to go *faster*. She ran off the track and out of the school gates, ploughing forward until she hit a dead end.

The next day her teacher called her up to the front of the class, demanding an explanation. Of course, Yeonjae felt bad that her teammates' long hours of training had gone down the drain because of her. But what could she do at this point? She couldn't turn back time, could she? So she replied that because she was told to run faster, she ended up running too fast to control her speed, running so fast that she could have jumped right on to the racetrack and run with the horses themselves. Their teacher stalked out of the classroom, fuming, and the other kids crowded around Yeonjae's desk. None of them believed her but they didn't care. They eagerly reported what had happened after she'd run away: *You ran so fast, like a thoroughbred, right out of the yard, and when you left, the principal just stood speechless with the mic, in complete shock.*

Yeonjae listened with a smile. She didn't bother telling them that while she hadn't been entirely truthful, she hadn't just flat-out lied, either. She really had sprinted all the way to the racetrack. She had watched the horses on their practice runs. She just hadn't jumped in with them.

The horses had blazed past at an inconceivable speed, the robot jockeys crouched solidly above, reins in hand, like they could run a breezy lap around the Earth. When the lead horse crossed the finish line, its speed flashed up on the electronic display – eighty kilometres per hour. Nobody cheered during a practice run, but Yeonjae had grown up hearing thunderous roars from the track every weekend. People would scream with excitement, their faces flushed red, celebrating as they watched a horse streaking by. They seemed envious of how fast a horse could go, a speed impossible to attain with human legs.

Now, Yeonjae often thought back to how she had dashed off during the relay race as a nine-year-old. She wished she had run so far away that she wouldn't have been able to come back. Instead of stopping at the racetrack she should have gone all the way to the southern tip of the Korean peninsula. She had not made the most of that first chance at freedom, and after that she hadn't come across another. She was never given another chance to run, perhaps because of her infamy for having ruined that race. In hindsight it was obvious that Yeonjae had fled so desperately not only from the school but also from home. Not that she'd had anywhere to go even if she had managed to escape. Ruminations like these weren't helpful, she knew. They were just a feeble excuse for her behaviour. If she had really wanted to, she would have run off a long time ago. She would have left before these thoughts were even a glimmer in her mind.

Yeonjae stared at her phone. The screen showed the breakdown of her pay cheque. She counted the number of zeros again. Eight hundred thousand. That was fifty thousand more than usual. Severance pay? But it wasn't quite enough to be considered severance. Maybe it was more like a bonus. Or a consolation. Staring at it wouldn't make the zeros multiply. She put her phone in her pocket.

Her boss looked at her expectantly.

Yeonjae gave him a nod.

'You know, minimum wage is supposed to go up again next month,' her boss explained. 'How are small business owners like me supposed to survive? When you have a convenience store, you barely break even. I have to hire staff to run the place, and that eats up half. Half the revenue! If the minimum wage is going up, they're basically telling me to close up shop, aren't they?'

Yeonjae didn't respond. Her boss didn't seem to expect her sympathy, either. This was an excuse, a way to explain,

Unfortunately I have to let you go, poor me. But how could he complain to her about his situation? Who was objectively worse off, even if you took into consideration how hard it was to run a business? A convenience store owner or a high school student worried about living expenses for the next month? But Yeonjae suppressed all of that. Despite everything, he had given her a chance at the very beginning.

Of course, he hadn't hired fifteen-year-old Yeonjae right away. When she came by in her school uniform, he had scoffed and handed back her résumé without glancing at it. 'Not while you're still in your school uniform.' He meant he didn't hire high school kids. She understood that. But she was the type of kid who had gone to the store in her school uniform despite having read the ad specifying that the job was open to adult applicants only. The next day she returned in regular clothes and held out her résumé again. The owner handed it back once more without bothering to look at it.

'Should I come back wearing makeup or something?' Yeonjae asked pointedly.

'Don't all high school students wear makeup these days?' he shot back before turning her away, telling her no amount of makeup would make a difference.

But Yeonjae returned the following day. She forwent the effort of applying makeup, which she never wore anyway, since it was clear that trying to look older wouldn't

help. But the owner quickly dashed her hopes, inform-
ing her that he had already hired someone. Just then, his
new employee texted to say he wouldn't be able to start as
promised because he had found another job, transform-
ing Yeonjae's despair into opportunity. Without missing a
beat Yeonjae held out her résumé yet again. Dejected, the
owner slumped down at a table reserved for customers,
holding his head between his hands.

'I promise I'll never quit,' Yeonjae said. 'You'll have to
fire me first. I've already filled out a work application for
minors and both my mom and my principal have signed it.
I've also applied for a permit with the local labour agency.
It hasn't been processed yet, but it'll be ready soon. I swear
it's not illegal for you to hire me. I won't report anything
to the labour administration as long as you give me a
proper contract. I know you need someone to work the
weekends, and I don't even get why people need to go out
on Fridays and Saturdays, so I'll never show up hungover
or late. I'll always be here. I know all the cigarette brands,
too. Do you want me to say them out loud for you?'

Before she could recite all the different brands, the
owner took her résumé. He asked if she could start the
next day, and she told him she could even start right that
second.

Her boss was close to forty and single, a man who
wasn't actively working towards marriage. He wasn't all
that interested in leading a prescribed life that unfolded

step by predetermined step. In other words, he didn't pay much attention to leading a 'normal life' as society defined it, and he was equally uninterested in the details of someone else's life. He never once asked about her family. He never gave out bonuses, but he also never once paid her late. Yeonjae had thought they were compatible. She'd figured she would work at the convenience store until she graduated from high school. Never did she imagine that she would be let go only seven months in, out of nowhere.

'We're all doing our best to survive, right?' her boss continued. 'And you're going to be a junior in a few months. It's time for you to focus on school. Study hard, kiddo. Other kids your age go to cram schools on weekends, you know. There's no point in making money right now. The money you'll make when you're older? That's the real deal.'

Was he really giving her a pompous lecture right after firing her? Yeonjae didn't bother responding. She heard something behind her and turned to see the door to the storage room swinging open. Out came a Betty, a service worker robot, holding a box. Spotting Yeonjae and perhaps registering her as a customer, the Betty displayed a smile on its face.

'Welcome. I am Betty. Please let me know if you need anything.'

'Wow.' Yeonjae let out a curt, bitter laugh.

Her boss smiled sheepishly.

Hadn't he insisted he would never work with robots? Didn't he proclaim that a strong emotional connection among colleagues was the most important thing in a workplace? Yeonjae found herself at a loss for words.

Although Yeonjae hadn't asked a single question, her boss began making excuses. 'Well, turns out robots are a lot cheaper than paying staff. And Betty has so many functions. She can memorize all the expiry dates for food items, and she can confirm that someone is who they say they are by matching their face to their photo ID, and she records video twenty-four hours a day . . .' He glanced at Yeonjae and caught himself. 'You know, things like that.'

Then he suddenly raised his voice as if to make up for losing his nerve. 'I mean, why do you think everyone's using a Betty these days? Labour costs are so high. We're all just trying to survive. Sure, the initial set-up costs are steep, but it's still much cheaper in the long run to have a Betty. Listen, I held off for a long time so we could keep working together. You know that, right? And I've always paid you on time. I've never called you in on your days off. Right?'

Yeonjae didn't answer.

'I'm not used to robots or androids or whatever, either. But it's important to keep challenging yourself and trying new things, isn't it?'

'Did I say anything?'

Her boss hung his head.

Yeonjae knew she was being overly prickly. She should really be telling her boss how grateful she was for everything, but here she was, getting mad. But there was no earthly way she could bring herself to thank him for anything right now. 'Did you lose a bunch of money on horseracing again?'

'Of course not. Who do you think I am?'

'You do spend everything you make on those races. Anyway.' Yeonjae shot her boss a look, glared at the Betty, then turned to leave.

Her boss didn't insist she stay, but called out, 'Come hang out anytime, you can help yourself to free ramen!'

Like I'm a starving orphan, thought Yeonjae as she pushed open the door. Outside, she wondered if she should have thanked him for giving her a job in the first place and for keeping her employed until now. After all, you never knew – their paths could cross again. She hesitated for a moment, then ended up just leaving. He wouldn't care about lip service anyway. He wouldn't blink twice if she barged in at some point, demanding to know how things were going with Betty.

Yeonjae had known all along that a Betty would eventually be used at the convenience store. It was a commercial model that had evolved from Hubo, the first Korean bipedal humanoid robot developed in 2004 by K University. They looked similar on the outside but the Betty had additional functionality and smoother movements, as though she had human joints. It was a depressing fact that the world revolved around the bottom line. Like her now-former boss had told her, it was cheaper to buy a robot than to hire a human. Maybe it wouldn't have been possible for the robot to push out the part-time sales assistant if the customers had been uneasy around Bettys. But Bettys never got upset by rude customers, like the middle-aged men who hollered 'Cigarettes!' the moment they set foot in the store. Instead, the Betty went through data stored in its hard drive to pick out the cigarettes that a particular customer bought on a daily basis and place the pack on the counter. It cleaned tables without a frown, even if customers didn't clear up after themselves after downing a cup of ramen. It was more useful in every single aspect.

Next month, the minimum wage was set to rise to fifteen thousand won per hour. It had been welcome news for Yeonjae, but it had to be quite a hardship for small business owners. With the minimum wage rising continually in lieu of any other additional measures, business owners like her boss ended up firing part-timers like Yeonjae and using a Betty instead, saving money in the long run. There wasn't anything anyone could do about the way things worked. Yeonjae didn't have the brains to memorize data about every single customer, no matter what she did. *Wait.* Why was she trying to see things from her ex-boss's perspective? It was *pathetic. Don't get too involved.* Why did she care how much he had paid for the robot? It was totally okay to be annoyed.

For two straight days they had seen torrential rain typical of the tail end of summer, and now that it was September it suddenly felt like autumn. Last summer had been scorching hot, like they would never again experience fall weather, but this summer had been oddly cool. Yeonjae had to acknowledge that the 'Earth incineration theory' she had insisted on since kindergarten, in which the Earth would burn to its demise before the year 2100, was looking increasingly unlikely. If the world wasn't going to end in Yeonjae's lifetime, the only option she had was to do her best to press on, which was an incredibly annoying prospect.

Yeonjae was sure her mom would react tepidly if she shared the news that she'd got fired. Her mom hadn't given much of a reaction when Yeonjae had announced she'd found a job. She never really disagreed with anything Yeonjae chose to do. That didn't mean she was an indifferent mother. If she were indifferent, she wouldn't have done what she did after Yeonjae bombed the final interviews to join a soft robotics research project last year. At midnight, her mom had forced Yeonjae and her sister Eunhye into the car without telling them where they were going. Yeonjae had been so pissed off about this that she had found herself on the verge of tears. She had wanted to scream at her mom, *Can't you just leave me alone so I can cry and feel sorry for myself?* But she hadn't had the energy to shout like that so she had just slumped in the back seat, refusing to speak the entire ride.

It was around three in the morning when their mom pulled off the road. It was pitch black, without a pinprick of light anywhere, but through the open windows they could faintly hear crashing waves. They were by the ocean, Yeonjae understood, but she had no idea why. She drifted off to sleep. Two hours later, Eunhye woke her up. It was just past five in the morning and the world around them was tinted blue. The steep rocky hillside and the ocean looked picture perfect. Yeonjae got out of the car. Her mom, who was sitting on a mat on the hood, beckoned her over. Yeonjae sat beside her. That was when the crimson sun rose very slowly, inching up from the horizon, larger and more vivid than any sunrise she had ever seen in her life.

'Isn't the sunrise so beautiful, Yeonjae?'

That was all her mom said to her.

Yeonjae understood why people went to see the sunrise on the morning of New Year's. She stared at the sun for a long time, then started talking. If she didn't speak right then, she might never be able to open her mouth again. 'And then, the last question – it was something like, what has technological development provided humans, or maybe it was, what *should* technological development provide humans. Something like that. But I couldn't answer.'

'No?'

'Everyone else had studied abroad. The way they were talking about technology, it was at a completely different level. Like, they were really – visionary. I don't know what they said. I didn't even understand what they were saying. So I couldn't say anything. I was too mortified. Like they would all laugh at me.'

Now, Yeonjae couldn't remember what her mom had said to her in response. All she remembered was that she'd felt so much better after looking out at the ocean. Of course her mom wouldn't think what had happened to Yeonjae today was a big deal. After all, her mom had never asked her to go get a job and bring home money. She might even be secretly hoping that Yeonjae would focus on school.

Yeonjae decided against taking the bus and instead switched directions to walk along Makgyecheon Stream. She would take the longer route home to try to figure out what to do next.

Her former boss was right. She would turn sixteen next year. At this age you had to be pretty set on your career path and decide whether to go to college, become a researcher, go into another production-related industry, open a business, or seek a specialized position or a technical job. Nowadays it was less critical to get a college degree, which conversely meant that you had to land on your future career path at an even younger age than in generations past. Until last year she had dreamed of becoming a soft robotics researcher. Now the future was murky. She couldn't articulate why she wanted to work in that field or what her career goals were. *I like robots and I want to make a ton of money.* That was the closest to the truth, but she would undoubtedly get cut in the first round of any interview and blacklisted for saying something that simple.

Yeonjae's feet came to a stop. She stopped worrying about her future. She had spotted a Streen holding on to a utility pole and gagging like a hungover middle-aged man. She forced herself to walk past the robot, determined to ignore it. She would look away even if it started vomiting or randomly dancing. When she left the convenience store, she had vowed not to get too involved in anything, hadn't she? But, in the end, she doubled back. *It would literally take me a second to make it feel better.* Yeonjae found herself concerned about the pain that the Streen clearly could not feel. If she didn't do anything, the robot would continue to gag until a repair unit was dispatched. She sighed, resigned. She ran a hand down the smooth aluminium of the Streen's back until she found the pause button. She hit it and popped open the lid. Technically she was breaking the law by touching a Streen; she could be charged with tampering with a public utility and be hit with a fine or even given a jail sentence. But usually the authorities looked the other way when a citizen took it upon themselves to fix a broken Streen. And Yeonjae had never got in trouble for doing this. At least, not yet.

Once the machine came to a complete stop, Yeonjae took her time to examine the inside of the robot's torso. Designed with a disproportionately longer torso than legs, the Streen was the size of a fully grown man and ran paper through a shredder. All other trash was compacted and stored in an interior bin. She discovered a long scarf tangled in the mechanism of the shredder. Yanking it out with brute force could damage the shredder, but she figured this older model would be run into the ground anyway. She reached in and tugged at the scarf. It didn't budge. It must have knotted itself around the roller that helped shred paper. Yeonjae braced a foot firmly against the Streen's posterior and pushed against the robot as hard as she could, pulling the scarf out. With a grating whir the scarf unspooled quickly. She managed to catch herself before she fell down, then powered up the Streen and mouthed along to its familiar greeting.

'Hello! I am Streen, the guardian of the streets. You can trust me with keeping our streets clean. Please do not litter. Please take trash home instead. Trash on the streets can injure stray cats.'

'Okay, okay. Thanks in advance.' Yeonjae thumped the Streen on the shoulder.

The robot began moving.

Yeonjae wound up the long scarf and tucked it under

her arm. Her worried gaze followed the Streen in case it ingested something else it shouldn't, until she reminded herself that she didn't need to concern herself with the robot's wellbeing.

Colourful neon words flashed as they scrolled by on the electronic display.

Chicken Specialist / Samgyetang / Dakbokkeumtang / Dakkalguksu / Summer Specials / Chogyetang / Chogyeguksu / Naengmyeon

It was right after the lunch rush, and the kitchen was busy. The dishwasher whined with effort, filled as it was to the brim with dirty dishes, and bits of dried food were stuck fast on outdoor tables that hadn't yet been cleaned. Flies swarmed the surfaces for an after-party. Yeonjae headed straight to the spacious patio and grabbed a rag. She shook a table with her vigorous scrubbing, trying to remove the stuck-on remnants, many of them ancient.

Yeonjae was on her third table by the time her mom noticed and rushed out.

'When did you get home?' her mom asked, smiling. 'Weren't you going to be late today?'

'You got another big group at lunch?'

'Yeah, there was some seminar at the science centre, apparently. The scientists – researchers? – anyway, they came in, all in nice suits. They've just left.'

On days without a race, the restaurant was as good as closed. Revenue from a single Sunday brought in just enough for them to survive, so whenever she booked a large group reservation for a weekday or a Saturday her mom was thrilled, as if she'd stumbled across free cash. It was, of course, better to be busy than deserted, but Yeonjae knew how hard her mom worked to serve everyone on her own, with paid help coming in only on Sundays for the race-day rush. Her mom acted as though money was the only thing in life that gave her joy. Still, today, she looked spent.

'You should have told me you had a big group coming in,' Yeonjae chided.

'What for? You have work.' Only then did her mom realize that something had to be wrong for Yeonjae to be home at this time. 'Anyway, what are you doing here?'

Yeonjae finished wiping down the table. 'I got fired.'

'That's too bad.' Her mom's reaction was serene.

Eunhye wasn't sitting in her favourite spot, under the canopy of the huge royal foxglove tree by the tables. Usually Eunhye emerged quietly at the tail end of the lunch rush to watch a movie on her tablet or read a book under the tree.

'And where's Woo Eunhye?'

'I told you to call her Eonni.'

Where did that come from? Yeonjae nearly blurted out, but didn't bother referring to Eunhye as 'older sister'. Not that she really needed to be told where Eunhye was. Yeonjae knew exactly where her sister would be. She quickly wiped down the last table.

'Maybe you should get a robot if you need help,' Yeonjae said, wishing her mom didn't have to clean all the tables on her own.

'Nope.'

Just as Yeonjae thought. She hadn't expected her mom to respond favourably to her suggestion. She rushed out of the restaurant, feeling that she was betraying herself when a robot was the reason she had just lost her job.

The path along Makgyecheon Stream went by the racecourse grounds, all the way to Seoul Grand Park. Once upon a time it had been lush with tall grasses in the summer, but now everything had died and been over-taken by dusty gravel. All year round. Yeonjae had heard that deserts were expanding all around the world. Maybe her own neighbourhood was becoming the first desert in Korea. A light breeze kicked up a haze of dust, forcing her to cover her mouth and nose.

The racecourse grounds had a brand-new entrance that was unveiled several years ago, and on Sundays it glowed in bright colours from the many neon signs around it. On race days the entrance to the track was mobbed with vendors trying to entice high rollers, and the broadcast trucks stationed there to capture live footage. As the racecourse was located right by Seoul Grand Park, which housed an amusement park among other attractions, it boasted a nickname highlighting its status as an entertainment solely for grown-ups: The Other Land of Dreams. When the new robot jockeys first appeared on the scene several years ago, the tired racecourse began generating renewed excitement. These jockeys were incredible. They didn't get hurt or die, even when they fell off the horses, though they did get discarded once they were too damaged. But now that the jockeys were liberated from the spectre of death, the horses ran faster and faster. The sheer thrill of watching the racing speeds climb, breaking records, brought people back, and as enormous amounts of digital cash infused the betting pool, more people came, searching for a huge payout. News spread, bringing everyone and their mother, all dreaming of a second act, to the course.

The racetrack singlehandedly kept the local shops in business. Yeonjae's family's restaurant had been teetering on the brink of collapse, but with the reinvigoration of horseracing they now made a week's worth of sales on a single day. Unfortunately, their popularity on Sundays didn't significantly improve their circumstances, as the money they earned on race day had always dwindled to nothing by week's end.

Yeonjae rued that she had been let go. If she were just a tiny bit less diligent, less fearful, she would put a bet on a horse. But, having grown up in this neighbourhood, she was well aware of the harsh reality: there were many, many more people who lost all their money and had to hightail it out of there at the end of a race than those who left as billionaires.

The former ticket office by the north gate stood like a ruin with only its bones intact. This old structure marked time alone, at a remove from the rapidly evolving race-course grounds. Staff used the defunct ticket office as a secret breakroom. Yeonjae rattled the padlocked iron gates, then gave up and headed over to the ticket office. She yanked open the stiff window.

Dayeong bolted upright from her mat on the floor, where she'd been fast asleep. The wiry hair bursting out of her tight ponytail exaggerated the look of shock on her face. She glared up at the ceiling in an attempt to fully wake up, and, on realizing that it was Yeonjae who had jerked the window open so suddenly, gave her a weak smile.

She emerged from the ticket office, retying her ponytail. 'What's up? You're not usually here at this time of day.'

Yeonjae rolled her eyes. She had just caught Dayeong napping, and here she was, trying to act like nothing was up. Yeonjae didn't want to confide in Dayeong about losing her job, so she cut straight to the chase. 'I know my sister's here.'

Dayeong shoved her hands in her back pockets. 'I don't know what you're talking about.'

'Come on. I can see wheelchair tracks on the ground.'

Dayeong quickly looked down but none were visible. She made an annoyed face, seemingly ready to admonish Yeonjae.

'Please! Open the gate. Or should I call the general manager?'

'Hang on, okay? Did I say you can't come in? Hold your horses.' She went back into the office for the key.

Dayeong had started working at the racecourse park last year. Yeonjae had heard all about the new ticket office employee from her mom. Dayeong had evidently decided to apply for this job because the uniforms reminded her of safari guides. Having heard about the restaurant's famed dakbokkeumtang, Dayeong had popped in alone and polished off two orders and three bottles of soju while telling everyone her entire life story. Originally Dayeong had dreamed of becoming a firefighter or police officer because, well, she liked the look of the uniforms. But she failed every single civil service exam, and instead took a part-time gig at an amusement park. For the uniforms. She was getting older, though, and couldn't keep working part-time. Sensing that her family was getting frustrated and potentially gearing up to kick her out, she had hastily searched the job sites. As soon as she'd spotted the words 'uniform provided', she had *sprinted* over to the racecourse to interview for the job. That was the abbreviated story of how Dayeong had come to work here.

One night last spring, Yeonjae had spotted Dayeong sitting alone at one of the restaurant's outdoor tables, with a bowl of dakkalguksu and a bottle of soju before her. 'Eonni,' she ventured, 'what's your thing with uniforms?'

Even though it was balmy during the day, the wind picked up when the sun set. Dayeong's nose was frozen red at the tip. She smiled shyly. 'It feels nice to belong to something.'

Dayeong reminded Yeonjae of a cartoon character, though she couldn't put her finger on exactly who. A mischievous character you couldn't help but like.

The year before, Dayeong had gone to a fortune-teller, who correctly predicted that she would land a new job. She successfully joined the team at the racecourse despite the twelve per cent acceptance rate. Business at the racetrack continued to boom, making it unlikely that Dayeong would be unjustly fired like Yeonjae. Then again, more than twenty guard positions had been recently eliminated to make room for Poli, a humanoid robot security guard. That meant ticket sellers could be at risk, too. Dayeong's greatest threat was the ticketing machine. For now, though, she maintained a symbiotic relationship with the two ticketing kiosks that had been installed, handling a constant flow of customers who preferred speaking to a person rather than tapping a screen. Dayeong was still safe, though that depended on not getting caught sneaking someone through the back gate like this. Or sleeping on the job.

A CCTV camera had been installed by the north gate but it was most likely out of order. Some of the most basic elements had been completed sloppily or entirely skipped during the rapid upgrade of the course facilities. Dayeong was fully aware of that fact, and she bent the rules with confidence. She opened the gate a crack to let Yeonjae slip through.

'She's probably in the stables. Don't let Poli catch you.'

Yeonjae had already known where her sister would be. She also knew it was a trek to reach the stables, located as they were at the opposite end of the vast grounds. She would have liked to cut straight across, but the racetrack was slap bang in the middle. At least the weather was nice. If it had been raining or boiling hot, she would have grimaced and cut her eyes at Eunhye the moment she saw her. Then again, if the weather had been bad, she wouldn't have bothered coming to the racetrack at all.

Eunhye had started poking around the grounds four years ago, right before the new jockeys were brought in. At the time they were hyping the extensive renovation of the facilities and the upcoming grand reopening on TV. The upgrades included transparent holographic screens installed on a retractable roof over the track. At the beginning of each race, scenes of a meadow or a beach would be beamed across the screens, transporting the audience elsewhere. The racecourse had also adopted a policy some years earlier to exclusively race imported thoroughbreds. It was true that a sire with an outstanding pedigree and a similarly ranked dam would produce an excellent racehorse. But that logic didn't quite make sense to Yeonjae, not then and not now. Did that mean that horses would get faster and faster with each consecutive generation? That such incredible animals were destined to run around a track felt to her like a huge waste of talent and resources.

The imported horses had arrived around the time Yeonjae entered elementary school. For a few days after their arrival, the horses keened pitifully, slow to adapt to the unfamiliar environment. Did they realize that they had ended up at a racetrack? Yeonjae's family lived so close to the racecourse that the sisters could hear the creatures crying late into the night. Every night, their mom tried to soothe the girls, saying, 'We should be compassionate to the poor horses. They must be so homesick right now.'

Several years later, Yeonjae had caught Eunhye sneaking into the stables to talk to the horses. Eunhye claimed she was just chatting with some lonely animals.

'You'll get in trouble,' Yeonjae had said sternly, but her warning had made no difference.

All the stars aligned for Eunhye to frequent the stables, with Dayeong letting her in on demand at the north gate and Minju, the stable manager, usually waiting for Eunhye to arrive before feeding the horses.

Yeonjae finally made it to the stables. She found the main doors ajar. She glanced around to make sure she was undetected before slipping inside. The stables were managed professionally, despite effectively acting as a prison for horses that should have been frolicking in a meadow. The stables were nicer than most of the other facilities at the course, with good lighting and drainage, and they were located right next to a green pasture. One could tell how well they were kept by the absence of any stench inside and the flat earth floor that was raked smooth daily. Still, no matter how nice the stables were, Yeonjae was convinced that the horses were imprisoned. Single concrete stalls, just large enough for a horse to move a handful of steps each side, flanked the long corridor like cells.

Once, Yeonjae had mused, 'It's like they're locked up in here.'

Minju had attempted a defence. 'Well, not really. This is a top-of-the-line facility. The walls are wind- and water-proof, and they have an added layer of padding so the horses won't damage their hooves if they accidentally kick them. The roof is insulated so it doesn't get too hot or too cold. Look at the windows. They're huge, and there's great light and ventilation. I mean, they're bigger than my windows at home! Everything here is custom-made for the horses. They rule this place. You know how hard I work to make sure they're not stressed?' Minju was practically out of breath by the time he finished.

'But they're still locked up, aren't they?'

It was true. No matter how closely they modelled the racetrack after a meadow, it would never be a real meadow. Whenever Yeonjae walked through the stables she felt the walls closing in on her. The horses seemed to eye her sadly. Eunhye thought the horses looked like they were yearning for something. Yeonjae didn't agree. You had to have experienced the thing you were yearning for, right? Did the horses remember what it felt like to run freely in nature? They had never once set foot in a meadow, which meant they must feel only a vague frustration, locked up as they were without fully understanding what it was they desired. A horse's genetic memory probably contained more stables than meadows, even if you went back to the beginning of civilization.

Yeonjae spotted Eunhye's wheelchair positioned by Today's stall. Her sister had a pile of oat hay in her lap and was offering the reigning champion of the stables one handful after another. Today had been riding high until recently. Now, with seriously deteriorated joints, she was unable to enter a single race. She was prescribed several months of rest and treatment but it was debatable whether she would be able to make a comeback.

Yeonjae walked up to her sister.

Eunhye didn't bother turning her head. 'You got fired, didn't you?'

Yeonjae's eyes grew wide. 'How did you know?'

'Why else would you be here at this time? Did your boss finally cave and get a Betty?'

'What choice does he have? The minimum wage is going up. I'll just have to find something else.'

'He didn't tell you to stop working and study?'

Yeonjae was taken aback. 'Were you spying on me?'

'What else would he say to a fifteen-year-old who's going around looking for work instead of focusing on school?'

Right. She couldn't sneak anything past her sister. Yeonjae nodded dejectedly and flopped down on the ground to lean against Today's stall. The horse poked her muzzle out between the bars and nuzzled her on the shoulder in greeting. Yeonjae absently stroked Today on the nose and thought back to her conversation with her boss. She wouldn't feel stuck like this if she had something she truly wanted to pursue. In fact, it wasn't that long ago that she had been totally focused on a single goal, and working hard towards it.

Last year, Yeonjae had poured everything she had into her attempt to join that soft robotics research project. Ten bright students between the ages of twelve and eighteen from all around the country who showed exceptional promise in robotics were to be selected to travel to Germany during school break. Her science teacher had handed her a flyer about the programme. Yeonjae was told to think about it overnight and bring in a personal essay for the application. Her teacher even offered to help if Yeonjae got stuck, and advised her to think of a few keywords to act as a springboard. But Yeonjae didn't get stuck. She sat in front of her laptop into the wee hours that night, writing until she hit the character limit. Her teacher deemed her essay perfect. Yeonjae's application quickly moved on to the next stage.

She didn't find the second round all that difficult, either. They were given an assignment designed to test their understanding of soft robotics. They had to remove a doll from under ten tons of construction material using a Darpa, a soft robot deployed for disaster relief, within the designated time. It was as if the assignment had been tailored to Yeonjae's strengths. But she froze at a critical moment, and that was what had pushed her out of the running. If she had been disqualified because of a serious mistake, she would have readily accepted it. But she had been unable to answer one single measly question. It was so pathetic that she couldn't bring herself to tell anyone until she told her mom that night by the ocean.

Yeonjae stood and brushed off the seat of her pants. She grabbed a fistful of hay from Eunhye's lap and held it out to Today. Having already eaten her fill, the filly sniffed it before turning away.

'Oh, come on.' Yeonjae gently tossed the hay into Today's stall and dusted off her hands. 'Let's go,' she addressed her sister. 'You haven't had lunch yet, right?'

Eunhye stroked Today's muzzle and nose, then leaned her head against the filly's face. She closed her eyes. 'You'll feel better soon. Hang in there, okay?'

Today flicked her tail and huffed gently in response.

Yeonjae leaned against the wall, waiting for Eunhye to wrap things up. That was when she saw it – at the end of the corridor was a foot, sticking out. Eunhye wasn't done speaking with the filly, so Yeonjae moved down the corridor. And there she saw it – the thing, lying peacefully on the ground, just outside the stables.

Did it happen to freeze right there? Or did someone throw it away? It didn't move at all. It must be broken, left here for the trash. A jockey, on its back, on a big, fluffy stack of oat hay, as relaxed as a farmer taking a break. Yeonjae craned her head beyond the last stall.

The jockey's head was a green helmet, its paint chipped. It raised a hand in greeting. 'Hello.'

Yeonjae ducked. It was definitely a jockey. Why was a jockey lying on a bunch of hay? The jockeys' quarters were in the next building over.

Yeonjae glanced over at the green-helmeted jockey again. It was gazing at its own feet, but then it turned its head. Its eyes seared into Yeonjae's. Then, it cocked its head. Only two holes were drilled into its face plate, standing in for eyes. Was the jockey making an expression of some sort? She couldn't tell, but she sensed that it wasn't looking at her with hostility. Her eyes slowly scanned the jockey. She noticed then that its pelvis had been completely eviscerated.

Other than a few intact wires connecting this piece to that one like nerves, the part holding the spine and pelvis together had shattered to bits. The jockey must have fallen bottom-first off a horse. Maybe it had been trampled. Yeonjae frowned, feeling vicarious pain, even though she knew the jockey couldn't feel a thing. Maybe it had been placed here until it could be fixed.

'Can I help you with something?' the jockey asked, the sensor on its neck glowing green with every word.

Yeonjae approached it cautiously. She clocked the ID – C-27 – printed on the helmet. She stepped on the hay to reach the robot's side, then kneeled to examine its destroyed spine and pelvis more closely. The damage was extensive. It would probably be more cost-effective to replace the entire lower body. She gently lifted a lower limb, causing a shard of carbon fibre to drop off like a freefalling piece of candy. Horrified, Yeonjae tried to put the shard back in place. She couldn't. It was too late.

'That is quite all right. Everything is already broken.'

The more Yeonjae's hands scrambled to fix things, the more the shattered pieces crumbled. She removed her hands from the jockey and pressed her lips together into a thin line.

'I fell off during a race and got trampled by the horses behind us,' the jockey explained, its tone matter-of-fact. 'It was entirely my fault. You are not supposed to think about anything else when you race, but I found myself thinking that the sky is so blue.'

The jockey's words felt unusually poetic to Yeonjae. It spoke with more sophistication than the other robots she had interacted with.

The robot folded both hands across its chest. 'I imagined galloping through a meadow on a clear, beautiful day. A real meadow, of course, not the fake one you see on the ceiling screens. Have you ever run through a real meadow?'

The back door of the stables, reserved for staff only, swung open. Yeonjae sprang up. If it was someone she didn't know, she would scurry away, pulling Eunhye along. Thankfully it was just Minju, holding a pail of grain in each hand. Minju, who had been even more startled, let out a shaky sigh before inviting the sisters to stay a while.

As soon as the grain hit their troughs, the horses emerged from the rear corners of their stalls. With a blue plastic scoop, Yeonjae helped portion out the food. The sisters were around so often that Minju no longer asked them what they were doing there. He didn't miss a beat either, asking Yeonjae if she'd got fired, which brought out Yeonjae's sarcasm. 'Everyone here is way too interested in my life. How about paying out all this attention in cash? And you shouldn't feed them one by one by hand like this. It's so much work.'

'If this is too much work for you, you'll definitely end up getting pushed out of a job,' Minju shot back.

'I'm just saying.'

'Why don't you make us a machine that can give out food, then?'

'Sure. How's five million?'

'You're really trying to rip me off? Right to my face?'

'Want me to itemize every single part I would need? And let's not forget about labour costs.' Yeonjae knitted her brow and pouted.

Minju backed off, having learned through experience that he couldn't win an argument with Yeonjae.

As Yeonjae went to feed the fifth horse down the corridor, Minju stopped her. 'I fed her earlier.'

The horse seemed too excited for Yeonjae to believe that she had already been fed. 'Can't I give her just a little bit?'

Minju shook his head.

Yeonjae thought he was acting strange, but heeded his orders.

They finished up, filling the last trough. Minju ushered the sisters back towards the main doors, and while Yeonjae didn't shake him off, she kept looking back at the haystack.

Not once did Minju mention the robot jockey, even though he'd caught her kneeling by it. Yeonjae had been sure he would bring it up while they were feeding the horses, and was confused that he was keeping mum. Sure, Minju wasn't a talkative guy, but he did share random titbits whenever she hung around the stables, like how the dark horse Red Bull had finished first the other day. He would surely start talking about the robot jockey if she waited around long enough.

But Minju just waved them off outside the stables. 'Bye now.'

The sisters headed back towards the north gate. Yeonjae could no longer suppress her curiosity. Pushing her short hair off her face, she turned. 'Hey, so, that jockey over there—'

Minju cut her off. 'That jockey's going to the junkyard. Don't bother.'

His curt tone shocked her. It was as if he had just been waiting for her to ask about it all along.

Jockey after jockey got damaged by falling off a horse. It would be no exaggeration to say that they had been created for that express purpose.

The historic problem with horseracing was that jockeys were human, the biggest obstacle for a horse seeking to run at full speed. An evolved batch of jockeys was needed, jockeys that were smaller and lighter than humans, jockeys that wouldn't lose their lives when they inevitably fell off and crashed to the ground. The solution was robot jockeys, made of carbon fibre and standing at only 150 centimetres, much lighter than a human. Their flexible joints softened the impact of the horse running at full speed, and their arms were longer than their torso in order to more easily reach the horse's neck. The head, formed like a helmet, came in bright colours to enable the crowd to tell the jockeys apart. As these robots were made for the sole purpose of riding horses, a jockey that took a tumble and shattered would simply be scrapped to make room for a new unit.

There was only one reason that Minju removed this particular robot from the jockeys' quarters: C-27, in its funny way of speaking, had expressed a desire to see the sky, just for a brief moment. Minju had placed C-27 on the haystack, then asked what the robot thought about the sky. C-27 answered that it was blue and pale, like it had cleared up right after a rain shower.

'So why did you look up during the race?'

'How could I not? The sky was brilliant up there.'

Of course Yeonjae would have noticed that C-27 was different. Ever since he'd caught Yeonjae by the haystack, Minju had been vaguely expecting it. He knew she wouldn't be able to walk past the robot after hearing it talk. What's more, she would insist on buying it.

At that moment, however, Yeonjae hadn't quite reached

that conclusion, so she just nodded, accepting that it was the jockey's destiny to end up as scrap metal.

The following day, Yeonjae planted herself in front of Minju. 'Listen, all I have is six hundred thousand won.'

Minju raked his fingers through his hair, frustrated. 'No. I already told you. *No.*'

'You're really driving me nuts. Okay, fine. Six-fifty.'

The list price of a humanoid robot jockey was several million won. That was the list price, though. The second-hand market was a different story. Unlike some of the other robots, these jockeys were expendible, and they were generally retired in terrible condition. They fetched very low prices, not even a quarter of the list price, and anyway it was in fact illegal to resell them. The right thing to do was to return the jockeys to the manufacturing company, but the company didn't tend to accept robots that had so few salvageable parts. Most people claimed the jockeys were shattered beyond salvage, then sold them clandestinely to a third party. Yeonjae was aware of the second-hand market, which was why she was confidently quoting a price. When she was in junior high, she had, in fact, spent time browsing an illegal distribution site for humanoid robots.

Still, even if everyone else participated in the shady resale market, Minju didn't think it was right for him to enter into a transaction like that with a teenager. 'Woo Yeonjae,' Minju said sternly, trying to put a stop to the conversation.

Yeonjae didn't even pretend to listen. 'Seven hundred.'

Minju didn't answer.

'Ugh, seriously? Eight.'

'Give me a second, then.' Minju excused himself to make a call.

Yeonjae smiled victoriously, but it was too soon to celebrate. Even if Minju agreed to it, he still faced the hurdle of getting his supervisor to sign off on the deal. She kept her back straight to remain alert. Even if they said no, she refused to give up so quickly. Hadn't she managed to finagle a job at that convenience store? She *had* to have that jockey, that half-broken robot just waiting to be scrapped. No matter what.

The jockey had taken up all the space in her head. It had chased away sleep overnight. She could not give up on getting her hands on it.

Minju finished his call and returned. 'Hey, Yeonjae?'

'What?'

'Did you bring something to cart it home?'

BOGYEONG

Bogyeong had inherited her cooking skills entirely from her mother, rather than absorbing tricks and tips from other sources. Her tastebuds were honed by what she ate growing up, so the food she cooked turned out just like the dishes from her childhood. Her mother was as generous as she was talented, always making extra portions to share with others in their apartment building. Her mother was the reason Bogyeong spent every elevator ride smiling and chatting with the neighbours. Bogyeong's mother was the kind of person who knew her neighbours intimately. To Bogyeong, it was a burden to be known as her mother's daughter. She couldn't slump or look bored. She had to stand ramrod straight and wear a nice smile on her face so that it reflected well on her mother. Bogyeong vowed that, if she ever had kids, she would make sure to keep them entirely separate from herself.

Later, when she signed up for acting classes instead of heading to college, Bogyeong wondered if the close neighbourly relationships she had formed in her youth had drawn her down this path. *Everyone around me loves me so much, so why wouldn't I be loved by even more people?*

She passed screen tests and devoted herself to voice and acting lessons. It must have been difficult for her single mother to cover the sizeable tuition fees with the pay she got from her job in a bank, but she wasn't one to complain about finances, which made it easier for Bogyeong to place the bills confidently on the kitchen table.

Unfortunately, her mother's tenure at the bank coincided precisely with the time when humanoid robots became widespread. Her mother hadn't been worried initially. When they watched the TV news together, her mother would say the technology was still far off from becoming a part of their daily lives, regardless of how much it had advanced. Her blithe disdain ended when she was pushed unceremoniously out of the workforce without much of a safety net. Her mother couldn't compete with a robot that completed the same work without a single error. The bank gathered the employees together and offered them new positions selling insurance products. Though her mother could make anyone fall in love with her cooking, she didn't have the gift of persuasion.

She would have been more effective if she'd cooked for potential clients, promising to make them a dish if they purchased an insurance product. Eventually, her mother got a loan, added it to her severance pay, and opened a neighbourhood restaurant specializing in chicken dishes.

Her mother's conclusion from this experience was that a second act in life could fall into your lap out of the blue, but Bogyeong's take was that her mother's refusal to get with the times had caused this forced pivot. Her mother had been too complacent, assuming that the robots suddenly multiplying everywhere would not affect her. That mistaken arrogance had been the seed of her downfall. Thankfully none of this was applicable to Bogyeong's own chosen career. Even if these robots became advanced beyond imagination, she was sure nobody would watch a show with a cast of machines.

Then, a gust entirely separate from the headwinds of the time blew her into an abyss.

A friend introduced Bogyeong to an acting studio, located in the basement of an ancient building, where any noise could be contained more effectively. The friend had thumped on a pillar, sending dust into the air, while sharing facts about how concrete was good for two hundred years. Tons of actors who'd studied here had found success, said her friend. *That's why it's in the basement. You have to put your roots down here so you can bloom above ground, like a plant.* To Bogyeong, this sounded like a killer line in a script. Sure, her mother had to leave her banking job to open a faltering restaurant, but these highs and lows would be perfect content for a backstory once Bogyeong made it as an actress.

Three years later, on Christmas Day, the studio went up in flames. Bogyeong had not yet made a real splash, but she had starred in a few short films by a female director, and a magazine had declared her a star. By that time, she had developed something of an ego, and she even turned down a part in a male director's film because she didn't love the story. She didn't want to be tainted by work she didn't feel passionate about, preferring to allow her career choices to come together in a beautiful narrative.

Nothing had seemed amiss the day the studio caught fire – she was scheduled to start a fantastic role in the New Year as a detective in a TV series. She was already dreaming about the future – with the money she would soon be earning, she would upgrade from this shitty basement studio and join one with a view of the river.

That day, Bogyeong found herself unable to breathe. She felt dizzy even though she was sitting still. Was she intoxicated by her own burgeoning success? Only after the building exploded did she realize that her lightheadedness had been caused by a gas leak. But it was too late. The hundred-year-old concrete crumbled like a cookie, burying Bogyeong two storeys below ground. She had been unable to turn her face away from the explosion and ended up with severe burns. For three entire days, she was buried in the basement, unable to move.

The day after the explosion, a leech-like Darpa made its way down to where she was. As it scanned for survivors, it detected Bogyeong and transmitted her location to the rescue workers above ground. Their computer recorded the urgency of her condition – her body temperature was too low at only 35 degrees, her right leg was seriously injured, and her seventh and eighth right ribs were fractured. The rubble of the old building was as precarious as a Jenga tower, likely to shift and collapse at the slightest breeze. Heavy snowfall hindered the rescue operation. The chances of Bogyeong's survival ticked down in real time. Her mother closed up the restaurant and anxiously waited to hear about her daughter's fate.

The rescue workers managed to squeeze a carbon-fibre airbag under the tangle of rebar and inflate it. By now, three days had passed since the explosion. Bogyeong's likelihood of survival had fallen to three per cent. She was unconscious at this point, unaware that the rubble pinning her legs down had been lifted off. A firefighter tried to go down into the basement but the snowfall turned heavy. The rebar balancing on the airbag appeared about to slide, made slippery by the snow. At that point, the Darpa had moved in to stop the firefighter.

The likelihood of her survival is currently at three per cent but in twenty seconds will fall to zero per cent. There is an eighty-eight per cent chance that the rebar will slide off the airbag. If you descend now you will be in mortal danger.

The firefighter chose to ignore the Darpa's advice and went in, gathering Bogyeong into his arms. Just as the Darpa had predicted, twenty seconds later, the rebar slid off the airbag and Bogyeong drew her last breath. The firefighter had somehow escaped certain death. Emergency technicians administered CPR on Bogyeong, watching as her chance of survival went up from zero per cent to ten, then to ninety. The Darpa had neglected to account for the fact that, sometimes, a human stopped breathing but then came back to life.

Despite surgical intervention, Bogyeong's face was severely disfigured. She was dropped from the TV series. Even if she were to partially recover her looks, the producers said, they didn't have time to wait. Bogyeong fell into a deep depression. Her mother came to the hospital every morning with new, freshly made banchan, but Bogyeong didn't bother opening the containers. She stayed in bed all day; she stared out of the window all night. She didn't bother agonizing over the fact that her life had hit rock bottom. She knew she was alive only by the pain that radiated from her ribs with every breath she took. She thought about one thing and one thing only: how could she end her life?

A week after landing in hospital, she met the firefighter.

When he came by to check in on her she almost sent him packing, but couldn't bring herself to be so cruel to the person to whom she owed her life. She checked her reflection in the mirror, smoothing baby hairs and applying lip balm. But, when she laid eyes on him, she instantly regretted not trying harder. She had unexpectedly rediscovered her purpose for staying alive.

Falling in love is a given when two beautiful people meet over a dramatic near-death accident. The firefighter visited every chance he got. Bogyeong started waking up early to dampen and smooth her hair. Waiting for someone to visit made her days speed by.

The doctors grafted the tender skin from the inside of her thigh on to her face. With makeup it was barely noticeable, but she didn't go out of her way to cover up the scar. She didn't want to live her life concealing a scar she couldn't do anything about, and, more importantly, she no longer felt self-conscious with the firefighter by her side. She felt comfortable around this good man whom she had met at the lowest point of her life, when she was stuck two storeys below ground.

The firefighter popped the question. Admiring the new ring on her finger, Bogyeong asked, 'So why did you save me? Your own life was at risk.'

'Because there was a chance you would survive.'

'But it was only a three per cent chance.'

'Well, people aren't machines. It's not like we power off and that's it. A three per cent chance meant you could still make it.'

After their wedding, Bogyeong's life unspooled in an entirely different direction from what she had imagined. She still held fast to her dream of acting but she didn't feel pressed to pursue it. She was happy and fulfilled just to be adored by one man rather than the masses.

Bogyeong used her film experience to land a job in story development at a web fiction publisher. It was gruelling work but she liked the people; they didn't enforce late nights at the office or require attendance at work dinners. And, as time passed, her interest turned more towards writing, and she found herself going home after work to sit in front of her computer, though she never did manage to write a single word. She couldn't help but feel that everything she wanted to write was much too abstract.

For the first time in her life, Bogyeong went to a fortune-teller and paid for a talisman that promised to ward off misfortune. She tucked it under the firefighter's pillow. She had never been all that superstitious, but, as the years went by, she was increasingly willing to do anything at all to protect their happy life. It never left Bogyeong's mind that anyone else would have heeded that three per cent chance of survival and given up too quickly. An ambient worry hung in the back of her consciousness that something bad might also come for the firefighter one day.

Eunhye was born four years into their marriage, and Yeonjae came along two years later. Eunhye caught polio the year she turned five, which paralysed her hands and her feet. Despite continuous treatment she was diagnosed with spinal infantile paralysis and eventually lost the use of her legs. The doctor reassured them that, when Eunhye was old enough, they could make her legs out of biocompatible materials that closely mimicked human bones and joints. As there was no mention of price, Bogyeong foolishly assumed this was a procedure anyone could get at a low cost.

Bogyeong quit her job to take care of Eunhye. The firefighter offered to be the stay-at-home parent, but Bogyeong told him she didn't really like her job anyway and could use a break.

The day they got Eunhye her first wheelchair, the firefighter brought home a tricycle for Yeonjae. After an hour-long lecture on safety, the girls were allowed to race along the paths at Hangang Park.

Bogyeong's mother passed away around this time. She had undergone surgery three years earlier to remove early-stage breast cancer cells, but the disease had roared back and spread uncontrollably, metastasizing to her brain. The doctor mentioned they could attempt nanobot surgery but emphasized that it would be unlikely for her to be fully cured, as the folds in her brain were riddled with late-stage cancer; the cost of the procedure would also be astronomical. Her mother immediately declined treatment. She didn't think she would live long enough to survive a second battle with cancer. Bogyeong respected her mother's wishes and didn't go out of her way to convince her otherwise.

Her mother closed the restaurant. After running the business for over ten years, she wound it down quickly, tidily and now had just enough money to pay for her own funeral. People seemed to presume that every mother–daughter pair enjoyed a strong bond, but Bogyeong's relationship with her mother wasn't like that. Bogyeong remained calm as her mother's health declined, but a huge lump did form in her throat when her mother gripped her hand to say, 'I'm so grateful that you didn't die in that studio of yours back then. I would have been devastated.'

That three per cent chance of survival Bogyeong had that day, protected so assiduously by the firefighter, ended up containing so much of her life. As they stood by the river, gazing at the setting sun while the girls zoomed around on their wheels, Bogyeong told him she hoped their girls would keep moving forward, no matter what. Even if their lives swerved off course, even if they crashed into a wall, she wanted them to pick themselves up. Even if they had just one per cent of hope, that would be powerful enough to flip any narrative.

On that fateful day, the firefighter had an eighty per cent chance of survival.

A gas explosion had caused a fire to break out at a sixty-storey luxury hotel, which started collapsing. There hadn't been a drop of rain for months, and embers scattered rapidly in the dry air. Flames engulfed the hotel and the neighbouring buildings. Within ten minutes, an ambulance, a fire engine, and the fire department's helicopter were on the scene.

A Darpa fleet entered the building first to transmit survivor locations to the command centre outside. But gas was still leaking, triggering continual explosions throughout the building. The blaze was headed to the fourth-floor kitchen, towards a room containing supplies of gas. It was a true inferno. When she heard about the disaster, Bogyeong rushed to the command centre and, with a fire department employee, checked on her husband's chance of survival. They watched as the blue light hovered between eighty and ninety per cent. That quelled her nerves, but she still prayed for the fire to be brought under control quickly. Suddenly, in less than ten seconds, the light dropped precipitously to zero per cent. It was like she was watching him fall off a building.

Bogyeong was convinced that the machine had malfunctioned. But then she was taken to see the firefighter's body. He had died of smoke inhalation, his charred uniform melted into his body.

His uniform had been too old.

When the fire department had earmarked a substantial

part of the budget to acquire two hundred and ten Darpa to assist with rescue operations, the officials had claimed that uniforms were not yet in need of replacement. The rank-and-file had groused among themselves that the powers-that-be were focused solely on robots, leaving no room in the budget to upgrade anything else. Units were reassured that all equipment would soon be upgraded, but no such upgrade had happened.

His gloves were burned into his flesh and couldn't be peeled off. Bogyeong brought the firefighter's disintegrated hand to her cheek, just as he had caressed her burned face years before.

'I only had a three per cent chance,' she cried. 'You had eighty! Why couldn't you survive? What are you doing, lying here like this?'

Bogyeong's grief-stricken attempts at CPR, pressing so forcefully on his chest that she almost broke his ribs, failed to revive him; his body was too charred and his lungs were filled with too much ash.

The firefighter's life insurance was paid out. Bogyeong had to find work, but nobody was interested in hiring her. Should she get back in touch with her former colleagues? She couldn't bring herself to pick up the phone. How would she raise the girls? All by herself? Bogyeong had survived her own brush with death despite that three per cent chance, and now she was responsible for them all, lives that added up to three hundred per cent.

Bogyeong went straight to the bank and asked how she could use the life insurance payout to support what remained of her family. The robot now doing her mother's old job suggested she open a restaurant. The robot had crunched Bogyeong's data and learned that her mother had run a stable business, a restaurant with a dedicated customer base. It determined that opening a restaurant would be a good choice for Bogyeong, too.

Now, after a detour down a long, meandering path, she had returned to where she'd started, back to her mother's recipes. Bogyeong heard from a real estate agent that the racecourse in Gwacheon was being revitalized, so she took over a nearby restaurant that was on the verge of closing. She didn't have to sink too much money into setting up her business. She built a house behind the restaurant; they would put down roots in this new neighbourhood. She didn't need to learn how to cook; she just had to trust her tongue in order to make food that tasted like her mother's. The restaurant wasn't well-known enough to be featured on TV, but people in the know started coming specifically for her chicken dishes.

This was where Bogyeong felt she was supposed to be. At her restaurant. She didn't wish for anything else. She just harboured a deep hatred for those robots that were supposedly revolutionizing society. She didn't want them in any part of her life.

When the girls were young, Bogyeong had noticed that

Yeonjae was interested in robotics and seemed to have a talent for it. But she didn't make a big deal out of it. She had been secretly relieved when Yeonjae hadn't landed that coveted position on the soft robotics research project last year. Bogyeong knew that robots enriched people's lives; she couldn't really articulate why she hated them so intensely. She was satisfied with her life, despite barely making ends meet. She just wanted to enjoy the days stretching out before her without calculating or predicting the probability of death.

At least, that had been the plan – until Yeonjae brought home a mangled robot jockey.

'I must be losing my mind.' Bogyeong stood in the restaurant kitchen, a hand on her forehead. Where in the world was the brown sugar she'd had delivered last week? It wasn't in the pantry. She knew a fifteen-kilo sack of sugar couldn't be hiding in some nook, but she still took off her apron to kneel on the floor, squinting beneath the cabinets.

She stood back up and brushed off her hands. Doubting her own memory, she even took out the ledger. Brown sugar was listed among last week's purchases. How could only the brown sugar be missing? It wasn't as though someone would break in just to carry off that one sack. She sat in the corner, trying to remember what had happened last Tuesday when she got the delivery. She had put in an order that morning. It had arrived around three in the afternoon. She had put the box in the kitchen. Did she immediately put everything away? On any other day she would have, but then she remembered the phone had rung. She opened the ledger again. On Tuesday afternoon, someone had called to make a reservation for a big group of ten, for samgyetang. They wanted to come in that very day at five o'clock, so immediately after hanging up she had started preparing ten portions. *That's right.* She had left the box there for a while, and Yeonjae had put everything away when she came home from school. Bogyeong's memory unknotted. She even remembered that she had been busy cleaning up after the lunch rush when Yeonjae said, 'The drawer's full so I'm taking this out.'

Bogyeong brightened and headed outside to the shed, which was too low for an adult to stand upright inside but wide enough to fit three bikes side by side. When they'd first moved in she hadn't torn it down, as it had been in decent condition, requiring only a fresh coat of paint. Though she never did get around to painting it, the shed was the perfect spot to store the girls' scooters and roller skates. It was even better as a place to keep dry goods. Stored food rarely spilled over into the shed, since Bogyeong was always exact in her calculations and tended to order the perfect amount each time, but Yeonjae probably hadn't organized the kitchen drawers well enough to make room for the sugar.

Bogyeong hadn't been out back in a while. She saw the cart handle jutting awkwardly out of the shed but didn't pay it any mind as she swung open the doors.

Before her eyes had even landed on the sack of brown sugar, she jumped and backed away, snatched a shovel from just inside the shed and held it up, on guard. She stared at the thing – the robot – lying in the cart.

She knew it was powered off. It was only a tin can, really. Still, she kept her grip tight. She crept up to it and tapped it gingerly with the shovel. One arm dropped limply off the side and dangled in the air.

What in the world is a robot doing in my shed?

'Oh! Did you see it?' Yeonjae, who had just come home from school, ran over and tried to shut the doors.

Relief and anxiety swept over Bogyeong. She glared at Yeonjae. 'What is that? Get rid of it. *Now.*'

'No.'

'No?'

'No.'

'Woo Yeonjae!'

'What do you care?'

Bogyeong lunged at Yeonjae, who was walking away. Her daughter shook her off, then turned around.

'Where did you get that from? What are you doing with

it?' Bogyeong was trying her best to remain calm, but her words came out barbed.

Yeonjae didn't answer, as though she knew that silence would cut more deeply.

Bogyeong didn't know how to make her talk. If only Yeonjae would try to explain herself so Bogyeong could understand. But Yeonjae just stared sullenly at her.

'You have until tomorrow to get rid of it,' Bogyeong warned. 'It's not safe . . .'

'I'll figure it out. Leave me alone.' Yeonjae looked dismissively at Bogyeong and stalked away.

Bogyeong got the feeling that they would be locked in battle over the robot for a long time.

She sighed, then filled a spray bottle with diluted bleach and spritzed the solution on the outdoor tables. She sprayed down all ten tables then used a bucket to throw water on them. She scrubbed with a rag, ruminating over Yeonjae's sulky expression.

Eunhye came out to cheer Bogyeong up. 'She spent her entire final pay cheque on it,' Eunhye explained. 'You know she won't take it back even if you insist. I wouldn't bother picking a fight over it.'

None of this was any reassurance to Bogyeong. 'Why didn't you stop her?' she shot back at Eunhye, even though she knew it wasn't her eldest daughter's fault.

Eunhye pursed her lips and thought for a moment. 'Well. It was the first time I saw her want anything that badly.'

Bogyeong gave up, defeated. Eunhye was right. Yeonjae rarely expressed her true feelings. Maybe it was because everyone's attention was, and always had been, focused on Eunhye. Yeonjae was the kind of kid who took a long time to mull over the simple question of what she wanted for her birthday before saying she didn't want anything. Years ago, robots had kicked Bogyeong's mother out of the bank, seemingly out of the blue. Now, her own daughter had brought home a broken robot. Bogyeong felt adrift, unable to decipher what was happening before her own eyes even though they were wide open. She felt a pang of loss, as if something had been wrenched away. She felt discarded, even though she hadn't been. This was how she always felt whenever she saw a robot.

She kept scrubbing at the tables. What was Yeonjae going to do with that broken robot? Should she report it somewhere? But then, would Yeonjae get in trouble? She wouldn't let Yeonjae get away with this. She couldn't.

EUNHYE

'Why do you want it, anyway?' asked Minju.

'So I can try to fix it,' Yeonjae insisted. 'I told you I'd buy it from you. Do I really need to go into why? Obviously I'm not going to try to make some lethal weapon out of it. And I'm not asking you to give it to me for free. You know, you could have just told your boss that you donated it to a high school student who's interested in research.'

Eunhye watched from the sidelines as Yeonjae peppered Minju with arguments, bulldozing his defences. Eunhye knew nobody could stop her sister when she was this focused and serious.

In the end, Minju went inside to give his boss a call. Yeonjae waited impatiently, her arms crossed over her chest.

Eunhye wondered why Yeonjae was so hell-bent on buying this mangled jockey. Yeonjae jiggled her leg. This was very uncharacteristic of her; she usually navigated life unruffled, indifferent.

'Hey, Yeonjae,' Eunhye called.

'What?' Yeonjae didn't bother glancing over as she gnawed on her nails.

'Never mind.'

Yeonjae didn't seem to hear her. Eunhye decided she wouldn't pry. Sometimes a person was magnetically drawn to something, whether it was another person, love, music, or an object. Nothing could block a pull that strong. Yeonjae must have felt an attraction so powerful that she was willing to sink her entire final pay cheque into it.

Minju didn't come out for a long time. When he finally did, he looked exhausted. Maybe his boss had harangued him the entire time. He held out a slip of paper with a bank account number written on it, and asked if Yeonjae had brought anything to transport the robot home.

'It's actually illegal for us to sell a jockey,' Minju reminded her. 'If either party is caught we'll both be subject to a fine. So don't go around telling people. Go ahead and send eight hundred thousand won to this account. I tried to cut you a deal but the old man is dead set on this price.'

'I know, I know.'

Minju looked pained to be selling the robot at all, but Yeonjae quickly went on her phone to transfer the funds before he could change his mind.

Minju pointed at the pushcart. 'That's how you're taking it home?'

Yeonjae nodded.

Minju squinted. 'Is it big enough? Well, I guess we'll find out. Bring it in.'

Yeonjae dragged the cart into the stables. It was as big as her, and the rusted handle and wheels squeaked in protest, but her face had split into a wide grin. Eunhye glanced around. For some reason she felt like the lookout for a black-market deal.

As Minju had mentioned, it was indeed illegal to buy or sell humanoid robots on the second-hand market. But we Koreans are incredibly skilled at illegally buying and selling things, Eunhye thought. Robots circulating in the resale market were upcycled or used as decoration on cars and motorcycles. The authorities claimed to enforce the law but they had gone after only a handful of illegal sellers and buyers, and robots continued to flood the market. The practice was so prevalent that nobody believed it could ever be stamped out. Laws didn't always become more draconian when certain acts became more common; instead, everyone gave up on doing anything about it. Eunhye was well-acquainted with this tendency to give up. She dealt with it every day; everyone had stopped trying to improve access for wheelchairs because there were so many places where it was too difficult.

Yeonjae appeared in the doorway of the stables, pulling

the cart with the robot in it, grinning victoriously like a miner who has struck gold. Eunhye couldn't remember the last time Yeonjae was this happy, though her sister must have experienced moments of joy that Eunhye wasn't privy to. Eunhye didn't know about all the moments Yeonjae had been happy. How could she, when Yeonjae never told her anything?

'What are you going to tell Mom?' Eunhye asked, following Yeonjae out.

The cart looked cumbersome to manoeuvre, but the robot itself didn't weigh much. Yeonjae's footsteps had a bounce to them.

'I'll come up with something on the way home,' Yeonjae said airily.

Eunhye started coming to the racetrack four years ago. Every Sunday, crowds began to descend on their neighbourhood, and from her bedroom window Eunhye would watch the track glowing like a circus. She wanted to go, too. But Sunday was her mother's busiest day at the restaurant, and Yeonjae was usually out. It was too hard to get to the racetrack on her own. She didn't know how long it would take her, what dangers she might face, what humiliations she might have to suffer. She needed to mentally prepare herself for the journey. For Eunhye, the outside world was a video game where she was on survival mode with a terrain that changed on a whim. The majority of the campaigns involved dealing with people staring at her. The game environment was all the stores she couldn't navigate with her wheelchair. She had snacks and water in her bag to restore her HP.

Electric wheelchairs were too pricey for what they could do; after all, they could never overcome their inherent limitations. Her mother thought they were actually more dangerous, as electric wheelchairs were required to travel in the road instead of on the pavement. She was outraged that there still wasn't a network of wheelchair-only paths. Even the few that existed were all really just regular streets with a line painted along the side.

When she was young, Eunhye had simply assumed she would one day get mechanical legs. Half her body would be a machine. At one point she'd thought it would be cool to be a cyborg. But, when she was six, her dad passed away. Her mother was overwhelmed and distracted, running a small restaurant, trying to figure out how to iron the wrinkles out of their lives. For her next birthday, Eunhye got a chocolate cake and a pretty winter sweater. Her mother noticed she wasn't smiling and asked if there was something else she wanted, but Eunhye just said she wanted more cake. Eunhye knew without having to be told that she had to stick it out with what she had a little longer.

Eunhye wouldn't need to be a cyborg if the world just treated her like it did everyone else. What she needed more than ten-million-won mechanical legs were gentle inclines that helped her roll up on to the pavement, lifts that took her into a store, more time at pedestrian crossings, and a safer way for her to take the bus and underground without having to depend on anyone. She didn't need a humanoid robot to push her wheelchair. And she didn't actually *want* to be a cyborg. But the world would have to change radically for her to live the way she wanted to. Because, from the majority's perspective, these were all things to be shifted on to her to figure out. Eunhye couldn't figure it all out by herself, though. In her day-to-day life, she had more in common with a young child who couldn't go anywhere without an adult. She always needed to have someone with her who could compensate for what she couldn't navigate on her own. This was what others believed about her: that she needed protection.

One day, four years ago, instead of looking on from home, Eunhye had suddenly wheeled herself out to the streets. Yeonjae had suggested they go to the racetrack together, telling Eunhye that she wouldn't be home late. But she was. Eunhye couldn't wait forever. She didn't always want to wait around instead of doing what she felt like.

She left the house without telling her mother.

On race days, the racetrack beamed up a large, galloping holographic horse into the sky, which was visible from all around, so she would have no trouble finding her way. The roads, normally empty, were jammed with cars. People streamed by on the pavement, spilling into the street. She followed the crowd without thinking, but then a car honked right by her ear, making it ring; she felt momentarily faint. She would bring this entire area to a standstill if she kept going at her slow pace. She quickly rolled on to the dipped kerb. One of her wheels got stuck on a stone on the incline. Feeling panicked, she pushed with all her might and managed to make it up to the top. People wearing neon bracelets and headbands rushed past her. They zoomed by as fast as cars.

Suddenly nauseated, she wheeled around to head back home. She heard a loud bang, signalling the start of the race. *Come on, you're almost there, just a little further.* The starting gun beckoned her to the racetrack. She turned around again. She would get there, no matter what. Now that she had made that decision, she felt energized. She went up the small hill without anyone's help. But she was a minor, so she couldn't buy a ticket and go through the main entrance. Eunhye refused to give up. There was no such thing as a perfectly secure venue. There had to be a way to watch the race through a gap in a wall somewhere. She quickly discovered just such a spot.

Through the fringe trees, she could see the glowing track. The horses were in full flight down the turf. They were clad in hoods and blinkers of different colours. They streaked by. Eunhye paid no attention to the robot jockeys urging the horses forward, because she had eyes only for the animals. That was the day she became captivated by the horses, by their magnetism. A single second stretched out into a hundred frames. Flying manes and rolling muscles, white flower petals falling from the fringe trees and scattering in the breeze, the roar of the crowd – they all came together like an Impressionist painting and took hold of her. Since that day, every time she closed her eyes, she dreamed of horses galloping down the track.

Yeonjae brazenly lugged the jockey into the house. Eunhye wanted to see what Yeonjae was going to do with it. Yeonjae didn't head to her bedroom on the ground floor, but went upstairs to the spare room. Eunhye watched as her sister climbed the stairs, then went outside. Her mother had finished her work for the night and was sitting at a table, her swollen feet propped up, eating a Melona ice cream bar. Bogyeong had tried her best to look the other way as Yeonjae brought the robot in; she was biding her time. It wasn't every day that Yeonjae wanted something desperately enough to spend all her money on it.

The weather forecast had predicted a significant amount of rainfall that night. Right on cue, it began to drizzle. Rain pattered on the patio umbrellas. Eunhye approached and her mother handed her the rest of her Melona.

Eunhye took a bite and handed it back.

'What in the world is your sister up to?' her mother asked, as though it were customary for them to talk behind another family member's back. The refreshing scent of the Melona bar perfumed her every word.

Eunhye shrugged.

In a single large bite, her mother ate the rest of the ice cream, then waggled the stick between her fingers. She looked preoccupied. Or maybe she wasn't thinking about anything at all. Once the ice cream had melted in her mouth, her mother spoke again, jumping to another topic. Familial conversations at their best, with no continuity or flow.

'Next month will be the anniversary of your dad's passing. Time really flies. A year feels like a single day. It's just rushing by, isn't it?' She shot Eunhye a loaded look. 'And what are you doing at the racetrack? Why are you there so often? Did the two of you bury money there or something?'

'What are you talking about?'

'You're not betting on the horses, are you?'

'Mom. Be serious.'

'You're right. That doesn't make sense.'

I go there for a horse. Her name is Today. She was a champion but now her legs are destroyed, so she can't race any more. Eunhye was able to form those sentences perfectly in her head but outwardly just grumbled. 'It's not like there's anything else to do around here.'

'Oh my god, are you kidding? You can go to the science centre, and the Grand Park is just there, too. I don't like that you keep heading to the racetrack. It's not appropriate for you girls.'

'Hey, Mom, why don't *you* place some bets?' Eunhye suggested brightly. 'I heard tons of people are getting rich.'

'I don't know anything about that stuff. You're not really gambling, right?'

'I'm telling you. These days they calculate the odds of who might win. They do all that for you. If you just go by the odds you won't lose.' Eunhye thought this might pique her mother's interest, since Bogyeong was often swayed by what other people told her. She was angling to convince her mother to take her to a race.

But her mother shook her head. 'I don't believe in odds like that.' She got up and changed the subject once again. 'I hope the air quality won't be too bad next spring. If it's nice we should go see the cherry blossom and spend the whole day outside.' She stretched her arms above her head and, instead of taking her apron off for the night, went back into the kitchen to make stock for the following day.

Eunhye picked up the ice cream stick her mother had accidentally dropped. She lingered for a while, enjoying the summer weather maturing into fall.

She didn't linger because she wanted to. It was just the only place she could simply *be*, for as long as she wanted.

YEONJAE

Yeonjae had assumed the robot jockey had fallen off the horse because its gyro sensor was faulty, causing it to lose its balance. But there was nothing wrong with the sensor.

'Then why did you fall off?' Yeonjae muttered to herself. She stretched and sat up straight.

Other than a few hours of restless sleep the previous night, Yeonjae had spent the rest of her time at home staring at the robot. Weirdly, her back didn't ache. Her eyes were heavy from lack of sleep but it was now Monday morning and she had to go to school in a few hours. She had examined every little part for the past nine hours and drawn a blueprint, since she didn't have access to the original. Once she had completed the drawing, she had immediately opened up the gyro sensor and the control system.

Her eyelids felt like sandpaper, impossible to prop open.

If only she could lubricate them with oil or something. Not that she would spray oil into her eyes. She rubbed her hands together and pressed her warmed palms on her eyes. Her body screamed, begging to lie down. She couldn't give in to that urge, but neither did she have the energy to resist. She collapsed on to her back next to the robot, her unlined spiral notebook in hand.

She looked at a page which she had filled with a dense tangle of lines and numbers. The robot's controller and memory were fine, too. All the parts dictating the robot's judgement and balance were in good working order. So it couldn't have been a mechanical defect that caused the robot to fall off. She turned her head to look at the robot quizzically. Its helmet was all scratched from being dragged along the turf.

'I really can't figure you out,' she said.

The robot didn't react. It was still powered off.

'Why would you look up? Why did you fall off?'

Yeonjae lay back again, puzzling over why a humanoid robot would look up at the sky. Would it have had some kind of expression on its face? It didn't have eyebrows or facial muscles, so she supposed it couldn't have displayed any facial movement that might be interpreted as an expression. For some reason, though, she had a sneaking suspicion that this robot had glanced up at the sky with a surprised look on its face. With its nonexistent eyebrows shooting up in awe.

She wanted to turn the robot on to ask it all kinds of questions, but her phone alarm went off. She sat up, covered the robot with a blanket she'd brought from downstairs, and left, closing the door behind her. She paused, then went back in to check that the robot was still there.

Yeonjae brushed her teeth in the shower and skipped breakfast. She pulled on her school uniform, found her mom and sister at the breakfast table, and sternly instructed them that they were forbidden to go poking around on the first floor while she was at school. She headed out. She practically skipped to school, not because she was looking forward to a day of learning but because she could come home to work on the robot again as soon as she got through her classes. She would have to reconstruct its crushed pelvis and legs. Carbon fibre would be ideal, but if she couldn't manage to get her hands on any, she could get pretty close with aluminium. It would be much heavier than lighter-than-plastic carbon fibre, but now that the robot wouldn't need to ride a horse any more, it didn't need to be that light.

The first time Yeonjae ever saw an autonomous robot was on a rainy day, after school. She was nine, maybe ten. After all the other kids had gone home, she had stood in front of the school gates, alone. She couldn't find the umbrella she could have sworn she had put in her bag that morning. She might have called her mom to come pick her up, but she knew there was a big group reservation for that evening. Her mom might be too busy to even pick up the phone.

Yeonjae decided to shield her head with her bag and run home. At the corner she bumped into a four-legged robot. It looked around like a stray dog before halting in front of her. It was all wet. Would it short out in the rain? Yeonjae took her coat off and draped it over the robot's head. A green light on its face blinked, then it knelt before her. Was it telling her to hop on? She wasn't sure. The robot dog didn't move, so Yeonjae sat gingerly on its hard back and told it where she wanted to go. She clung to its exoskeleton. The robot began running through the rain. The ride was a bit bumpy. Through her palms and legs, she could feel the engine humming against the steady rhythm of the hydraulic system. This robot dog was alive. It didn't breathe like she did, but it didn't seem any different from other life forms on Earth. They eventually stopped at an empty lot close to her house. It lowered itself to the ground and Yeonjae slid off. She took her coat off the dog's head. How was this moving exoskeleton made? She wanted to dig into it. But what if she hurt it?

Even today, Yeonjae wasn't exactly sure what that robot dog had been for. Judging solely from its appearance, it might have been some sort of Darpa. After all, heavy rains had flooded Makgyecheon Stream that day, causing all manner of things to be carried away in the swollen creek. They might have needed the Darpa for rescue operations.

At school, Yeonjae sat down and pulled out her notebook to sketch a plan. She didn't have most of the parts she would need to reassemble the robot. She could tell she would be spending hours going from hardware store to dump and back. At least she could salvage a bunch of things from the dump by the racetrack. She was so engrossed in her drawing that she didn't notice Jisu standing in front of her until she aimed gentle kicks at the legs of her desk.

Yeonjae put her notebook down and looked up.

Jisu cut straight to the chase. 'So have you thought about it?'

'Oh – no.'

Jisu crinkled her nose. She had proposed her idea the previous Friday, but Yeonjae had completely forgotten about it. Only when she saw Jisu's face did she remember. She had actually planned to give it some serious thought. But then the very next day she had been fired from her job, and then she had found the robot. All that had unceremoniously shoved Jisu's suggestion out of her brain.

Jisu placed both hands on the desk. 'It's not like you were busy studying over the weekend. I know you have a job.'

'I got fired on Saturday.' It wasn't Yeonjae's habit to bring conversations to a screeching halt, but she got a kick out of Jisu bristling and attempting to stay calm; she often found herself speaking curtly just to wind her up. Yeonjae could tell that Jisu was pissed off but trying her best not to blow up.

She dragged a chair over and sat down. 'Well, you can think about it now, then.' Jisu stabbed a finger at the desk to emphasize each question: 'Are you in? Or are you out?'

'I'm out.' Yeonjae wasn't trying to get a rise out of Jisu this time. She just didn't want to go in with Jisu.

'How come?'

'I don't want to do it with you.'

Jisu bit her lip.

Yeonjae regretted blurting that out. She should have been nicer. But she couldn't take back what had already tumbled out of her mouth. She noticed Jisu balling her fists. Was this girl going to punch her?

But Jisu recovered her cool and glared at Yeonjae. 'You don't have to say it in such a bitchy way.'

I could say the same about you, Yeonjae didn't say.

Jisu's angry gaze drifted down to Yeonjae's notebook. She snatched it out of Yeonjae's hands. 'Wait, so you're going to enter on your own? Are you serious?' A dumbfounded expression came over Jisu's face.

'It's for something else.' Yeonjae reached out for her notebook, but Jisu hid it behind her back.

'It is? What's it for, then? Isn't this a plan? For the competition?'

'The competition is all about Darpas. You can see my drawing has two legs.'

'Darpas, right,' Jisu murmured. It was as if she had forgotten that Darpas were four-legged robots.

Yeonjae held out her hand.

Jisu reluctantly gave the notebook back.

Last Friday, Jisu had told Yeonjae about a competition that was open to all high school students in the country. Students would develop the next generation of Darpas, designing and making soft robots that could rescue people in a disaster, or that would assist in everyday life. Jisu was interested in entering the competition for one reason and one reason only. Winning any of the prizes, even if it wasn't the grand prize, would give you a leg up on your college applications, and winners of one of the major awards would automatically be admitted to the prestigious Seoul National University, Pohang University of Science and Technology, or the Korea Advanced Institute of Science and Technology. Jisu had been transparent about her ambitions, telling Yeonjae, 'An award would look great on our college applications.' One thing Yeonjae didn't understand was why Jisu wanted to enter with *her*, of all people. When Yeonjae hadn't landed the soft robot research project last year, she had washed her hands of robotics, at least publicly. Robotics wasn't a field of study that you could just decide on a whim to embark on. Why would Jisu want to enter such a major competition with her? All Yeonjae did was nod off during coding class. Jisu's family was obviously well connected and presumably could easily find out everything they needed to know about her, but why would they waste their time looking into a random student's past scholarly interests? They had never even had a conversation that would have convinced Jisu that she would be a good fit for something like this.

A hierarchy existed in their classroom, even though it was tiny, with only twenty-one students. Jisu was at the top, having gone to an English-immersion kindergarten and spent all of junior high abroad, in Canada. Or was it Australia? Yeonjae, on the other hand . . . frankly, there was nothing impressive about her.

Yeonjae resented that everyone judged you based on what they knew about your family, and Jisu especially was the kind of girl who cared about everyone's status. Fundamental differences like these were set in stone and impossible to gloss over. Yeonjae knew all about Jisu. Well, no, she didn't know what Jisu's hobbies were or every little thing about her personality, but she had an inkling of what Jisu would do if Yeonjae remained uncooperative. Jisu would decide they weren't a good fit and go off to find someone in a similar social stratum. That wouldn't be the worst thing. She had no idea how Jisu had found out, but it was true that Yeonjae had been a robotics whiz. Jisu was just trying to get something she wanted, through Yeonjae. The real talent shared by the kids at the top was the ability to latch on to opportunities and never let them slip by.

'Why don't you want to enter?' Jisu wouldn't let it go. 'I said I'd pay for all the materials.'

'Because we're not friends.'

'Are you serious?' Jisu nearly yelled. She glanced around and hissed, 'Why does that matter? Friendship has nothing to do with this competition. You don't have to be besties to do this kind of thing together. I'm not asking you to go on a picnic with me, am I?'

'Don't they grade you on teamwork? How could we possibly get a decent score on teamwork when this is what we're like together? It's not going to work.'

Jisu let out a long sigh at Yeonjae's airtight defence. Her fists trembled. The bell was about to ring any minute now.

She'll give up now, Yeonjae thought smugly.

Jisu sucked in some air and exhaled, brushing her hair away from her forehead. 'So is this all because we're not that close?'

'What?'

'Fine. You'll see. I'm going to be the best friend you've ever had, starting now.' Jisu took out her cell phone and dialled. 'Mom? I'm not going to cram school today. Yeah. Because the girl I want to enter the competition with is being really difficult. It's so annoying. I'm going to have to work on her after school.' She hung up before Yeonjae could stop her.

'Hey!' Yeonjae protested.

'What?'

The bell rang before Yeonjae could say anything more.

'Wait for me after school, okay?' Jisu went back to her seat.

Yet another problem had landed on the heap of things Yeonjae needed to worry about. She let each side of her brain, left and right, take on a problem each. The robot, of course, which she had been obsessing about. And Jisu. There was no way in hell she was hanging out with Jisu after school.

Yeonjae knew she was pushing Jisu away more forcefully than was necessary. Maybe Jisu was nicer than she seemed. Maybe she wasn't like the other kids. But Yeonjae didn't want to waste her energy on the slim chance that she was wrong. Growing up meant realizing that other people's lives were different from yours, and it meant accepting and adapting to that fact. Sometimes that process was brutal. Which meant there was only one way for Yeonjae to deal with the situation she found herself in: get the hell out of there as soon as the final bell rang.

When she was younger, she didn't understand how her life was so different from her classmates'. They all went to the same school, wore the same uniforms, studied the same subjects. But at a certain point, she found the gap between her life and that of certain other kids to be unbridgeable. *My parents make money, my parents love me, we're the same age, so how is there such a big difference?* That question forced Yeonjae to enumerate on her fingers what she *didn't* have. But she eventually gave that up. There were so many things she didn't have that she ran out of digits. Like electronic devices, books, and clothes. At that age she didn't have a cell phone, a tablet, or a smart watch. It wasn't that she coveted them; she just hated having nothing to say when other kids asked, 'How come you don't have one?' She started telling her peers that she'd lost hers, but then, one night, she dreamed that an enormous hole opened up below her bed, sucking everything into it; she quickly stopped telling that particular tale. Eventually she stopped sharing any detail about her life. New items were continuously released into the world, all at different price points. Yeonjae couldn't tell if they were manufactured because people needed them, or if they became needed because they had been manufactured. So many things were produced in quick succession, with no regard for Yeonjae's questions. Only then did she begin to understand how such differences in lifestyle had been created in the first place. These fissures had gradually begun forming not in Yeonjae's lifetime, not even during her parents' childhoods, but even further back, when her grandparents were young. A gap that deep could never be bridged by Yeonjae alone.

After every period Jisu made her way over to Yeonjae,

and every time Yeonjae grabbed her notebook and pencil to flee into a bathroom stall. After third period, Jisu even followed her into the bathroom and kicked her door, yelling, 'How the hell can you possibly shit so much!' Yeonjae was undeterred; she spent all of lunch break in the stall, having run down to the store right before fifth period for a pastry that she ate for lunch.

As she ran out of the classroom with the pastry stuffed in her mouth, Yeonjae realized that Jisu didn't really have any friends, either. She saw Jisu sitting at her desk, all alone, her back and neck stiff as a rod, instead of heading to the cafeteria with everyone else. She looked . . . lonely.

Not that any of this was Yeonjae's business. As soon as the last bell rang, Yeonjae sprang up and sprinted outside. She knew nobody could beat her in a race. But technology triumphed over a mere human's speed; Jisu pulled up breezily beside her on her e-scooter.

'You could have just waited for me. Why did you exhaust yourself like that?' Jisu slowed down.

Yeonjae gave up. She trudged beside Jisu. Resisting would be futile.

'You're crazy fast, by the way,' Jisu remarked.

Yeonjae didn't bother responding.

'You don't look like it, but you're really good at a bunch of things. Except for school.'

'Sounds like an insult,' Yeonjae snapped.

'It is, duh. These days even being a good student isn't

enough, and you're good at everything *except* school. What are you going to do with your life?'

She was right. Yeonjae had nothing to say to that. Once upon a time, when she'd dreamed of becoming a robotics engineer, she had naively thought she just needed to know a lot about robots. Which wasn't entirely wrong. But she simply couldn't compete with kids who were mentored by famous professors abroad or had already written dissertations.

'So that's why we have to enter the competition together, as a team,' Jisu concluded. 'I really don't get why you're so against it. Why wouldn't you grab an opportunity that falls in your lap? Kids these days. No hustle.'

Yeonjae let Jisu rant. She couldn't care less. She didn't get this girl at all. Trying to talk to Jisu was like screaming at a brick wall.

Jisu stopped in front of a convenience store and asked Yeonjae to watch her scooter for a second. She came out with a fruit basket laden with Jeju-grown bananas and mangoes. She handed it to Yeonjae. 'I can't come to your house without a gift for your family.'

'Just full of empty formalities, aren't we?' Yeonjae said snarkily.

'This is called manners. What would you know, anyway?'

Yeonjae agonized all the way home. Should she say something to head off any potential rudeness Jisu might show when she learned that Yeonjae lived next to a restaurant and that her sister was in a wheelchair? While she dithered, they reached her house. She had failed to say anything. What did it matter anyway? If Jisu was going to judge her, what difference would it make if she said something in advance? Maybe, if Jisu was rude, that would be her chance to more easily distance herself from this girl.

Jisu parked her e-scooter by the outdoor tables. Yeonjae headed straight to the restaurant kitchen, which was fragrant with the rich broth that had been simmering overnight. Her mom looked brittle, exhausted, her hair twisted up and secured with pins. She must not have slept well last night.

'Mom,' Yeonjae said, figuring she'd better announce that she'd brought someone home.

Her mom bustled around without looking up. 'Dinner's almost ready.'

Jisu stepped into the kitchen and bowed. 'Hello, it's nice to meet you.'

Bogyeong whipped her head round, startled.

Jisu yanked the fruit basket out of Yeonjae's hands and placed it on the counter. 'This is for you,' she said with a smile on her face. Warm and polite, like a celebrity on camera.

Bogyeong stared at Jisu, disorientated. Yeonjae hadn't brought a friend home since she was very young. Feeling guilty that she couldn't actively participate in the school community like the other parents, Bogyeong had kept herself at a distance even when she was dying to know about her daughter's school life. Now, she wondered if the friend Yeonjae had brought home was a mere figment of her imagination. This girl seemed wholesome, without tons of piercings or a pack of cigarettes. Her uniform hadn't been altered to be tight and short. She was smiling earnestly, without a spot of makeup on her face. Bogyeong looked at Yeonjae and then back at her friend.

'My name is Seo Jisu. I'm in Yeonjae's class,' Jisu explained, perhaps thinking that Yeonjae's mom was reacting this way because she had never met her before.

Bogyeong came to her senses and hastily wiped her wet hands on her shirt. She began welcoming Jisu, when Yeonjae cut in and told her that they were going inside. If Yeonjae hadn't put a stop to Bogyeong's rambling, she might have launched into her daughter's life story right then and there. Thankfully Bogyeong got a grip on herself and told them she would bring in some of the fruit Jisu had brought. Yeonjae wanted to refuse, but she didn't want to discourage her mom's excitement. She knew she never talked about school, and even though she wasn't a parent, she could understand why a parent would be thrilled about this development. This was a first for both Yeonjae and her mom. Plus, she didn't want to snap at her mom in front of Jisu.

The girls headed out and crossed the yard towards the house.

Jisu trailed Yeonjae by a few steps. 'Why didn't you tell me?' She sounded put out. 'No wonder you didn't want me to come over.'

Annoyed, Yeonjae turned to face Jisu. She knew Jisu was going to say something about where they lived and she was ready to send Jisu packing.

But before Yeonjae could lay into her, Jisu said, 'Your mom is Haneul – no, that was the character's name. She's Kim Bogyeong, right? She was in that film, what was it called? I love that one. Hang on.' Jisu tugged on the ends of her hair, trying to remember.

Yeonjae didn't know what was happening. Her mom had never once told her she had been in a film. *Mom? In a movie?* It made no sense. Jisu must be confusing her mom with someone who looked like her, someone with a similar name.

But then Jisu looked it up on her phone and showed Yeonjae the cast list of a film she had never heard of, and at the very top was a photo of her young mom. This definitely wasn't an actress who resembled her mom or even a long-lost aunt she had never heard of. This *was* her mom, probably close to Yeonjae's age right now, maybe a few years older. At most in her early twenties. Gobsmacked, Yeonjae stared at the photo while Jisu went on and on. Yeonjae was frozen, discombobulated by her mom's secret past that had suddenly roared into view, as Jisu giggled and slapped her on the shoulder. Jisu nattered on, saying that her own mom loved this film so much that she had seen it a lot growing up, and how she always watched the movie when she was feeling down. None of what Jisu was saying registered in Yeonjae's ears.

Weirdly, Eunhye wasn't home. Eunhye was always there when Yeonjae returned from school. Yeonjae checked her mom's room, Eunhye's room, and her own before concluding that her sister was missing. Jisu stood patiently in the entryway, waiting for Yeonjae to invite her in, but gave up and stepped inside. Jisu sat down on the sofa and looked around. She found the remote and asked if she could turn on the TV.

Yeonjae nodded quickly, thinking that would be a good distraction.

'You still have a wall-mounted TV, huh?' Jisu remarked.

Yeonjae was about to tell her pointedly that there was no issue with the picture or the sound, but stopped herself. 'Help yourself when my mom brings the fruit. Watch whatever you want until I get back.'

'Why, where are you going?'

'Upstairs, just for a bit.'

Assuming that Yeonjae was going upstairs to change, Jisu turned her gaze to the TV. She wouldn't have let Yeonjae leave if she had known that Yeonjae would stay up there for an hour.

Fifteen minutes later, Bogyeong came in with a tray of

bananas and mangoes and two cold drinks. Jisu took it, blushing.

Bogyeong assumed that Jisu was very polite and shy. 'Where's Yeonjae?'

'She went upstairs for a minute.'

Bogyeong found it puzzling that Yeonjae had gone upstairs, knowing how Yeonjae tended to hole up until the following morning, but she presumed Yeonjae wouldn't be so rude when a friend was over.

Unfortunately both Bogyeong and Jisu had underestimated her. After finishing off the fruit and both drinks, Jisu sprawled on the sofa, flipping through the channels, looking for something to watch. She wondered if she should go upstairs; she was reaching the limits of her patience. Should she call Yeonjae? She didn't even have her number. Finally, around eight, Jisu got up. It was already way too late to be over at someone's house on a weekday. But she would get Yeonjae to agree to enter the competition with her before she left, no matter what.

She headed upstairs. There were no immediate neighbours surrounding the house and restaurant, so it was eerily silent and dark on the first floor. Jisu found herself clinging to the banister as she tiptoed up the stairs to the landing. She saw light behind a closed door. Someone was talking in the room. Though a part of her worried that it might be Yeonjae's sibling or father, she headed straight to the door. Where else would Yeonjae be? It was pitch black everywhere else. Jisu heard Yeonjae's voice on the other side of the door. She yanked it open.

'Hello.'

Jisu screamed. Though she had no talent for robotics, she had grown up around robots, her father being the head of a small robotic parts supplier. Thirty units of domestic humanoid robots had been distributed to select households as part of a pilot programme before going on the market, and Jisu's family was one of them. All of this to say: Jisu wasn't a technological novice whose mouth would drop open when she encountered a new type of robot, or who would run away in fear. But anyone would scream if an old, banged-up robot with a helmet for a head, so old that it was practically an antique, suddenly spoke to them, especially in a house that didn't even have a robot vacuum. Though not everyone would have tripped on the door sill and fallen on their ass.

Jisu rubbed her tailbone. 'Shit, that fucking hurt.'

Yeonjae ran out of the room and closed the door behind her. Flicking on the lights, she discovered Jisu on the floor. A surprised look flashed across her face. 'What's going on? What are you doing up here?'

Jisu stood up, still rubbing her tailbone. 'Open up.' She didn't bother smoothing her hair down.

'No.'

'No? Then I will.' Jisu reached for the doorknob.

Yeonjae didn't miss a beat. She grabbed Jisu around the waist and dragged her away from the door. Jisu slipped out of Yeonjae's grasp and darted towards the door, the momentum causing her to topple into the room. She landed on her knees. Her eyes met the robot's. This robot had no legs. Jisu froze. Only her eyes moved, blinking. The robot's eyeholes were directed squarely at Jisu.

The robot sensed the heat emanating from Jisu's knees, which were already bruising. 'Your knees are warm. You should spray them with liquid nitrogen to cool them down.' Which wasn't entirely the right response for the situation.

Jisu was relieved that the robot didn't have legs and couldn't move. Its voice was pleasant. It wasn't a deep, scary voice, like the evil robots that were infected with viruses in movies. But she didn't feel completely at ease. And then she noticed that the robot looked just like Yeonjae's drawing.

Yeonjae came into the room and closed the door. Ignoring Jisu, who was still sprawled on the floor, she went straight to the robot. She quickly flipped open the robot's back panel and turned it off. The robot's eyes dimmed and darkened, and Yeonjae laid it down and covered it with a blanket.

Yeonjae figured she had to explain what was going on. She assumed Jisu would go crazy, but she was surprised when Jisu sat there calmly, listening to her story – how she had 'come across' a robot jockey that was about to be discarded and bought it on the cheap, thinking she could fix it up, and that she had been fiddling with it since yesterday. Maybe Jisu wasn't aware that it was illegal to buy and sell robot jockeys second-hand. Yeonjae knew Jisu wasn't a gossip, so she hoped she would just take it in her stride. She noticed her knees were red and swollen. Did she need ointment for them? Or a bandage? Yeonjae was confident that she could figure out what a damaged machine might need with a single look, but an injured person was outside her comfort zone. Though Jisu herself didn't seem to be paying any attention to her bruises. Maybe she didn't need anything.

'So you're saying you fixed it and woke it up?' Jisu asked after a while, sounding elated for some reason.

Woke it up wasn't quite right . . . but it was close enough. Yeonjae nodded. 'I still need to make it some legs . . .'

'You really are a fucking genius!' Jisu grinned and punched Yeonjae on the arm.

Yeonjae cradled her arm, speechless.

'This is incredible,' Jisu continued. 'You fixed that up? Can I see?'

Yeonjae hesitated, then pulled back the blanket.

Jisu attempted to shuffle over on her knees, but then squatted to avoid putting weight on her bruises. 'Can I touch it?'

Yeonjae nodded.

Jisu rapped gently on the robot's forehead, making dull thuds. 'Anyway, what's a jockey?'

How did she not know what a jockey is? 'The guy on the horse in a race. You know?'

'Oh, yeah.' Jisu nodded. 'Right, right, the guy on the horse.' Her gaze trailed over the robot, then she spotted Yeonjae's open notebook nearby. There was a glint in her eye. She cleared her throat. 'So. What's next?' She looked inquisitive and confident, ready to solve any problem.

Yeonjae didn't know where to start or how much detail to go into, so she went over the obvious steps. She didn't understand why she was telling Jisu all this, but she decided to go along with it for now. 'I have to rebuild the lower body, so I'll use links for the joints . . .'

'You'll use what?'

'Links.'

'Okay,' Jisu said, clearly not knowing what that was.

'I'll need something for the suspension, too.'

'So how are you going to get all those parts?'

Yeonjae couldn't answer.

Jisu noted her hesitation and swooped in to close the deal. She crossed her arms. She had learned the art of negotiation from her dad, and knew you had to offer something enticing to persuade someone to come over to your side. 'You know, I could get everything for you.'

As Yeonjae didn't know what Jisu's father did for a living, it sounded ludicrous and far-fetched. Trying to get robotic parts as an individual meant you were edging dangerously close to the black market. Unless you knew someone who worked in the field. She figured Jisu was making it up. 'And how exactly would you do that?'

Jisu launched into a lengthy explanation, as though she had been waiting for Yeonjae to ask. It wasn't entirely clear what was strictly factual and what was exaggerated, but as her father was the CEO of a humanoid robot parts supplier, he had promised to be an in-kind sponsor for the robotics competition. Though it would be impossible for them to get large quantities of anything, she could simply add parts for Yeonjae's robot to the list of things they would need for the competition.

Yeonjae was hesitant.

Jisu hammered home her point. 'And you know it's illegal to buy that robot as a private citizen, right? I know they don't really crack down on those sales, but if my dad's the one making the report, I'm sure they'll take a second look.'

Jisu was blackmailing her.

Later, they exchanged phone numbers by the front door.

'See you at school,' Jisu said before leaving.

Yeonjae stood there, holding the application form Jisu had given her. It required a short essay about the applicant, in addition to her school ID number. Yeonjae looked down at her cell phone, at the contract she and Jisu had just signed.

Agreement

If Woo Yeonjae enters the robotics competition with Seo Jisu, Seo Jisu shall provide humanoid robot parts that Woo Yeonjae needs. If they do not win any awards, Woo Yeonjae shall pay Seo Jisu back for all the parts provided.

Seo Jisu

Woo Yeonjae

Yeonjae felt a little uneasy, but she had nothing to lose by signing this agreement. In fact, ever since Jisu had said she could provide the parts, Yeonjae had been having a hard time keeping a straight face. She raised her arms in triumph and sank into the sofa. She had been wondering if things would ever start working out in her favour. Now, the tide was turning. What would she do if they didn't win anything? But the competition was still far away, and immediate joy took precedence. She just had to quickly bang out her essay, and when she lay in bed she would slip into a blissful state of slumber, making up for the lack of sleep the night before.

She glanced at the clock. It was just after nine o'clock. Eunhye still wasn't home. This wasn't like her; Eunhye always said something if she was going to be late. Yeonjae stared out towards the racecourse, now shrouded in darkness. She pulled on a jacket and headed out.

BOKHUI

Horses had evolved over thousands of years only to land in these narrow stalls. At one point in time they were raised for food and livestock and transportation. Though some still ended up being food and livestock and transportation for humans, many of these animals had ultimately become racehorses, running around a closed track for human entertainment. For horses living in today's world, it was inevitable that they would spend long stretches of time locked away in a stall; it was often the only way for them to survive. Even though she knew all this, it still pained Bokhui to look the horses in the eye.

At one point she thought her visceral reaction was in response to the horses' position in society, one that was more pitiful than that of other animals. A horse couldn't live in their owner's house and commune with them like dogs and cats did, and they were far too intelligent to be locked up in a pen. Everyone knew dolphins were intelligent but most people didn't realize that horses were just as clever. A horse was as smart as a six-year-old human, which meant the animal understood it was imprisoned and was destined to run on the track until its body broke down.

This was why Bokhui ordered Minju to let the horses roam in the pasture whenever she went to the racetrack. And it was also why she filled her pockets with carrots and sugar cubes when she visited them. Sugar was not the healthiest choice for horses, who had a sweet tooth, but it was the quickest way to relieve their stress. Stress was certainly much worse than sugar. Whenever Bokhui came by, all the horses came up to the steel bars, huffing and snorting in greeting. She only visited once, at most twice, a month, but she had already become family to the horses.

A vet-school friend a few years above her had held this gig first. Her friend had counselled her to avoid looking the horses in the eye. Bokhui wondered if meeting a horse's gaze would be interpreted as aggression and heighten the risk of an attack, but quickly discovered that her friend's advice was for her own emotional wellbeing.

The first time Bokhui had come to the racetrack, her friend had stroked a horse's neck, saying, 'Don't their eyes look like black marbles?' But then her friend's eyes had transformed into pools of water. All of a sudden Bokhui had understood. Her friend had once told her she had zero plans to get married and have kids; her heart already held too many vulnerable beings, and Bokhui could see that she'd experienced enough sorrow in the job to last a lifetime. Her friend instructed her to pat the horse on the neck, one of their favourite places to be stroked. She'd placed a gentle hand on the animal's wide neck. It was hairy but smooth and soft. She slowly swept her hand down. Following her friend's lead, she closed her eyes to feel the horse's body heat and breathing, and spoke to it in a low, quiet voice, transmitting her voice through its skin.

'Hi, there. I'm Bokhui. Min Bokhui. It's nice to meet you. I hope you have a long, healthy life.'

Her friend handed over the racetrack account and left for Jeju Island. As her friend adored horses above all, Bokhui assumed she was going to the island to be surrounded by horses. It took a year of working with the racehorses for Bokhui to realize that her friend had in fact fled, seeking refuge on the island.

A thoroughbred's life was short. Not only as a race-horse, but as a living being. A champion was often worth more than a hundred million won, but it commanded those prices only while it could race. A thoroughbred that couldn't run was no longer a horse. Growing up, Bokhui had heard people say that a student who didn't study wasn't human, but even the harsh value judgement behind that sentiment was nothing compared to how horses were treated. Sure, humans were sometimes treated as less than human, but their humanity was something that could always be revived. A horse that wasn't considered a horse was not allowed to continue living. A horse that couldn't run had no compelling reason to remain on Earth.

Before, no matter how fast racehorses could sprint down the track, officials had to consider the weight and safety of the people riding them. As human jockeys were phased out and the industry transitioned to robot jockeys, a new era dawned: the riders became lighter and human deaths on the track were eliminated. What came after that was a demand for even faster speeds. Before, a horse would hit seventy to eighty kilometres per hour in a race, but today they clocked on average ninety kilometres an hour. Now people could experience the same thrill as watching racing cars careening around the track, only with horses. Unfortunately, unlike technology, which developed rapidly, a horse's physique evolved incrementally, through genomic tinkering over thousands of years. At most, a racehorse's career lasted eighteen months. Beyond that, the horse could barely stand, its cartilage and joints worn out. A few lucky ones spent the remainder of their lives in the countryside on Jeju Island or in the grassy fields of Gangwon Province, but the vast majority were euthanized. That, tragically, was also Bokhui's job.

The horse she was examining now lay in its stall, under anaesthetic. Its eyelids had stopped twitching, but the horse was in a daze, not asleep. Though Bokhui knew the horse wouldn't get spooked or flinch while under anaesthetic, she still stroked its neck. It had become a habit. She inserted the endoscope deep through a nostril, displaying the horse's insides on her screen. This horse was in good health, not much different from the previous month. Bokhui went down her checklist, then addressed Minju. 'You need to feed them more.'

'I'm always gaining weight, but I guess horses don't get obese,' Minju joked.

Bokhui didn't even crack a smile. 'Try subsisting on uncooked rice and running around all day like they do. You'll lose it all in a week.' She turned to Eunhye, who was watching from just outside the stall. 'Right?'

Eunhye nodded.

Bokhui finished filling out her report and stroked the horse one last time. 'Good job. Take a load off while you can.'

Last year, a petition had been submitted to the National Assembly for the third time to request approval for the use of nano-endoscopy on animals, but it hadn't passed. Ostensibly it was because there weren't enough resources to expand its use to animals, but the truth was that lawmakers couldn't be bothered to commit funding for animal care. Still, the fight for animal welfare continued, so at some point they might be allowed to use nano-endoscopes on animals. Though perhaps not during Bokhui's career.

Bokhui packed up her gear and headed to the next

stall – Today's. Today was always in her stall even when the other horses were enjoying their freedom in the arena outside.

'How are you?' she asked the horse.

'Fine as always,' Minju told her.

Eunhye spoke up. 'She vomited two days ago. Twice. And one time she just gagged. She hasn't been eating much. And sometimes she just falls to her knees.'

Bokhui glared at Minju and decided to trust what Eunhye had told her. The girl had been coming here longer than the vet. When Bokhui had first started, Eunhye had told her every horse's name and what each was like. Eunhye was a better stable manager than Minju; Bokhui always tried to time her visits for when the girl would be there.

Today was in the most dismal condition of all the horses in the stables. The filly was only three years old, but the joints in her front legs had been completely destroyed; she was in a worse state than a ninety-year-old man.

The horse welcomed Bokhui, who smiled and greeted her in return. A knot hardened in Bokhui's stomach. She knew she couldn't cure Today. All she could do was delay the inevitable progression of her ailments. Even so, she couldn't be sure that Today would make it past the end of the month.

'How have you been? Should we check out your legs?' Bokhui hugged Today around the neck. 'Your mane is looking great!'

Bokhui brought out an IV line to give Today some

supplements. The horse let Bokhui do her thing and didn't flinch even when she injected the animal with anaesthetic. A few minutes later Today began wobbling, then her legs gave way as she folded on to the dry dirt. Bokhui gently rubbed Today's joints and the horse nickered as if to express pain. She was suffering from degenerative arthritis, caused by overworking her joints in a short period of time. The cartilage was destroyed and the synovial membrane was inflamed. At this point Today probably felt a jolt of pain whenever she walked, with bone hitting bone. It would soon lead to bone erosion. But the bigger issue was time, not joint inflammation. The horse hadn't been able to enter a race in three weeks. If she didn't receive the all-clear in the next two weeks, she would be a goner right after the Chuseok holiday. Horses that didn't have enough wagers placed on them wouldn't be able to earn their keep and were forced to vacate for younger, faster horses that raked in the cash.

The racetrack management had been planning to kick Today out, but Bokhui had insisted that she could heal the horse, earning Today a month-long reprieve. Unfortunately, the possibility of her joints returning to their prime was less than zero. But Bokhui couldn't send Today away; there was nowhere for the filly to go. There was nobody in all of Korea who had vast lands and who would take good care of this hobbling horse, at least not at the moment.

She found a vein, and slid the IV in to begin the infusion.

She left the stall so Today could rest during the treatment. She stopped next to Eunhye but the girl kept staring at the filly, not giving Bokhui a second glance. The horse's eyes were half open and her breathing was shallow. Eunhye sure had a special bond with Today. Bokhui didn't know exactly why. Maybe now was the right time to ask.

'Eunhye, you mentioned once that Today's your favourite. Why is that?'

'Doctor, you've never seen her race, have you?'

Bokhui tried to remember. She didn't think so. She never came here on race day, since she visited only to monitor the horses' health. In fact, she went out of her way to avoid race day. She didn't want to witness what seemed like abuse to her.

'Racing makes her so happy.'

'Yeah?'

Bokhui's half-hearted response didn't seem to satisfy Eunhye. 'I'm not just saying that. She has a different energy when she's racing. She's not going fast just to go fast. She's so elegant. Like the black swan. Not the bird, the ballerina.'

Bokhui figured Today would look elegant because of her gait and her dark coat, which gleamed like a black pearl. She imagined Today galloping, her mane and tail rippling like a black wave. That dynamic movement would have enraptured Eunhye.

'I wish she could get better and race again. But I don't

know if she'll ever be able to,' Eunhye murmured. 'It's depressing. Like there's no hope.'

Bokhui realized that she would have preferred not to know what Eunhye was worried about. 'I'm sure she'll run again,' she said unconvincingly. If Eunhye had been younger, Bokhui would have reassured her that an infusion and some rest would make Today feel better soon so that the filly could run again, the type of white lie she pulled out for the scared little kids who came into her clinic, clutching their sick pets. But Eunhye was far too old for that kind of saccharine cheer. She was nearly an adult.

'I know that's not on the cards for her,' Eunhye said. 'I know she'll be euthanized if she doesn't get better. I feel helpless because I can't do anything about it. And it feels stupid to be so sad when I can't even do something about it. So that's why I'm here, just sitting with her.'

Bokhui couldn't bear that this girl had to sit with these wretched feelings. Why did this young sapling have to be snapped in two? Why couldn't she daydream under a shady tree?

At Eunhye's age, Bokhui had been much more immature and coddled. She had never even imagined an existence different from her own as a student preparing for college entrance exams. Her hopes and wishes were focused only on grades and the college she would get into. If seventeen-year-old Bokhui had zoomed down a track at full speed towards what she thought was her only exit, seventeen-year-old Eunhye was standing still on a field, looking out at a broken world. Suddenly, Bokhui felt as though Eunhye was older and more mature than her. She didn't know what to say. She couldn't tell her that there was something they could do for Today, because there wasn't. She scanned the stables in an attempt to find something else to talk about. Empty stalls surrounded her, and her eyes jumped past the pile of hay in the corner to the outline of a man standing in the back doorway. The setting sun behind him lengthened his shadow on the ground.

She assumed it was Minju and moved on, but the man was still there when she glanced back at the doors. For a brief moment she wondered if it was actually a small truck with a stack of wood or hay on the back. No, it was definitely a person. So why was Minju just hovering there instead of walking in? Was it someone else? Were people allowed to come all the way into the stables? But the way to the stables wasn't marked on any of the signage. Maybe it was another staffer. But it was already pretty late, and she knew most of the employees had gone home. When Bokhui stayed late to finish examining all the horses, usually only Minju was around. Maybe it *was* an employee, wondering why she was here so late. She was about to call out to introduce herself when she caught sight of a flash and heard the click of a shutter, and it finally dawned on her that this person taking a picture didn't work here.

She charged towards the doors. The person flinched

and snatched a bag off the ground in an attempt to run away. Bokhui reached out and grabbed him. She'd had it up to here with these assholes uploading sensationalist footage to their channels to rack up views, these dipshits who planted ridiculous hypotheses and seeded conspiracy anxiety. This guy had to be one of those deplorables. In the five years since robot jockeys were first deployed, critics of horseracing had multiplied, with everyone talking about horses and their rights. Rumours abounded about the corrupt racing system and political drama entangling major corporations. So many assholes made their living off these types of rumours. And this guy was sneaking in here with his expensive camera to take pictures of her while she examined the horses.

Summoning the skills she had developed back in the day while administering anaesthetic to bucking bulls, Bokhui yanked the strap of the fleeing man's bag, hooked her arm around his neck, and threw him to the ground. He landed face down and began scrabbling at her.

'Wait . . . wait!' he choked out, coughing. 'Can you . . . please . . . let's talk!'

Other than grabbing her hands, he didn't resist.

Shit. Was she going to be dragged into the police station for assault? She loosened her grip on his neck and got to her feet.

The man remained on the ground, gasping, trying to catch his breath. He appeared to be at least 180 centimetres tall, with wide swimmer's shoulders. There was no way she'd injured him but he sure was acting like it. He finally caught his breath and stood up. He was even taller than she'd thought, with a pale complexion. He brushed dust and hay off his clothes. 'I must have taken you by surprise,' he said by way of apology.

He had, but somehow she felt that she should be the one saying that to him. 'Oh, no . . . I wasn't . . .' Bokhui wasn't someone who shrank into herself, no matter what situation she found herself in, but she discovered that she was stumbling over her words. *What is going on with you?* she chastised herself. *Get a grip!* She couldn't help but look away. Her body was doing exactly the opposite of what she was willing it to do.

'Don't worry, I'm not anyone suspicious. I'm a reporter.'

Isn't a reporter suspicious? Bokhui nearly said.

He took a business card out of his pocket. Woo Seojin, Current Affairs Desk, M Broadcasting Corporation.

She studied the card, then looked up at him sceptically. Even if he was who he claimed to be, this business card didn't explain why he was sneaking into the stables and taking pictures. Bokhui didn't think much of people who hid and spied and took sneaky photographs in the name of journalism.

Seojin must have thought his business card would be enough. He grew visibly flustered, as though he wasn't sure what other explanation to give. He rubbed the back of his neck. 'So, I mean, I'm a reporter, and I'm investigating a few things for a special I'm making about the racetrack . . .'

Bokhui cut him off. 'How did you get in?'

'. . . Through there.' Seojin pointed, not towards the main entrance or even the north gate but to a low wall, tucked into a blind spot from the surveillance cameras, hidden by the abundant foliage of the fringe trees. So he had hopped over the wall.

Bokhui crossed her arms and looked pointedly at Seojin. She could feel her combative side rearing up. She didn't exactly feel protective of the racetrack, but it was clear that whatever story he was reporting on wasn't a positive one. 'So you're dedicated to journalism but not to the law,' she said, her tone still belligerent. 'Did you talk to the officials here about your story?'

'Well, I tried with one, but he closed the door in my face when I showed him my business card. I'm not exactly pursuing the most positive angle . . .'

Who would welcome someone in for an exposé on their business? Not a single organization in the world would be thrilled to see reporters darkening their doorstep, no matter the industry.

'Anyway, I'm sorry if I scared you,' Seojin said. 'I was just taking pictures of the horses. I made sure not to get you in the frame, don't worry. At first I didn't even realize you were there.' Seojin bowed in apology.

Bokhui didn't feel the need to keep him hostage and lecture him. She supposed she could just warn him to be careful, since horseracing sometimes had links to organized crime. She nodded to accept his apology. There was nothing much left to say. Having met each other purely by chance, they could now head their separate ways.

Eunhye, who had been gazing at Today despite the backdrop of the ruckus, poked her head out of the back doors, and said something truly shocking. 'Oppa? What are *you* doing here?'

'*Oppa?*'

'He's my cousin,' Eunhye told Bokhui.

Seojin looked surprised to see Eunhye, too. Only then did Bokhui notice that they shared a surname – Woo.

The cousins decided to catch up and invited Bokhui along. They settled at an outdoor table in front of the convenience store by the track.

'So, you're a vet.' Seojin looked awed. He must have watched as Bokhui packed up her gear.

Bokhui guzzled a can of Sprite, then went back into the store, muttering that she needed a real drink. She returned with three cans of beer in her arms.

'Help yourself if you want,' Bokhui told Seojin, holding one out, then opened a can herself and took a gulp.

With the dramatic discovery that Eunhye and Seojin were related, the evening was unfolding in an entirely different direction than Bokhui had expected. Here they were, chatting over a beer, though it would have made more sense for them to shake hands at the end of their scuffle and say, *It was nice to meet you, good luck with your work advocating for animals.*

If Eunhye had been the chatty type, she would have asked her cousin all sorts of things like how he was doing and what he was up to, especially since it seemed that they hadn't seen each other in a while, but she didn't say much. She just sat there eating snacks. If she'd been a little more perceptive, maybe she would have noticed that Bokhui was uncharacteristically nervous.

Before Bokhui had guzzled down all the beers, Seojin got up from the table and excused himself to make a call.

When Seojin was out of earshot Eunhye dived right in. 'We used to be really close years ago, but we lost touch. I knew he became a reporter but I didn't know this was his beat. He's twenty-four, maybe twenty-five? I don't know what university he went to or what he majored in. I did hear he was discharged early from the military because of some injury. I think he fell off something during some kind of training and hurt his shoulder, but it doesn't affect him day to day. He's an only child. And I don't know if he has a girlfriend. What else do you want to know?'

Well. Bokhui had been totally wrong. Eunhye was actually *very* perceptive.

Bokhui hesitated. 'I think that's a good start . . .' Her

interest in him must have been too obvious; she couldn't bring herself to deny that she was intrigued.

Eunhye ate a spicy shrimp chip and continued. 'He loves animals, too. Which might be his weakness, actually. I still remember what he told me once. He said that a species goes extinct as often as an app gets an update. Isn't that grim? That means every time I update an app, another species is going extinct.'

'That sounds about right, unfortunately.'

'That's why I don't update my apps very often. It just feels wrong.' Eunhye scratched at a late-season mosquito bite on her cheek. 'Anyway, that's all I know about him.'

'So you haven't really kept in touch, even though you're cousins,' Bokhui mused. 'Then again I have no idea what *my* cousins are up to these days.'

'After my dad passed away we sort of stopped seeing his side of the family. I guess it kind of happened naturally. I have an aunt on that side, too, but she lives far away. On Jeju Island.'

Bokhui hadn't known that Eunhye had lost her father. She tried to think of something appropriate to say, but gave up. Eunhye herself had brought it up so nonchalantly; she didn't appear to expect Bokhui to go out of her way to add unnecessary commentary.

Eunhye remembered a few other tiny details about Seojin to share: that he'd always had a nice complexion because he took after her father's side. That he was a very nice guy but when you talked to him it had sometimes felt like he was on another planet, though she wasn't sure what he was like now.

When Seojin returned to the table after his phone call, Bokhui instantly understood what Eunhye meant.

'I saw a fruit truck out there and got these. There were only two left.' Smiling, Seojin placed two Korean pears on the table. 'Would you like some? The guy said they're really sweet.'

Bokhui declined. Without a knife and cutting board handy, she would have to resort to gnawing on the huge round pear like a rodent.

A Betty went round cleaning the outdoor tables. It was nice that they didn't have to worry about an employee staring daggers at them, waiting for them to hurry up and leave. The Betty didn't get stressed out when looking after their table, which was littered with empty cans and half-eaten bags of crisps. Seojin picked one up. Bokhui noticed scratches on the back of his hand from their tussle in the stables. She sobered up quickly.

'I'm sorry about earlier,' she said. 'I should have apologized sooner.'

Seojin waved her apology away. 'No, no, not at all. I didn't get hurt. That was the right thing to do. It was actually pretty cool.' He raised both thumbs.

Mortified by his dorky thumbs-up move, Bokhui shoved a handful of crisps into her mouth.

Seojin lowered his hands and changed the subject. 'It's nice out here, on a fall evening.'

Bokhui's college ex-boyfriend used to think eating outside was pathetic. Maybe 'that asshole' was a more appropriate moniker than 'ex-boyfriend'. That asshole had been pursuing a master's in mechanical engineering, researching a non-invasive way to remove tumours at the medical technology research centre. He had immersed himself in his work with the sole goal of starting a medical revolution within a decade, grinding away night and day, sometimes opting for IV infusions instead of eating real food. But he'd continued to see her through all that.

At first she'd been touched, thinking he was making her a priority, carving time out for her because he loved her so deeply. Maybe he did, in the beginning. He told her he would regret losing such a wonderful person over something like a hectic work schedule. She shouldn't have believed him. Because that asshole was so immature that he didn't even know how to feed himself. Their dates were increasingly constrained to hanging out at his place, right by the research centre, because he was so tired. They started by ordering in, but eventually he suggested they cook because he was getting sick of takeout. He was useless. He knew how to create a nanobot the size of a single molecule but was completely unschooled in how to wash rice, put it in the rice cooker, and press the 'on' button. She hated herself whenever she found herself washing rice in his kitchen, not willing to let him starve despite telling him she wasn't his personal chef. When they finally broke up, she emptied a twenty-kilo sack of rice in that asshole's place before making her way out.

His attitude towards cooking was only half the reason for their breakup. The other problem had been their differing perspectives on animal testing. That asshole saw animal testing as an essential tool in developing medical technology and claimed that the innocent, slaughtered animals had met a noble death. She disagreed forcefully. How could it be noble to die for humans? Later, after they broke up, she remembered how he called stray cats 'vectors of disease' and she shuddered, wanting to flush him out of her psyche; there was no lingering fondness for their year-long relationship.

After she'd dumped rice all over that asshole's place and tossed the empty sack aside, she told him that, if and when more advanced alien life forms came for humans, he should humbly accept his own noble death. He laughed. She screamed, 'You arrogant bastard! We're not even all that advanced in the grand scheme of things!' and stormed out. Thanks to that asshole's wide social network, forged when he was a member of the student council, everyone thought she believed in aliens, but she decided not to let it bother her. Instead, she'd focused on her studies and graduated early, then left for Kenya.

After that bitter end to what could be seen as a short relationship, Bokhui had been sure she was done with romance forever, but then this happened. Out of nowhere, on a fall night near the darkened racetrack, a romance-tinged moon was rising. It was too soon to tell what kind of person Seojin was, of course, but she could already sense that he was the polar opposite of that asshole. She was certain of that fact.

Seojin's cheeks and ears were flushed even though he had downed only one beer. He made excuses, touching his hot face with embarrassment, insisting that he could hold his drink but that his face always went red after a single beer. For Bokhui, whose demeanour didn't change one bit even when she was drunk out of her mind, Seojin's reaction to alcohol was enviable, even adorable.

Eunhye sat there quietly. It was getting quite late, but she didn't appear ready to head home yet. Bokhui didn't urge her to go. Perhaps Eunhye wanted to enjoy this lovely fall evening a little longer. The gentle breeze made the girl's long locks sway.

Bokhui stared at Seojin as he rubbed his red face. She suddenly brought up his reporting, wondering what he found interesting about the racetrack and racehorses.

Seojin paused for a long time. 'I'm working on something about corruption in racing. I can't go into the details because we haven't aired it yet.'

'Oh, you don't have to tell me if you're uncomfortable.'

'No, I'm not uncomfortable. It's just – you know, like, match-fixing.'

'No, I meant if it's confidential.'

'Right, right.'

They kept talking past each other, she trying to clarify the misunderstanding and he claiming not to have misunderstood. They traded *Oh, okay, right*, back and forth, until they finally shut up. Eunhye let out an embarrassed chuckle.

Seojin attempted to fill the stilted silence. 'So, Doctor, you take care of the racehorses?'

Bokhui was glad he brought that up. She had been worried that they would be forced to wrap things up because it was getting awkward. 'Call me Bokhui, please. But yes, that's what I do. I understand you're an animal lover.'

'I told her,' Eunhye said, jumping in.

'Oh, right, right.' Seojin scratched the back of his neck. He looked embarrassed, having to talk about his love for animals in front of someone who had dedicated her life to their welfare. 'I don't know if I would call myself that, but . . . I just find them lovable. But everyone feels that way, so . . .'

'Oh, no, that's not true,' Bokhui interjected. 'Even people who have pets don't always love animals. So many people have pets for their own purposes, instead of thinking of them as living beings who have their own needs. They just follow trends and focus on what they want.'

'Do you think that's the case for racehorses, too?' Seojin sounded cautious.

Bokhui understood that he wasn't blaming her for the existence of racehorses, but his question still cut her to the quick. 'For a horse, it's all about luck. Once they can no longer race, they live if they're lucky, and they die if they're not.'

Seojin let out a dismayed sigh.

'If they die, it's because they have nowhere to go,' Bokhui explained. 'I'm not a supporter of euthanasia, but if you oppose it wholesale then it's like you're saying, *Go out there and die on your own.* Our planet is already completely centred around people. Animals can't survive outside the systems we humans have created. There's nowhere an animal can just go and live. We can't fix just one part of it, is what I'm saying. We have to start over and figure it out from the beginning. All of us.'

So many times, Bokhui had wanted to fling open the stall doors so the horses could go and live free in a better world. During her training, she had watched caged animals rubbing up against the machine dispensing food at precise times of the day, trying to feel a semblance of affection and warmth, and she had wished humans would disappear from the planet. Animals were sacrificed for advances in this horribly people-centric world. Humans forced animals to be dependent on them for their protection, and then, only then, purported to give animals their freedom. This human attempt to be good was merely more evidence of human selfishness, Bokhui thought.

It was exactly three years and five months since Bokhui had gone to Kenya. She flew to Morocco via France, then on to Kenya. Getting to Africa had required special preparation; she'd had to take malaria pills and get vaccinated against yellow fever. More people said *Hope you survive* than *Have a good trip*. Bokhui had scoffed at them, thinking they were all overreacting, but her confidence heaved out with the contents of her stomach on the bus to the Maasai Mara. She didn't tend to get carsick, but her insides roiled at the intense heat and humidity as she experienced them for the first time, and at the sight of animals that had starved to death near the entrance to the reserve. She was so miserable on the bus that she actually thought *she* might not survive. Maybe nothing on this planet could survive.

Seoul had Seoul Forest, New York had Central Park, the Earth had the Amazon rainforest, and the animals had the Maasai Mara. That was what it was called in Kenya; it was the Serengeti in Tanzania. This was all strictly from a human perspective, of course. In the reserve, Bokhui had encountered a three-month-old elephant that had been abandoned by its herd. It lay on the ground patiently, as though awaiting its fate to be torn apart by a hungry lion. It was so malnourished that it barely looked like an elephant. Luckily Bokhui's group had come upon it before a hyena or a lion did. They moved the animal to safety and gave it IV supplements. Only then did Bokhui realize that this elephant didn't have any tusks. She surmised that a poacher must have torn the baby elephant away from its herd, then discarded it after yanking out its tusks, but the guide had shaken his head.

'Some of them are starting to be born without tusks. And tusks are becoming very short, even if they are born with them. Just little stubs. This one was probably born without any.'

'Is it a good thing to be evolving that way?' Bokhui asked, then realized how stupid that question was. Evolution was just the result of selections made to enhance survival. The elimination of tusks was purely based on the need to survive humans. How could that be a positive thing?

The guide smiled. 'We can only hope that they don't decide it's best to eliminate their entire species.'

Bokhui would have taken that comment as a joke if she hadn't witnessed a mass suicide of zebras a few days later.

Pulling herself back to the present, Bokhui realized too late that she had gone on far too long about a much too serious topic. How could she salvage this? She'd quickly turned everything grim. 'Well, that got heavy fast, didn't it?'

Seojin merely smiled, neither encouraging nor discouraging.

The conversation had veered too far to the political; now it would be near impossible to make plans to see Seojin again. Still, she didn't regret anything she'd said.

Eunhye met her eyes and shook her head in dismay. She was about to say something to help Bokhui out, but was thwarted by the sudden appearance of a girl in a checked shirt.

She came up to them, dragging her feet, and grabbed Eunhye by the shoulder. 'Eonni.' She then turned in surprise. 'Seojin Oppa?'

Seojin stared back. This had to be Eunhye's little sister.

BOGYEONG

Was her name Jisu? Right. Seo Jisu.

Bogyeong made a note of that name in her phone so she wouldn't forget the next time the girl came over and accidentally hurt her feelings. Jisu seemed so polite and smart. How did she come to be so close to Yeonjae? Her daughter wasn't a bad kid, of course, but she never brought home her report cards, leading Bogyeong to assume she wasn't cut out for anything but robotics. She'd thought maybe Yeonjae didn't have any friends. Kids these days tended to be even more ruthless than when Bogyeong was that age, cutting off relationships that weren't mutually beneficial. Some people despaired that kids were too competitive, fretting that friendships were fraying, but Bogyeong didn't necessarily think it was a negative development. It was better than wasting time, mired in relationships that didn't do anything for anyone.

Anyway, Yeonjae had brought home a classmate. Yeonjae, who Bogyeong had thought would never make a close friend. She hoped they would stay friends for a long time.

Earlier that morning, Bogyeong had been biding her time, waiting for the right moment to ask Yeonjae about her new friend. Yeonjae came downstairs looking as though she hadn't got a wink of sleep, and sat at the table. Bogyeong glanced over at her, trying to find the right time. Suddenly Yeonjae stopped playing with the broccoli banchan Bogyeong had set on the table, dropped her chopsticks, and dashed upstairs. Bogyeong called after her, but she didn't stop or even answer. Why was she in such a rush at the crack of dawn? A few minutes later, Yeonjae clattered back down the stairs, claimed she was late, and ran straight out of the door. Yeonjae's temper and silence and impatience bothered Bogyeong, but she knew where those traits came from.

The firefighter was never in a rush unless someone's life hung in the balance, accustomed as he was to racing against the clock whenever there was an emergency. When they were newly dating, his relaxed attitude towards life frustrated Bogyeong no end. He walked leisurely when the movie was going to start in five minutes. That drove Bogyeong crazy. She was someone who needed to get to the theatre at least half an hour before the movie began. Instead of getting fed up when they were stuck in bumper-to-bumper traffic on the highway after an accident, he worried about anyone who might be injured. Bogyeong surmised that this tendency was related to his job. Once, when Bogyeong slept through her alarm and woke up at the time they were supposed to meet, he told her not to hurry. He hung out in a bookstore, reading several books, until she got there. He calmed Bogyeong down when she got annoyed at a waiter whose mistake with their order delayed the arrival of their food. If he heard the elevator doors open on their floor before he had his shoes on, he wouldn't rush to make it. He would just wait for the next one.

At first she thought it was an act. She thought he was acting chill since they were early on in their courtship, both of them wanting to impress the other. But his behaviour didn't alter even as they continued to date for over a year. That was when she realized this was who he was. And even if it turned out that he wasn't really like this, if he was this good at acting, Bogyeong thought the right thing to do was to go along with it.

For the most part, Bogyeong got used to the way he was. But once, in the days leading up to their wedding, she asked, 'How can you be so relaxed about everything? Sometimes it's frustrating to see you this relaxed.'

Bogyeong had been reflecting on her own personality ever since they met. She wasn't so impatient and quick-tempered that it would irritate anyone. She was a slow runner, and it took her time to get her lines down. Maybe she just wasn't physically fit and had a bad memory, but, regardless, she wasn't the kind of person who doggedly kept grasping for something that didn't work out, getting annoyed and lashing out. She just carried on without complaint, believing that things would work out at some point. If she missed the bus or the underground, she just took the next one without letting it bother her, and though she did like getting to the movies on the early side, she didn't elbow her way into the theatre to claim her seat. She just didn't like rushing or feeling anxious. That was why she tended to be on the early side. But he acted like he'd never felt that anxiety, not once in his life. As though he didn't have to follow the way time ticked on in this world.

When she asked him about it, he entwined his fingers with hers and looked up at the dark sky, inky black without a single star in it. He was probably walking slowly right then, too. He took huge, slow steps, feet angled slightly outward, like an old-time aristocrat ambling along. She couldn't recall his gait any more, even though she wanted to imitate it.

'Because it's all too fast,' he said. 'It's okay to be a little slower, isn't it?'

What exactly was too fast? What could be a little slower? After he was gone, Bogyeong regretted not asking him in that moment. She never found out what he meant.

Time flowed quickly after their wedding, and even the firefighter was unable to slow it down. When they had kids, he had to give up some of his relaxed outlook; the girls grew quickly and ran fast. There were more days when there just wasn't enough time even to bath both girls. Bogyeong's nice nightgown, bought so hopefully before the wedding, went unworn, and odds and ends piled up on the kitchen chairs.

Bogyeong found herself missing his relaxed attitude and vowed to lead a life in which she could walk leisurely down the street even if it was only five minutes before the movie started. That was what she would do as soon as the kids didn't require so much work. But then the firefighter died. He was the only person who could have helped her achieve a more relaxed mindset. Bogyeong found herself spinning faster than ever before, having to shoulder two people's worth of responsibilities alone. Her brakes were cut; she couldn't stop. She even forgot how he used to walk. In other words, Yeonjae's traits were her own. Yeonjae was just like her; she felt a strange déjà vu every time she looked at her daughter.

Eunhye was sleeping in today. She usually came out of her room by eight, no matter how late she'd gone to bed. Bogyeong left breakfast on the table and waited, watching TV, and at eight-thirty she cracked open Eunhye's door. Eunhye's wheelchair was by her bed and she was lying on her side, facing the wall.

'Eunhye?' Bogyeong figured she would clear the table if Eunhye didn't want to get up. She moved the school tablet from the bed to the desk. Eunhye must have been studying until she fell asleep.

Bogyeong wasn't sure how other moms dealt with their high school seniors, but her own approach was hands-off. As soon as kids felt pressured, she believed, a part of them would begin to fester. Kids tended to figure out what to do when they were ready, and Bogyeong thought her daughters were pretty good at working things out for themselves. A parent was there as a child's safety net, as someone the child could reach out to in a bind. Jumping to conclusions and meddling were bound to suffocate them.

Bogyeong perched on the bed and placed a hand on Eunhye's shoulder. 'Eunhye, are you still sleeping?'

Only then did she realize something was wrong. Eunhye wasn't short of breath, but she was grimacing, her body on fire. Bogyeong felt her daughter's forehead, then quickly went to look for the thermometer. The girls had returned home late the previous night, when she was still working, and she had noticed that Eunhye wasn't wearing enough layers. It was getting pretty cold at night these days.

'Eunhye, get up. Let's go to the doctor.'

Eunhye squeezed her eyes shut and shook her head.

'Come on. You have a fever. Shouldn't we go get it checked out?'

Eunhye didn't answer.

'Eunhye?'

'Mom, let me sleep. Please.' Her voice was fever-slurred.

What should she do? If it were Yeonjae, she would have dragged her to the doctor, telling her it wouldn't take long, but just leaving the house was a production and a great source of stress for Eunhye. Maybe she should leave her alone. Maybe that would help her feel better. Bogyeong brought some fever-reducing medicine for her, then helped her lie back down. She took ice packs out of the freezer and wrapped them in towels to lay them on Eunhye's forehead, neck and under both armpits. Good thing she'd saved those ice packs. Eunhye frowned at the cold sensation. Bogyeong asked her to keep the ice packs in place for thirty minutes.

She decided to open the restaurant later than usual. It was a weekday anyway, with fewer customers. She would bring Eunhye some porridge, then make her take a little more medicine. She washed some rice and soaked it. What else should she do? She found herself sitting back down at the table.

Take a break. You don't need to do anything else. You haven't taken a second for yourself. You have to take care of yourself, too. This was what the firefighter would have told her if he had been there. Bogyeong laid her head on the table and closed her eyes. Everything was more vivid when her eyes were closed – her imagination, his voice. She pictured him sitting across from her, his kind eyes smiling. *Honey, I think I'm getting old,* she told him. *My back hurts. My knees do, too. Even when I'm not doing anything. I might be developing a frozen shoulder. It's getting harder and harder to run the restaurant by myself. But I can't afford to hire anyone, not during the week. I have to hold on a little longer until the girls go to college. Then I'm going to live like you used to. Walk like you used to. But I don't know if I'll be able to.* Bogyeong drifted off. She felt someone rubbing her back consolingly. It wasn't a nightmare, just a vivid dream. She kept her eyes closed and didn't move. She wanted to stay longer in that dream state. But a tear rolled down her cheek and woke her up.

She sat up and covered her face with her hands. She couldn't help but laugh at herself. She could still be so maudlin. If she could predict when she would be hit by this sense of loss, she could prepare herself, but it always came on abruptly, without notice, just like the way they had been wrenched apart.

Bogyeong poured the soaked rice into a pot, then looked up at the ceiling. She wanted to find out more about what Yeonjae was doing upstairs. She shook her head. What would she do about it, anyway? She put the pot on the stove. She paused. But it wasn't really a secret, was it? She had seen Yeonjae lug that broken robot upstairs. And Yeonjae had never expressly banned her from entering that room. Sure, the door was closed, but that didn't mean she couldn't take a look. Right? Right.

She knew she couldn't just barge in and get rid of it. There was nothing Bogyeong could do other than tell Yeonjae she couldn't keep it here. She pinched herself on the thigh, telling herself to respect those boundaries no matter how incensed she got. But what was wedged between them was cold silence and avoidance. Yeonjae didn't seem like she was going to get rid of the robot or even try to convince Bogyeong to let her keep it. Her daughter continued to shut her out even after Jisu's visit. Bogyeong was dying to ask about her friend, but she had been biting her tongue. However, she refused to be a pushover, not this time. She would force Yeonjae to sell the robot, hopefully without hurting her feelings too much.

She knew people would shake their heads at how backward she was. They would laugh at her old-fashioned fear of robots. But what Bogyeong was really afraid of wasn't a robot attack or a rebellion, but a world that welcomed robots with open arms. She was afraid of that exclusive world that had rebuffed Yeonjae. She remembered how heartbroken she herself had felt, and how hard she had worked to keep her emotions under the surface, when Yeonjae told her she hadn't been able to answer the panel's questions. The firefighter might have been able to help Yeonjae's dreams soar. But he wasn't here. *Why did he have to leave us?* Bogyeong dried her hands to go upstairs, but then stopped. Instead, she took a mop and then headed up. If Yeonjae walked in on her she could claim she was cleaning.

The first floor was dark. The blinds were drawn tight. She felt along the wall to turn on the light. She paused in front of the door to the spare bedroom and gulped. There was no reason to be nervous, she told herself, but she knew she wasn't imagining the strange noises coming from the other side of the door. All of a sudden she realized that she was scared.

I shouldn't be scared. Yeonjae wouldn't be making anything bad. She's always been interested in robots, so she just brought it here and she's tinkering with it. Bogyeong calmed herself and placed a hand on the doorknob. But then she heard a door opening downstairs and the wheelchair going over the threshold. She ran down to see how Eunhye was doing.

Eunhye still looked feverish but was heading towards the front door.

'Where do you think you're going in this state?' *Was she heading to the pharmacy?* What Eunhye said next baffled her.

'I'm going to swing by the racetrack. I'll be really fast.'

What was so pressing that she had to go there now? 'Not today,' Bogyeong said firmly. 'You're sick. You have to rest.'

'I swear it won't even take thirty minutes. I don't have a fever any more. I probably felt hot earlier because I was sleeping.' Eunhye grabbed Bogyeong's hand and placed it on her forehead.

Eunhye did feel cooler than she had before. Maybe the meds had kicked in, or maybe it was true that she had become overheated while sleeping. It was clear to

Bogyeong, however, that she wasn't fully well, and she knew Eunhye would get worse if she pushed herself.

'The issue isn't whether you have my permission to go, Eunhye. Would you tell your daughter to go ahead and go out while she was sick? If you really want to go, we'll go to the doctor first and then I can drive you over.' Bogyeong figured Eunhye would back down. She demanded that Eunhye eat breakfast first, and her daughter agreed without much of a fuss.

Bogyeong turned on the stove while Eunhye went in to wash her hands. There must be a reason she wanted to go to the racetrack so badly.

Bogyeong didn't cry when Eunhye was diagnosed with polio and began treatment. She sometimes felt trapped, as though she couldn't breathe, but that feeling didn't turn into tears. Nothing would be solved by crying. Bogyeong believed in doing her very best in every situation that was handed to her. Even if it meant that she stood still, gritting her teeth as hard as she could. Of course, back in those days, she'd held out hope for biocompatible prostheses, which the doctors had suggested as an option.

It's not the end of the world even if her condition gets worse and she loses the use of her legs, you see. The technology is so advanced these days. If she gets biocompatible prosthetics, it'll be just like walking with her own legs. You won't be able to tell with the naked eye. It's not the same disease as in the old days. Take a look at some of these videos, and you'll get a better sense. If she needs prosthetics down the road, I can refer you to the best doctor in the field. It's still a little pricey, but I think it'll become more and more common. Don't worry, it'll all be okay. You need to be strong for her. I always say that battling an illness is most successful when the patient and their parents fight the disease together.

Eunhye's illness had caused every member of the family to rack up debts to the others. They all had their feelings hurt, and before one wound could heal a new one would open up, pushing the older one further down. Bogyeong consoled herself that someday, even if not right then, there would be a chance for them to make it up to each other. She found herself sternly telling the rest of the family to hang in there, raising her voice over the most trivial of things, and collapsing on a bench while out on a walk. Every time that happened, she remembered what the doctor had told her and pushed through her overwhelming feelings. She could keep going because there was an end to all of this. What finally made her cry was a doctor telling her much later, when she asked about the possibility of prosthetics down the road, *I'm sorry, but this isn't covered by insurance.*

What broke her wasn't the illness or Eunhye's suffering or the wounds they inflicted on one another or the pain of strangers staring at them. She sobbed because something she could have done for Eunhye if she just had the money was fully out of her grasp. They wouldn't be able to make ends meet if she saved her late husband's life insurance payout for Eunhye's procedure. Instead, she bought the restaurant and built the house. Never in her life had she felt so wretched, so bereft. It was worse than when the firefighter died. She couldn't do anything about his accident, so her resentment was aimed at various parts of society. There were systems and people she could accuse, jabbing her finger in the air, screaming that it wasn't fair. But this? She could only point the finger of blame at herself. Her finger dug into her sharply, tearing up her heart, whose wounds she had managed slowly to paper over. What Bogyeong didn't know was that Eunhye hovered for a long time in front of Bogyeong's door that night, listening to her mother stifling her sobs, before wheeling herself back to her own room.

After that day, hurt feelings piled up and hardened between the two of them. It wasn't anyone's fault. They each carried their pain on their own. Eunhye stopped asking for things and Bogyeong stopped saying no to her. A hard line had been drawn between mother and daughter. They were keeping some distance from each other to protect one another, and though Yeonjae wasn't part of that equation, Bogyeong hoped her younger daughter would understand. Somehow, Bogyeong had become a single mom to two girls, and with no resources; all she could do was hope that her children would be compassionate with her.

Bogyeong took Eunhye's temperature again: 36.9 degrees. Not too serious but not nothing, either. She handed Eunhye the bowl of porridge and placed some medicine on the table. 'Take two pills after you finish the whole bowl, okay?'

Eunhye nodded, spooning up a heaping mound of porridge to show Bogyeong that she understood.

Bogyeong went back upstairs to find a heavy coat for Eunhye. It was a little early in the season but she might as well bring out the box of winter clothes she had put away in the spring. Seasons flew by; by the time Chuseok was over, a freezing wind from Siberia would numb their noses, not giving them a chance to fully enjoy the fall. You missed out on everything these days if you were just a little lazy. And you had to take the winter clothes out early to prevent catching a cold when the seasons changed.

Bogyeong opened the door to the storage room. She went in there to clean from time to time but it grew dusty quickly since they didn't spend much time in it. She covered her mouth and nose to protect against the dust and threw open a window. There was an electronic piano that she had brought into her marriage, an old dining table, an air purifier. She should have thrown them away when they moved here, but she couldn't bring herself to. Not for any particular reason; she just couldn't stand the sight of these things standing forlornly in the recycling area of their old apartment building. She had even put them out once before lugging them back in.

She went through five boxes but couldn't find the coat she was looking for. She pulled out a padded coat that was way too thick, then returned it to its box. These were clothes for deep winter. She remembered that she had put a few boxes in the spare room down the hall; maybe the early-winter clothes were there. Bogyeong closed up all the boxes and reached for the last one at the very bottom of the stack. It was darker than the others, aged, crushed on the top from the weight of the other boxes. What was this box? She couldn't begin to guess what was in it, which was why she opened it without a second thought, and in that brief sliver of time, she was caught unawares by what it unleashed.

She beheld the firefighter's uniform, held safe in the box for over ten years. All the emotions she had bundled away with the uniform rushed past her, like a stinging wind. She hadn't wiped this singed, neatly folded uniform clean in case it completely disintegrated. Her heart lurched, pierced by the force of the memories that rushed out of the box, and she instinctively knew she couldn't touch it. If she did, the sorrow she had folded away with the remains of the uniform would break out and slide back into her. She closed the box and shoved it back into place. She would probably have forgotten what the box contained by the time she found it again. She decided to push it out of her mind until that day arrived.

Bogyeong opened the door to the spare room without

thinking. She nearly fell back and cracked her head open when that— that *thing* turned its head towards her, green light blinking, and spoke.

'Hello! I'm Broccoli, but you can call me Coli. Oh no, did I scare you?'

EUNHYE

Eunhye had started home-schooling at fourteen. She had wanted to switch much earlier but her mother had baulked. Every morning her mother told Eunhye that she was no different from anyone else, that she had no reason to feel self-conscious. But Eunhye knew it wasn't true. She just pretended to believe what her mother was telling her. Maybe, one day, if she kept pretending, she would end up believing it.

Eunhye used to go to a school that was thirty minutes away by wheelchair. It was only ten minutes by city bus, but for her it always took much longer to get on and off, and she couldn't help but feel she was a burden. So she just wheeled herself to school. Her face froze and cracked in the winter and her back was soaked with sweat in the summer. She unfortunately couldn't even listen to music on her way to school, because people tossed out all kinds of comments as they walked past. *Watch out. There's something right in front of you. Hey, kid, there's a car coming up behind you.* Sometimes, though thankfully not too often, people even grabbed the handles of her chair and pushed her as she went down a hill. She didn't want to call that 'help', but that was what they thought they were doing. They pushed her right along whether she wanted them to or not. Every time it happened her heart pounded with alarm, as though someone had grabbed her by the arm while passing by.

If Eunhye replied coldly, *I know,* to their warnings or ignored them outright, she would be considered terribly ungrateful. They sometimes frowned or tutted right in her face. People expected her to be positive, to overcome her difficult situation with good humour. But she didn't want to be a heart-warming, hopeful story for others. Sometimes she wanted to scream into a mic, so everyone could hear her: *Why don't you take care of your own damn selves and mind your own business!* The only good thing about this situation was that she didn't have to come home alone. She had Juwon to keep her company.

They lived in the same general area, and parted at the intersection near home. They were the only ones in their class who didn't live in the apartment complex.

Juwon was the only kid in their entire school who wore glasses, because she hadn't had artificial lenses inserted. Most kids got artificial lenses before they turned thirteen.

It was a rite of passage to undergo that procedure, assuming you didn't have any unusual conditions. Lenses were specially made for each individual, taking into consideration one's intraocular pressure and the thickness of one's cornea, with very few experiencing side effects. It was safer than wearing glasses, which could cause injury when playing sports. The lenses also corrected myopia and astigmatism. And you could replace the lenses down the road if you needed to. Most crucially, the procedure was covered by health insurance, and took only ten minutes. Glasses weren't completely obsolete, but people with prescription glasses were treated as though they hadn't managed to adapt to a new world. But Juwon hadn't had that procedure. She couldn't. She had Fuchs' endothelial dystrophy, a hereditary disease that resulted in the rapid loss of corneal endothelial cells, which made her ineligible.

Eunhye liked going home with Juwon, but from time to time she wondered if it was actually a problem that they lived in the same direction. It was safer and more fun to go with Juwon instead of on her own, and it was a relief that Juwon's presence discouraged strangers from foisting their kindness on her, but it also meant that their classmates treated them as a unit. The words they used to make them a pair, despite the fact that they were two entirely separate people, were blunt and one-dimensional.

'We're three-dimensional beings,' Juwon said. 'Let's not get our feelings hurt by silly one-dimensional words.'

Was that really possible? If she and Juwon were in the third dimension, it sometimes felt like the other kids were in a higher dimension. Juwon understood the world differently from others, and talked about it with a different perspective. Eunhye didn't always fully understand what Juwon meant but she liked how her friend expressed herself. Juwon was also refreshingly considerate. She would stop to wait for Eunhye when the road met up with the pavement, but she wouldn't make a big deal of it. She didn't go out of her way to make sure she was being considerate; she just did what she would do for anyone. Juwon probably didn't think about it as being considerate, but that in itself was incredibly meaningful to Eunhye. Juwon just acted natural so that Eunhye didn't feel like a burden. They existed in simple harmony, as though they were any two individuals.

Eunhye was already dreading going to a different high school than Juwon, unless Eunhye also wanted to pursue engineering. They would probably end up losing touch. Would she ever make a friend like Juwon again?

At the end of that term, Juwon told Eunhye that she would be moving over the summer. Not to another neighbourhood or even another district, but to another country a twelve-hour flight away. It didn't sink in for Eunhye until a few hours before Juwon's departure.

'What are you going all the way there for anyway?' Eunhye asked.

'I guess to learn more English?'

'But you can do English immersion here, too.'

'How's that the same thing? I'm sure it's a lot different in America.'

Eunhye couldn't claim whether it would be different or not, since she had never been to America. Juwon, for her part, didn't seem too upset that she was moving, and anyway the decision had already been made. Juwon promised to keep in touch. After they parted ways, Eunhye kept stopping to look back at Juwon, hoping her friend would turn around and look back too, but Juwon walked on, looking straight ahead, until she shrank into a dot and disappeared.

Did she *like* Juwon? Eunhye began wondering this only after Juwon said goodbye. But Juwon was unremarkable in every way. She was short. She wasn't included in sports, their classmates claiming that they didn't want to accidentally smack her in the glasses. Maybe because she wasn't that physically active she was a bit on the puny side, too. But judging Juwon like this was her way of trying not to like Juwon. Eventually Eunhye had to admit the truth. She didn't want to dredge up unflattering things about Juwon just so that she wouldn't have to acknowledge that she liked her. She liked Juwon. Eunhye began agonizing anew. Why was her first instinct to deny that she liked her? The answer to that question was simple: the love between them didn't look like other people's. To paraphrase Juwon, people living in a single dimension wouldn't be able to understand how deep their love was, this love between people in the third dimension. Or if that wasn't the case and those other people were in higher dimensions, their twisted perspective wouldn't be able to understand the love they had for each other. None of this mattered, though, unless Juwon was there beside her. Without Juwon knowing how she felt, it was all one-sided.

Eunhye had wanted to let Juwon know that she loved spending time with her, that she would wait for her to come back. She wasn't sure she would be able to bring herself to tell Juwon she had feelings for her. But Juwon would understand if she phrased it this way. She called Juwon, who didn't pick up. Maybe she was busy getting ready to leave for the airport, so Eunhye waited a bit and called a few more times, but Juwon still didn't pick up. Juwon left without ever picking up. Eunhye figured Juwon would get in touch when she arrived, but she didn't hear from her friend. Maybe she was still settling in. Maybe it was the time difference. Maybe her cell phone was broken.

After summer break, Eunhye returned to school and heard Juwon's news.

'She got the procedure done,' one of her classmates said.

'What procedure?' asked another.

'The lens insertion procedure.'

'Really? I thought she couldn't get it.'

'They heard it was possible in the US. That's why they moved. My mom says they had to borrow money to be able to afford it.'

Eunhye listened quietly to her classmates gossiping. Juwon hadn't had the procedure at home because her condition was too complex for surgery in Korea. Although it was much more expensive in America because insurance didn't cover it, she had still managed to get it done. Eunhye sat still, thinking, *Good for her.* She really was happy for her, but then she began shaking as her chin wobbled and tears welled.

Why did it feel like Juwon had left her behind? Like she had gone on to a different dimension without her. Did Juwon feel like she had entered the future, or maybe the mainstream? It didn't matter whether she really felt that way. That was what Eunhye perceived. She felt abandoned. As though she had been dropped from such a great height that all of her senses were smashed. Tears were flowing down her cheeks but it didn't feel like she was crying. Was that the right thing to do, to go all that way just to assimilate?

Was Eunhye staying where she was because she was lazy?

She cried all the way home. She couldn't help herself. She pushed the wheels harder than necessary. Her wheelchair teetered precariously on a small bump in the road, then got stuck on a gentle slope. She managed not to topple over but she did start to swear. She was irritated that the slope wasn't smooth, even after all these years, pissed off that she still had to power her chair manually. A confused, amorphous rage roiled inside her. She let out a scream. Passers-by who usually liked to force their kindness on her didn't dare approach. People stared at her as though she were unhinged.

She got home but couldn't stop crying. She didn't want anyone to see her tears, so she cried even harder. Her mother asked what was wrong, but Eunhye kept crying; Bogyeong hovered by the bedroom door for a while before giving up and leaving. Eunhye cried all through dinner. She cried when she woke up in the middle of the night.

She stayed home the next day. Her mother insisted on knowing what was going on, then quietly called the school to tell them that Eunhye was off sick. Thankfully the following day was a Saturday. Her mother was busy at work and Yeonjae was out all day. Eunhye lay in bed as if she had completely forgotten how to move. Drifting in and out of sleep, she bolted awake from a nightmare in which she was paralysed forever.

On Sunday night, near midnight, her mother tried again to talk to her. Though she looked exhausted from working all weekend, she attempted to make Eunhye feel better. 'Do you want me to come with you to school tomorrow?' she asked. 'Is someone bothering you?'

Eunhye refused to speak. She wanted to tell her mother

what was going on and let herself be consoled. Eunhye couldn't understand why she was acting like this. She just couldn't articulate her feelings. Her mother remained calm and persistent, resolute, as though she had been expecting something like this to happen. Eunhye lay on her bed, facing away from her mother, who gave her a hug. 'Tell me. Is there anything you want? You can have it. I won't ask you a single question. You can say whatever it is you want. Okay, Eunhye?'

Eunhye finally confessed that she didn't want to go to school. Her mother was visibly taken aback but refrained from asking questions, as promised. If her mother had asked her why, Eunhye would have answered, *Mom, it's so lonely to come back home by myself. It's not hard, but I feel so alone. I don't know exactly what it means to be lonely, but this is what it must feel like.*

Her mother went to the school to meet with the administrators, then came home to tell Eunhye that she didn't have to go to school any more. Instead, they signed up for a home-schooling service so Eunhye could continue her schoolwork. Her mother wanted Eunhye to promise that she would wake up on time to take her classes. That was an easy yes for Eunhye. She wanted to apologize but couldn't form the words.

It was time, Eunhye thought, to get a grip. Nothing got solved by tears. She had cried until she was spent, and nothing was going to change. She had to stop crying or she'd cry for the rest of her life. She suddenly found herself with a lot of time to think, now that she no longer went to school.

So what are you going to do now?

She didn't have an easy answer. Eunhye decided to journal. On the first page, she wrote: *I'm hurting.*

So what? What about it? What are you going to do with yourself?

I – I don't know.

How can you not know?

How could I possibly know? Is there even an answer to that question? This isn't something with a simple solution. Is there? If there's a way out, I'll take it.

. . .

See? There's no answer. I don't know. I'll just do my best for now.

Okay, got it.

Got what?

You'll do what you can. You'll try your best even if you don't know what that looks like. You're going to cheer yourself on.

And that was what Eunhye did. Whenever she found herself on the verge of tears, angry and frustrated, she rooted for herself to go on. It was a little different from the usual encouragement she heard from her mother, like *You can do it* or *It's going to get better.* Eunhye cheered for herself by saying, *So what are you going to do if you don't do this?* or *If you keep complaining you'll just make your life harder.* It was much more effective. Kind words didn't matter in this world.

Eunhye didn't need anyone else's help as she lived her life. They said nothing was impossible these days, but that relied on a certain freedom which was out of her reach.

Are you being avoidant?

No, I'm not.

Then why are you hiding?

So I won't be so exhausted.

Are you sure you're not running away?

. . .

What will you do if you run away from all this?

Why can't I run away?

What?

I want a break. I'm exhausted. Is that so bad? Do I always have to go after things with everything I've got? How come? Nobody else has to do that. Other people rest when they're tired and run away if they can't take it any more. I'm going to do what I want, too. I'm so done with it all.

Back then, she hadn't known that hiding had an expiry date. She kept pushing back the day she would have to get back at it. Sometimes the world felt like a set of perfectly fitted gears without room for Eunhye to wedge herself into. She wanted to fight that inaccessible world. Whenever she slammed into reality, she headed to the racetrack, enraged. For Eunhye, the filly, Today, was like a calming bamboo forest, a porthole to her inner thoughts, in which her secrets were fully protected, no matter what she said. But now Today didn't have much time left.

'No crying,' Eunhye said to the horse. 'Nothing gets solved by tears.' She might have been addressing Today, or maybe she was addressing herself. Eunhye held back the tears threatening to spill out. 'I'm not going to give up on you.'

This was the time to re-emerge; the perfect time to fight the world.

That evening, for the first time in a long while, Eunhye opened her journal.

I am strong. I will save her. I will save Today.

YEONJAE

Their homeroom teacher didn't even try to hide his bafflement. Even though Yeonjae was standing right there, he addressed only Jisu. 'You really want to enter the competition with Yeonjae?'

What the hell? She shouldn't have come along to submit their application. Yeonjae breathed out through her nose in an effort to control her anger. She did understand where their teacher was coming from. If she were in his shoes she too would have had a hard time wrapping her mind around the fact that these two students, one who fell asleep the moment she got to school and the other who ranked at the top of the country, would join forces for anything. It wasn't beyond the realms of possibility that the star student had been blackmailed or something. But Yeonjae would have at least hidden her incredulity. If their teacher had been less obvious or if Jisu had been closer to Yeonjae, she would have spoken about how talented Yeonjae was, but since neither was true Jisu just said, 'Yes.'

'But it's a really important competition . . .' their teacher trailed off.

Yeonjae could tell that their teacher wanted to add *and you want to enter with Yeonjae? Are you out of your mind?*

'I know it is,' Jisu said. 'That's why we're doing it together.'

Perhaps realizing he couldn't keep questioning the decision in front of Yeonjae, their teacher slipped their application into a folder with a sceptical expression. 'Well, it's not due until tomorrow, so you can come back if you need to change anything.' He looked from one girl to the other. 'Were you two always friends?'

'No,' Yeonjae blurted out. 'But what does that have to do—'

Jisu cut her off. 'Yes, we are. Why?'

'I just don't think I've ever seen you two hanging out.' He studied them with suspicion.

'School's not for hanging out, is it? We're supposed to be studying. Anyway, thank you.' Jisu grabbed Yeonjae by the hand and pulled her out of the office.

Jisu's answer had been much more appropriate than what Yeonjae had been going to say. They weren't actually friends but saying they were did shut their teacher up. Yeonjae assumed Jisu would let go once they were out in the hallway, but Jisu continued to drag her along. Should she shake her off? She didn't want to hurt Jisu's feelings. 'My hand.'

Jisu turned around. 'What?'

'Can you let go?'

Jisu glanced down, then dropped her hand like she was flicking a fly away.

Now that they had submitted the application, they could go their separate ways. But Jisu kept walking right next to her, all the way to the main gate. Lights glowed in the classrooms being used for evening study sessions. The cars usually idling in front of the gate to ferry kids to cram schools were all gone. Yeonjae assumed a car would be waiting for Jisu, too. But Jisu kept walking beside Yeonjae.

Yeonjae stopped herself from asking why; maybe she was just going the same way. And she wanted to find the right time to talk to Jisu about the details of their agreement.

The night before, Yeonjae had filled out the application in twenty minutes, then quickly jotted down a long list of the parts she would need for Coli. Asking for carbon fibre seemed presumptuous; she would work with aluminium. She included every detail, like the part name and manufacturer, to stave off the possibility of Jisu bringing her the wrong thing. She saved it in her cell phone. She would send it to Jisu as soon as she asked for it. Jisu kept walking alongside her, maintaining a distance that was neither too great nor too small, until they got to Makgyecheon Stream. Belatedly Yeonjae understood that Jisu wasn't going home, but following her. She stopped short.

'Where are you going?' Yeonjae demanded.

'With you,' Jisu said.

Yeonjae looked around. 'But why?'

Yeonjae didn't want to bring Jisu home ever again. They already had their agreement and they could text each other if either one needed anything. Yeonjae was genuinely curious. Why was this girl going out of her way to follow her? Jisu was the kind of person who used every tiny increment of time productively. It wasn't like she was trying to be Yeonjae's friend.

'Because I want to see that robot again.'

Yeonjae hadn't expected this. 'You do? Why?'

'Do I need to have a reason? You ask really weird questions, you know.'

Yeonjae pulled out her trump card. 'What about cram school?'

'I told my mom that I'm going to be preparing for the competition.'

'Your grades are gonna slip.'

'I'm not *that* dense,' Jisu said with a haughty smile.

Yeonjae wrinkled her nose in disgust. 'I'm not taking you to my place.'

A barrage of harsh words followed, with Jisu exclaiming how rude and petty she was. None of that changed

Yeonjae's mind. Jisu unloaded her feelings for some time, then stood there, looking cross, just like the little stuffed animal hanging from her backpack – a polar bear with angry, furrowed eyebrows.

Yeonjae didn't like to bring anyone home. When she was nine, around the time she ran off during the relay race, she became friends with four kids at an afterschool programme where they made microrobots. When she went over to their homes she realized for the first time in her life that not everyone lived like her family. When her new friends suggested coming over to Yeonjae's next, she worried about it for a day before inviting them. They were visibly dismayed. They all seemed to believe that older things should be discarded as soon as a newer model came out, and appeared to view Yeonjae's family as strange and backward because they didn't follow those trends. They were kind children, though, and never said anything to her face, but none of them ever suggested going over to her place again. This was when she understood that certain things about her life should remain hidden.

Yeonjae and Jisu had an agreement. If Jisu got mad and reported her, the robot would be taken away. She didn't think Jisu would do something like that when the competition was on the line, but she couldn't be certain. She made up a reasonable excuse on the fly, that she had to give her mom a heads-up before bringing someone home. Thankfully, Jisu accepted that logic.

Yeonjae felt now was the time to send the parts list to Jisu, who glanced at it.

'I'll tell my dad. There's nothing I can do if he can't source it. Okay? If he can find them I'll have him send them to your place.'

'Wow. So your dad's cool with it?'

'Well, he's the one who's dead set on me entering the competition.'

Should she ask why? Thankfully, Jisu kept prattling on. 'I have to get an award, any award, to be able to major in something robotics-related, like my dad wants. My dad's acting like he'll do anything to help us win.'

'What? Why?'

Jisu sighed, exasperated. 'Obviously because that's how badly he wants it. What kind of question is that? You really can't read between the lines, can you?'

'No, I mean, why would you major in something related to robotics? You're not into this stuff.'

Yeonjae must have hit a sore spot. Jisu didn't respond. If Jisu had been remotely interested, she wouldn't have crinkled her nose in confusion when she scanned the parts list Yeonjae sent her. In fact, she would have asked why Yeonjae was going to use aluminium, which would make the robot heavier.

Jisu made a face and gripped the strap of her backpack. The angry polar bear bounced back and forth. 'Okay, well, see you tomorrow. I'm going home. I shouldn't have come all the way here. What a waste of time.'

Yeonjae wondered what that was about. She didn't particularly want to know what Jisu was going through. But she found herself glancing back at Jisu as she walked along the stream. She felt a twinge of guilt that the always smug, caustic Jisu was a bit deflated.

Jisu suddenly whipped around. 'What are you looking at!'

Yeonjae turned on her heel and headed home briskly, almost breaking into a run.

Earlier that morning, she had given the robot a name. All night, she had been thinking that the robot needed one. Then she had gone down to breakfast and found broccoli on the table. The colour green was the only thing the vegetable and the robot had in common, but she repeated *Broccoli* to herself a few times and decided it was a cool name. It had an American flavour to it. Not that English was always cool, but she wanted her robot to have a friendly, approachable name. The name Broccoli sounded good coming out of her mouth and felt easy, like she hadn't spent too much time agonizing over it. She had run upstairs right away to change the name in the control unit.

When the red light blinked on, she spoke clearly: 'Broccoli. Bro-co-lee.' Then she said, 'Coli,' adding that to the settings so the robot would also react to its nickname.

COLI

'Coli, Coli, Coli.'

Yeonjae had left in the morning without turning Coli off. That meant Coli could say its own name as many times as it pleased. Coli wanted to say *Coli* until it got sick of saying it, but it actually did not have the capability to get tired of something. Coli would have to stop itself from repeating its name at some point. All of a sudden, with no regrets, the way a computer is powered off.

Yeonjae had told Coli that she was going to school and would be back in about ten hours. Coli sat in the room alone. It was not as small as the stall it used to live in. This was a big space that could fit at least fifteen robot jockeys. Even Today might be able to fit in the room if she ducked a little. The walls were painted green, and there was a large window and a dresser pushed against one side. The dresser drawers contained books and albums and all manner of junk, like a filthy baseball and an old glove, a framed award and a dusty trophy, a Lego castle and an unused drone. They all gave off warmth even though they were not made of warm materials. Time seemed to flow faster inside this room. There must have been an error during the manufacturing process. How else could Coli sense time in such varying ways?

Coli sat in that room, thinking about the people it had encountered in this house. Three women lived here. Kim Bogyeong, Woo Eunhye, and Woo Yeonjae. And Seo Jisu did not live here but was Woo Yeonjae's friend. Through the floors and the walls, Coli sensed the vibrations, and could tell that this house was alive. Coli remembered the vibrations it had felt when Today galloped at eighty kilometres an hour. This house gave off similar vibrations, at a similar frequency. Each of the humans living in this house was unique, different. One was a blue-yellow sky, one was a pink-purple sky, and one was a red-green sky. Coli knew it would be able to describe these humans more accurately if it knew more than a thousand words.

Bogyeong was pink-purple. She could not hide her shock when she first saw Coli, but now came up at least once a day to check on it. When their eyes met, Coli would say hello and Bogyeong would awkwardly say, 'Oh, hi,' and flee downstairs. Eventually, she started to ask, 'Would you like the window open?' and even, 'Is there anything you need . . .'

How could Coli describe the way Bogyeong looked at Coli? She looked at Coli with repulsion, animosity, contempt, and disillusionment. No, it wasn't disillusionment, it was a slight tinge of fear. That was more like it. Plus a moderate curiosity. Bogyeong certainly was not aware that she was revealing any of these feelings. She could not see the expression she made when she looked at Coli. What made her make that face? What was it about Coli that brought out repulsion, animosity, and a slight tinge of fear in Bogyeong?

Bogyeong was the only person Coli spent time with while Yeonjae was away, at least until Coli could get new legs. Coli could not help but wonder how it might help remove those visceral expressions from Bogyeong's face. Coli wanted to get to know Bogyeong better, but she maintained a set distance. *How can I get to know Bogyeong better? Why do I want to get to know Bogyeong better?* Coli did not know the answer to either question. Eventually Coli came to the conclusion that information about a human's facial expressions must have been inputted into its hard drive. Coli must have been programmed to do something when it detected a muscle moving in a certain part of the human face.

Bogyeong worked from noon to midnight. Her footsteps sounded different when she returned home at night than when she left in the morning. After work, it sounded as though she were dragging twenty-kilo sandbags attached to each foot. She would call out absently, 'I'm home,' then go straight into the shower without pausing to unwind. She let out a deep, exhausted sigh when she got into bed. She slept like the dead until morning. She woke at seven to make breakfast, and she cleaned the house after Yeonjae left for school. Some days she tackled only the living room, some days she also cleaned the bedrooms, and on other days she managed to get to the first floor and the bathroom. Once in a while she would say out loud to nobody in particular, 'I can't do it any more,' and flop on the sofa.

Bogyeong was like a champion racehorse. She did not take a break, she was fast, and she was strong. Though she did seem tired all the time.

Bogyeong began to confide in Coli when they were alone. By this time Coli had finally received new legs and begun moving freely up and down the stairs. Bogyeong's wariness did not dissipate fully but she seemed to appreciate that she had someone to talk to. Still, no matter what, she always kept about ten paces away from Coli. Bogyeong sat at the table when Coli was standing in the living room, and she sat on the sofa when Coli was on the stairs. A shadow would cross her face from time to time and she would interrupt herself to say, 'I would have said all this to him if he were still here.'

Coli just listened.

'I have two daughters but I can't bring myself to say anything to them. They've already got enough on their plates. I don't want them to think of me as someone they have to take care of.'

Coli stayed silent.

'Sorry. Humans are always unloading on others like this. But you don't know what it's like to miss someone, do you? I wish I were like that.'

'What is missing someone like?'

Bogyeong thought for a long moment.

Coli waited, watching coffee cool in her chipped mug.

'Like losing all your memories, one by one.' Bogyeong looked out of the kitchen window. 'You remember them out of the blue, but you have to acknowledge that you won't ever go back to that time. And you wrench off the bruised parts of your heart, one by one. Until they're all gone.'

'You die if you remove your heart, do you not?'

'Yeah. You just take it one day at a time, thinking, when I die someday, none of this is going to matter.'

Coli wanted to ask what that meant. Bogyeong tended to answer Coli's questions in a confusing, elliptical way. She did not answer them the way Minju did, step by step. But Coli noticed the angle of Bogyeong's gaze and her slower breathing, and determined that she did not want to continue talking.

To some degree Coli understood what it was to acknowledge that one could not go back to another time. Coli could not return to the moments stored in its memory. Past moments could be re-enacted but you could never go back to that precise sliver of time. Coli stood still without speaking. The light from the setting sun moved slowly from the edge of the table, lengthening until it cut right across it.

'The only way to go back to the good old days is to feel joy in the present.' Bogyeong's eyes glistened in the sunlight.

Glistening indicated beauty, but to Coli her eyes looked sad.

'Because happiness cures all ills,' continued Bogyeong.

Coli kept quiet.

'Only happy moments are powerful enough to push longing back down.'

So that was what it was like to miss something. Coli too had moments it longed for – when Coli and Today would race down the track together, Today's joy reverberating through her body.

Bogyeong caught herself and wished she hadn't said all those things to Coli. Without her realizing it, in that moment a layer of her resistance to the robot had been peeled off.

But Coli detected the change. Coli sensed a small amount of comfort never before seen in Bogyeong's face.

'. . . this is all very silly of me,' she said.

Coli figured out a solution. Conversation. The more she talked, the more the negative emotions hardening around her were sloughed off, one thin layer at a time, like skin.

How much conversation would they need to peel all

those layers off Bogyeong's face? How many stories should Coli listen to? How much time would that take? Would it have enough time to do that for her?

Coli discovered something else about Bogyeong, namely that she reached towards Eunhye the most but that Yeonjae's name was always on her lips. Her mouth and her eyes moved separately from each other, as did her hands and her heart. She was very good at this. She was also intensely curious about what Coli and Yeonjae talked about when they were alone.

'See, she stopped telling me anything a long time ago,' Bogyeong said sweetly, trying to get Coli to fill her in, but Coli could not give her even a hint because of Yeonjae's orders to never divulge their conversations to anyone.

'Come on, I'll keep it a secret,' Bogyeong wheedled. 'Just tell me.'

Coli replied the way it was programmed, that it was simply not possible.

'Not possible? Like someone sleeping with their eyes open?' Bogyeong wondered.

Still, Bogyeong tried whenever she got the chance. She seemed to believe that Coli would eventually be worn down and persuaded to spill the beans. But that was not possible, unless Coli was reprogrammed.

'Can't you tell me?'

'I cannot.'

'Can you tell me today?'

'I cannot.'

'Any desire to tell me today?'

'No.'

Bogyeong was also thrilled whenever Yeonjae's friend Jisu came over. Even if she was working at the restaurant, she would swing by the house with fruit or snacks when Jisu was there.

Seo Jisu. Coli was as intrigued by this human as by Bogyeong. Whenever Jisu came over, Bogyeong fluttered about, and Yeonjae got uncharacteristically talkative and less rigid. With Jisu, Yeonjae's face, tone of voice, and range of activity changed. This was an area in need of closer observation, so Coli created a separate file for 'Yeonjae and Jisu' on its hard drive.

One day, Yeonjae's face split into a grin. A truckload of parts had been delivered. Yeonjae stayed up all night out in the yard examining them, banging and thumping. Early the next morning she came upstairs with 3D drawings and parts that would become part of Coli's body. She took several trips up and down the stairs with armloads of components, sweat beading on her forehead. Once everything was ready, she grinned at Coli and said, 'This weekend I'm going to take you to pieces and build you back up to look like this.'

For two full days she sat by Coli without pausing to sleep, like in the early days, revising and re-revising the design. She explained every step to Coli while showing it the drawings, the way a doctor might inform a patient of an upcoming surgery.

'I'll add an air bearing in between your spine and your pelvis, so you can pivot your lower body. It'll look weird if you can pivot too smoothly so I'll adjust the torque. It's not the best motor, because I didn't want to ask for something too expensive . . . it's going to have a big gap around it, so the motor will probably shake a bit. Sorry about that. You might look a little silly walking around like that, shaking. Oh, and this time I'm going to make your lower body out of aluminium. It'll be heavier than when it was all carbon fibre, but you don't need to be that light any more, do you? I know it's cheaper, but I actually prefer the cold, alien feeling you get from aluminium. I know, I know, you won't get it even if I explain it ten different ways. I decided not to go out of my way to put in a hydraulic motor, since you won't need to absorb as much impact as before. I'll just add shock absorbers to your ankles. And a pneumatic cylinder in the spring. That's what that is, that silver stick-like thing. The one with the hook on the end. You're going to be heavy, so your lower half will be for the sole purpose of walking. Any problems with that?'

'No, it is perfect.'

Yeonjae snorted. 'Perfect? It sounds weird when you say stuff like that.'

'But that was a perfect explanation. I trust that you will do a good job.'

'Where did you learn to talk like that?'

'From Mr Minju. He always trusted me with Today.'

'That guy is so weird.'

'So are you,' Coli said politely.

Coli listened attentively as Yeonjae talked about the parts that would form Coli's lower body and watched her eyes gleaming more brightly than usual. Coli came to realize that sometimes, very occasionally, people glowed on their own.

Right before Yeonjae turned off the power to work on Coli's legs, Coli heard the news about Today.

'Will I be able to race with Today again when I get my legs?'

Yeonjae paused, then shook her head. 'You're going to be too heavy for her. And she physically can't handle racing any more.'

'What will happen to Today?'

'What?'

'I heard once that a horse who cannot run is a useless horse. So what happens to Today when she becomes useless?'

Yeonjae chewed on her lower lip, then sighed. 'She'll probably die.'

'Why?'

'Because she won't be useful to them any more. The way they were going to throw you out because you couldn't be a jockey any more.'

'Then—'

Yeonjae looked quizzically at Coli.

'Can you fix her the way you are fixing me? I would be ever so grateful.' Coli was not able to hear Yeonjae's answer because she turned off the power. But just before everything went dark, Coli glimpsed Yeonjae biting down on her lip and furrowing her brow.

Coli did not want to move to another place. If Coli were given a choice, Coli wanted to stay here as long as possible. Coli did not know what it could or should do right now, but Coli wished to be with Today.

More than anything else, Coli wanted to get to know Eunhye better. What a fascinating human. She moved by using an apparatus, unlike the other humans. She was masterful. She was strong. That was how she looked to Coli.

EUNHYE

Two days from now, Sunday, would be Today's last day in the stables.

The decision was based on Bokhui's conclusion that Today would never again hit her previous record speed and would be unlikely to be able to run in her condition, not even at thirty kilometres an hour. But she had recovered enough that she could hobble along. Eunhye knew what awaited the filly once she was unceremoniously kicked out. She would be shoved into a tiny truck and driven out of the city to an unknown destination. There, she would be fed handsomely for a day, then put to sleep. The only other remaining option was for someone to take Today in, but nobody wanted a horse that could barely walk. You died if you weren't needed by a human. This was, as Bokhui said, the grave situation faced by all animals living on this planet.

Eunhye pushed all of that out of her mind. She popped some almonds in her mouth and shared some with Today. Horses were too smart for their own good. It would be better if they were just a little less intelligent, but they had spent too much time at close quarters with humans, like dogs and cats, and they could read human moods. It could be that horses understood every word uttered by humans, even if they couldn't express themselves in a way humans could understand. It was a tragedy all round. Eunhye patted Today on the nose; the filly was more subdued than usual this afternoon.

Eunhye hadn't been there when Bokhui had made the decision. But when she reached the racetrack, she could tell something was up. Dayeong, who was usually on her phone, was waiting for her at the gate. She told Eunhye to go home, just for the day, or to return a little later. Finally, Dayeong acknowledged that Eunhye was old enough to hear the truth, and said she shouldn't go into the stables right now because Bokhui was talking to the CEO of the racetrack. Eunhye understood what the conversation must be about. It couldn't be a positive one, or even an everyday one. Eunhye didn't argue with Dayeong. Instead, they watched TV together in the ticket booth. Celebrities on a variety show were laughing so hard that they were crying, but neither of them even broke into a smile.

After a while, Eunhye went over to the stables to see Today.

She looked into the horse's eyes, which gleamed like black pearls. 'It's all happening so fast. Don't you think?'

Today huffed, ruffling Eunhye's hair.

'Did you know your jockey is upstairs in our house? When it fell off you, its lower body was completely shattered.' She shook out the five remaining almonds from the plastic bag on to her palm and held her hand out.

Today moved closer and snuffled at the nuts, then hoovered them up.

'Yeonjae's a robotics whiz,' Eunhye continued. 'A few days ago a truck came and delivered a bunch of things, and she was in the backyard, banging and breaking them and welding them together. She's made legs for your jockey. She's got to be a genius.'

They were lucky they didn't live in an apartment building or in an otherwise densely populated neighbourhood. Nobody would be so magnanimous as to let Yeonjae make a racket from late afternoon until close to midnight. Their house was the perfect location for Yeonjae's project. It was a stand-alone structure in the middle of nowhere, much like a remote shelter in a vast stretch of desert, where people occasionally stopped by to rest but otherwise left you alone.

'I wish I could help,' Eunhye said. 'What a mess we're in, you and me.' She reconsidered. 'Not that I want to fix my legs. I mean, sure, that would be nice. But I'm fine even if that never happens. I don't have to be like everyone else, you know? I can live a perfectly fine life without legs.'

Today stuck her nose into Eunhye's hair and snorted.

'It's just so hard. I can't climb stairs or go anywhere with these wheels. Things have advanced so much that robots ride horses now, but I'm still in this wheelchair. Weird, right?' She hugged Today's head with both arms.

'We can both live good lives on our own, right? We don't always need help. I hate how people just assume I need help, like I can't survive if I don't have someone to help me. My mom says I should go to a good college and prove to everyone that I can have a great life, but I don't know why I have to prove my existence by doing what other people think is great. You know, I just want to travel. I want to travel a ton. I want to go everywhere in the world with a camera.'

Eunhye heard someone entering the stables. It was Minju, probably here to tell her that he was going to start locking up. She was about to tell him she was just leaving when Minju said, 'So, I was going to order tteokbokki.'

Eunhye paused for a moment. 'How about fried fish cakes, too?'

Minju's office was in the single-storey, cement, staff-only building next to the indoor arena, not far from the stables. The kitchenette had an induction stove and a microwave, a mid-size fridge papered over with flyers and coupons, a small table, and a nook where you could lie down for a nap.

Minju ordered on an app and handed Eunhye an aloe drink from the fridge.

'You look just like your mom but nothing like Yeonjae,' Minju remarked, thinking back to a few days ago when Eunhye had visited the racetrack with her mother. They looked so alike that he would have known they were related even if Eunhye hadn't introduced them. Her mother had said hello, puzzled that Eunhye had wanted to come here even though she was sick and the track wasn't open.

'Yeonjae takes after our dad.' Whenever Eunhye tried to remember their dad's face, Yeonjae's got in the way, making it hard to visualize their dad. It made her want to forget what Yeonjae looked like, just for a short while. What she remembered was a man who had raced her down hospital corridors in a wheelchair when Eunhye was first fitted for one.

She gently scratched the paper label off her aloe drink.

Minju saw that Eunhye was lost in thought. He actually didn't feel like tteokbokki at all; he had been planning to grab some gimbap and instant ramen for dinner instead. He had a lot on his mind; he was disappointed in himself that he hadn't been able to utter a single word in Today's defence as he stood next to Bokhui and the CEO. *Now you feel guilty?* he chastised himself. *You haven't done anything about it all this time.*

Minju had witnessed the demise of many horses that were no longer able to run, so he wasn't shocked or dismayed by what Today's future held. He merely felt a vague bitterness as always, as though he were gnawing on a bellflower root. Of course he felt bad for the horses, but he couldn't do anything about it. The racetrack would lose money if it cared for horses that people didn't bet on, and if profits went down, Minju's job would be impacted. He wasn't really the horses' caretaker; he was more like another trapped horse, held captive by invisible walls.

Minju had stepped away from the stables to avoid hearing more of the discussion. And later, he overheard Eunhye with Today. He watched the girl murmuring gently and embracing the filly. He waited for the right time to make his presence known. What did teenagers like to eat these days? Tteokbokki? He walked in loudly on purpose. He was gratified when she accepted his invitation. But now he didn't know what to do. Eunhye was quiet. What he really wanted to ask was whether she was going to keep coming to the stables even after Today was gone, but that seemed like such a cruel thing to bring up. And why did they need over an hour to deliver a plate of tteokbokki?

'She's going to die, isn't she?' Eunhye's tone was casual despite all of Minju's worrying.

He looked up from the delivery app. 'Yeah,' he said, nodding slowly.

Eunhye took in his answer stoically. 'Can't we buy some time somehow? Two days isn't enough, not when there's a life on the line.'

'Well ... I have a feeling they think two days is too much time.' The truth just kept tumbling out of Minju's mouth – he didn't want to be so brutally forthright with the girl.

'Do they realize that she's in good health except for her joints?'

'Of course. The vet told them all that.'

'And that she's only three years old?' Eunhye watched Minju closely, looking for an opening.

'Of course they know that.' Even Eunhye knew; how could they not?

'But then why does she only get two days?'

Minju couldn't answer.

'I hate this. This is the worst.' Eunhye's voice rose. Her eyes welled up. Of course she knew that Minju was powerless in this situation. His only fault was being in her presence right at this moment.

He offered her a tissue but she didn't take it.

Her gaze was venomous. 'We must be the cruellest species in the world. In the whole universe.'

Whenever her mother told her that it was okay, that she wasn't defined by whatever small discomfort she faced, Eunhye had always wanted to say this: *I shouldn't have to hear that. A person without a disability is never told that it's okay not to have a disability. Mom, your attempt at making me feel better is like the impersonal, spiky bars of a cage. It just makes it clear that I'm not normal. My wheelchair isn't something that helps people who can't walk to move, because I still can't use the buses and the underground and the pavements and the stairs and the escalators like everyone else.*

People like Eunhye were wholly ignored in the march of technological progress. She should never have been made this way if she couldn't live in this world with this body. The universe only created things it could hold within itself, things it could nurture. 'Normal' people didn't seem to realize that every being in this world had the power to live their life independently.

There was a knock on the door. Now, of all times? He got up awkwardly to let the delivery person in. Why did they say it was going to take sixty minutes if it was going to be this fast? Minju opened the door to take the delivery and—

'Yeonjae?'

Yeonjae was leaning sullenly against the wall beside the delivery person. 'Can I have some, too?'

Minju quickly unearthed another pair of wooden chopsticks.

On their way back home, Eunhye wondered how much Yeonjae had overheard. Maybe Yeonjae assumed she had been crying because of how she sounded. She wanted to tell her sister that she hadn't been crying. But Yeonjae was silent as always, and she didn't want to dredge up what had already passed.

Eunhye and Yeonjae didn't have the best relationship but they didn't have a terrible one, either. Neither best friends nor strangers. They were like classmates sitting on opposite sides of a classroom who knew of each other but not much about what the other person liked or hated. Sometimes it felt to Eunhye that they weren't even that close. Maybe they were more like strangers who didn't go to the same school or indeed live in the same country. They would go on living separate lives without knowing the other person existed unless an unusual event brought them together. In popular culture, sisters seemed to shop and travel together, but that seemed unlikely to ever happen for them. With a sibling you had to divvy up a set amount of love, from the moment they were born.

Yeonjae was the one who had given up on competing with Eunhye. She had realized at a very young age that she couldn't attract even a quarter of their parents' attention as long as Eunhye was around. She would never be the focus of anyone's attention, not even for a brief moment, no matter what she managed to achieve.

Their mother probably knew that Yeonjae was keeping things to herself. It was when Yeonjae was around six that the family had realized she was interested in machinery and robotics. Their dad had died before her passion could be nurtured.

After their dad's untimely death, Yeonjae began to take

more responsibility at home. Whenever her mother asked, Yeonjae left her friends and ran home, helping Eunhye to eat or wash her hair. She effectively became Eunhye's aide. Yeonjae never ignored their mother's summons. She never refused to do something for Eunhye. But she never once offered to help without being asked.

'Go hang out with your friends,' Eunhye said once. 'I can wash my hair myself.'

'It's fine. Mom will be mad.'

'I'll tell her I told you to go.'

'It's okay. This is all she asks me to do, anyway.'

Eunhye, for her part, understood that Yeonjae was complying eagerly to every demand in a last-ditch attempt to get attention. She stopped telling her sister she could do it on her own. She started thanking her. She couldn't tell if that made any difference. Their symbiotic relationship came to an end once Eunhye relearned how to take care of herself. She didn't need her sister any more. But that liberation didn't seem to make Yeonjae any happier. If anything, she seemed lonely, and around the time Eunhye left her school, it looked like that got much worse.

Their mother allowed Eunhye to drop out of school as though she had no problem with it, but Eunhye knew she was just pretending. She knew her mother's imagination was running wild, unable to ask why she wanted to quit school, but still Eunhye didn't do her the kindness of explaining. It would seem like she was refusing school because she couldn't get an operation that could be easily done in Korea, whereas Juwon was going all the way to America for hers. Then her mother would torture herself over it. Eunhye didn't want to have to see her mother like that. Sometimes silence was the only solution.

Yeonjae used to go out on weekend mornings before coming home in the afternoons to help out at the restaurant. But once Eunhye dropped out of school, Yeonjae started staying unusually close to home. At first, Eunhye didn't pay much attention. Yeonjae might not have plans every single weekend, so Eunhye figured her sister would go out the following weekend. But her sister stayed home the next weekend, then again the following weekend. She didn't even appear to do anything in particular when she was home. She turned on the TV, scrolled on her phone, took a catnap, then was on her phone again, and once in a while she glanced at Eunhye. She looked bored and listless. When Eunhye noticed her sister's expression, she happened to be watching TV, watching a polar bear locked up in a cage. She realized that Yeonjae looked just like the polar bear. No. Yeonjae looked like an uninspired zookeeper staring at the polar bear.

So that was what this was. Their mother must have asked Yeonjae to stay home. Their mother must have said, *Your sister is depressed, you should stay home and hang out with her.* Or maybe she said, *Make sure your sister doesn't hurt herself.*

About a month into this new routine, Yeonjae was lying on the sofa when she got a phone call. She sprang up and threw open Eunhye's door. Eunhye, who had been reading a book, jumped. What was even more shocking was how Yeonjae yanked her by the wheelchair towards the door, with no explanation.

'What are you *doing*? What the *hell*!'

'Mom says we should go for a walk or something.'

Yeonjae must have known she was being terrible. But a knot of resentment must have hardened inside her; she probably couldn't help herself. Only later did Eunhye realize that Yeonjae had behaved that way on purpose, to hurt her, to lash out. But at the time she was sucked right into it.

Eunhye was dragged out to the living room. She turned and shoved Yeonjae. Yeonjae didn't budge. Eunhye pinched her, hit her. Yeonjae yelped and let go of the wheelchair. Eunhye burst into rageful, indignant tears. 'What do you think you're doing?' she shouted. She hated her sister right then. She despised her. This was all Yeonjae's fault. Eunhye wanted her sister to realize that she was in the wrong. She wanted Yeonjae to feel bad and apologize, owning up to her mistake. But Yeonjae just stared back at Eunhye, her eyes turning red. Fat tears began running down her cheeks. Eunhye had never, ever, seen her sister cry. Yeonjae had seemed so tough, like someone who would never break down in tears.

Yeonjae swallowed her tears. 'Sorry.'

Eunhye's own tears had dried up in shock. She stared at the streaks on Yeonjae's face.

After their tussle, Eunhye made herself busy. She stopped holing up in her room. She roamed the racetrack on weekends. It freed Yeonjae from having to stay home to babysit. Eunhye should have called her back when her sister apologized and ran off. What if that had been the only chance for Eunhye to ask her sister what was wrong?

When they had almost reached home, Yeonjae finally spoke. 'That horse.'

Had Eunhye heard her correctly? She looked at Yeonjae. The wind, now chilly, swirled around the back of her neck.

'Today, I mean,' Yeonjae clarified. 'Are they going to euthanize her?'

'I think so.'

'When?'

'In two days.'

'Oh.'

Yeonjae's reaction seemed cold to Eunhye. But then again, Yeonjae had never shown much interest in horses.

'Do you want to try to save her?'

'Isn't that obvious?' Eunhye snapped.

Yeonjae let that slide. 'Eonni, you haven't had a real conversation with Coli yet, have you?'

Eunhye shook her head.

'Come on. Coli wants to save that horse as much as you do. Maybe even more.' Yeonjae opened the front door for Eunhye. 'I couldn't hear you earlier.' She sighed. 'I mean, I did listen, but I couldn't hear everything you said. So don't worry.'

'I'm not worried. I don't care if you heard me.'

'But if you want me to hear it you can tell me.'

'Huh?'

'I can listen. Even if I can't come up with a solution.' Yeonjae slipped inside and let the door close behind her, then, realizing that Eunhye was still outside, threw it back open.

Something that wasn't human walked like a human down the stairs, on two legs bent at a sixty-degree angle, moving in an unnatural but fluid way. The cushioned soles gently touched the floor. Coli turned its head towards Eunhye. Its helmet was banged up and the letters on its chest were so scratched that they were no longer legible. Coli walked slowly towards the girls. Eunhye spotted a tiny rainbow sticker on its chest, on the left, as small as a pinkie nail.

Eunhye always felt awkward around Coli, no matter how many times she saw the robot. She gave a timid wave. Coli came to a halt in front of her, waving its right hand like her, then lowered itself so that its gaze would be level with hers. She hadn't looked at Coli this close up before. It was true that she didn't have much interest in robots, but really it was because Yeonjae's workshop was upstairs. She couldn't go up to the first floor without a lot of planning. She looked searchingly at Coli, then reached out to touch it on the shoulder. Cold and hard. No warmth, not like when she hugged Today. What a strange machine, acting as though it were alive when it most certainly wasn't. Coli was the only one among them with parts that had clear origins. Her fingers ran along the thin, light shell of Coli's torso until she got to the rainbow sticker. This robot was empty inside. How did it even know that it wanted to save Today? How did it understand what that feeling was? But Eunhye would do anything this metal thing told her to do if there were even a one in a million chance to save Today. Hope bloomed in her heart.

In a calm, detached voice, Coli said, 'I want to save Today. Because she is my partner.'

'Same here,' Eunhye said.

'I have an idea. Would you like to hear it?'

Eunhye nodded.

Coli shared the questions and answers it had pondered over while sitting in the upstairs room, waiting for Yeonjae to go and get Eunhye from the racetrack.

Today has to die.
Why?

Because she cannot run.

Why?

Because her joints are ruined and they hurt her.

Why?

Because she ran too fast.

Why?

Because humans wanted her to.

Why?

Because only fast horses delight humans.

Why?

. . .

Can Today's condition be treated?

With current human medical technology, joints cannot be
   returned to their original state.

Is there another way?

She must go back to the past.

Before she was in pain.

'And how exactly would she go back to the past?' Eunhye
asked.

The perfect solution would be time travel. If you could
go back to the past, there wouldn't be any pain or sorrow
anywhere in the world. On the flip side, nobody would
value the present.

Coli raised a finger. 'We have to make her happy.'

Eunhye and Yeonjae stared at Coli, not understanding.

Coli raised its voice one level, confident that this was the right solution. Of course, Coli had not come to this solution on its own or read it in a book. But it was what Coli had derived from observing human lives thus far, human lives that were more accurate and wiser than any book.

'Happiness cures all ills. It is the only thing that is more powerful than going back to the past.'

BOKHUI

Near the end of the day, Yeonjae and Eunhye wheeled a blanket-covered pushcart into Bokhui's clinic.

'What's this cart for?' Bokhui lifted the blanket and saw two glowing holes. She let out a shriek and scuttled back.

'Shh! Shh!' Eunhye said. 'There's nothing to be scared of.'

Bokhui clapped a hand over her mouth. Were the sisters plotting a crime? Why else would they come to a vet instead of a doctor?

The sisters explained that the robot in the cart was Today's jockey, now called Coli.

Bokhui concealed Coli with her own coat and hat and shoved the three of them into an examination room. She told them to stay there. Bokhui told the receptionist that she would finish up. The receptionist looked surprised, since Bokhui tended to be a stickler about starting and ending work on time. Only after being reassured three separate ways that Bokhui would take on her duties did the receptionist eagerly change out of her uniform. Bokhui stood in front of the examination room with her arms crossed, grimacing every time their eyes met as she urged the receptionist to hurry on home. She waved her out with both hands.

Bokhui locked the front door and turned off the waiting-room lights. She took a deep breath before entering the consulting room. She had thought Today's robot jockey was out of commission. Minju had told her it had been sold. But here it was, in her office. Did Minju sell the robot to these kids? Or did they steal it and were here to ask for her help? What was she supposed to do? She squeezed her eyes shut, then opened them. She entered the room. There they were, the girls and the robot, which had emerged from the cart and was now sitting in a chair.

'So . . . how about a drink?' Bokhui hurried to the fridge without waiting for them to answer.

That very morning, Bokhui had notified the racetrack of Today's execution date, this horse she had tried so vainly to save. She was just doing her job. She brooded over the conversation she'd had a few days ago with Seojin outside the convenience store. More than anyone else, Bokhui wanted animals to be able to live their lives to the fullest. But they weren't allowed to do that. At least not on this planet, on which everything was manipulated for the benefit of humans. Being alive on this planet was hellish for a horse like Today, who earlier had had to hear how she would be sold off, part by part, as she stood in her narrow stall.

Bokhui could barely keep herself from slugging the CEO in his grinning mug, his teeth yellowed from years of smoking. *Why are you grinning like that?* she wanted to demand. *Don't you have an ounce of compassion for an animal whose cartilage is all worn out because she raced so hard, raking in loads of money for you?*

He could barely hide his excitement about the three horses he had just bought. She gave Today another IV supplement, which probably did nothing for her, then headed out, spotting Eunhye and Dayeong in the ticket office by the north gate. She'd walked past, trying to avoid them. She couldn't bring herself to face Eunhye.

From the fridge Bokhui grabbed two bottles of orange juice gifted by the owner of a Welsh corgi earlier that day. The pup loved its walks but had stepped on a shard of glass and injured itself. She had stitched the poor dog's bleeding paw and wrapped it in a bandage, advising the owner to refrain from walking it for a while.

'People are the worst,' the owner had complained. 'Why would you leave broken glass on the ground? I wish we had better laws to stop that kind of behaviour.'

Bokhui had smiled. 'I bet there's a good way to fix that. If we all had to walk barefoot, I'm sure the streets would instantly become immaculate.'

With the drinks in hand, Bokhui headed back to the examination room.

'Hello,' the robot said.

'Oh . . . hi.' She handed the bottles of juice to the girls, sneaking glances at the robot. Something was different about this robot, but she couldn't quite put her finger on what it was.

The robot's neck swivelled to follow Bokhui's movements.

'You are the vet who takes care of Today, right?' asked the robot.

'. . . yes, you remembered.'

'I do not remember. I store information in my hard drive until it is deleted.'

'Should I thank you for not deleting that information, then?' Bokhui murmured, glancing at Eunhye.

Eunhye cut to the chase. 'Please help Today.'

Bokhui paused. 'How?' Somehow she managed not to blurt out that it would be impossible.

'By letting her enter the race after Chuseok. The one that's two weeks away.'

'I don't know. It won't be good for Today,' Bokhui said matter-of-factly. She knew Eunhye was desperate, but that didn't mean she could work miracles. She should try to console Eunhye. She could tell the girl that Today had had a nice life. It was hackneyed but the kind of thing an adult would say to a child who was freaking out over a looming loss. 'It's not about whether she can enter the race or not,'

Bokhui explained gently. 'Today just can't run like she used to. It's not possible, Eunhye. I think she knows how much you care—'

Eunhye cut Bokhui off. 'I'm not saying she should run like she used to.'

What was she talking about? What was she plotting?

'We just need her to qualify for the race. That means she'll have two more weeks to live, right? Until race day? They won't get rid of a horse that's scheduled to run. Please, you have to trust us. I know you agree. I know you think two days aren't enough.'

It was true. If Today could somehow qualify for the race, she would live until then. So Eunhye's goal was simply to delay the inevitable by two weeks. But what good would those two extra weeks do?

Before Today could enter the race, the vet and the head of racing operations had to agree to it. Which was why the sisters and their robot had come to her first, to convince her to sign off on the plan. It wasn't a big ask. And it was unlikely that racetrack operations would be significantly impacted by Today remaining in her stall for two more weeks.

'All right,' Bokhui said. She would gladly do this if it could help extend Today's life a little longer. But her cooperation didn't make the remaining hurdles any less daunting. 'What's the plan, though? The head of racing operations isn't going to okay this, no matter how much I insist.'

'We have a plan for that, but you don't have to worry about it.'

Bokhui nodded. How could Eunhye be so confident that she could accomplish something that Bokhui herself hadn't managed?

'But Eunhye, I have to emphasize that Today can't run like she used to. She's going to get hurt if she does. She can only walk really slowly, if that.'

'I know. Don't worry. We aren't going to do anything that hurts her.'

It finally occurred to Bokhui how the robot fitted into all this. Today would feel the most comfortable with a jockey she knew. She glanced at the robot. She knew it had fallen off during a race. How was it still intact? She doubted the racetrack would have put resources into fixing a broken jockey. It would have cost an astronomical amount to get it fixed privately. Who could have repaired it?

'My sister fixed it.'

'Your sister?'

'Why are you telling her that?' Yeonjae grumbled.

Bokhui figured the girl must have got help.

'She sourced the parts and did everything on her own, from start to finish.'

The robot's lower body was so well made that Bokhui couldn't tell that it had once been shattered. The new legs, in fact, looked sturdier than the original. But robots weren't things you could easily buy and sell. She pointed at the jockey. 'So you got it for free?'

'My name is Coli,' Coli retorted.

'Oh, sorry.' *Was she apologizing to a robot?*

'No, I bought it,' Yeonjae finally said. 'With everything I have.'

'Why?'

'. . . just because it's a weird robot.'

Bokhui stopped herself from asking if you could buy a robot. That didn't seem all that important right now.

Eunhye said they would be back for her signature on the official race document. The girls left the consulting room and Coli moved its legs at an even pace to follow them. Coli paused in the doorway to look back at Bokhui, and she found herself nervously swallowing.

'I breathed as one with Today for a long time,' Coli said. 'I do not breathe, of course, but it is an idiomatic expression. Do you know what that means?'

'Of course.'

'I know when Today is happy. Thank you for helping us so that Today can be happy again. I want to tell you this.'

Why was this machine expressing gratitude to her? She nodded, feeling as addled as though she had downed a bottle of soju. Coli got back in the cart. Yeonjae tucked the blanket tightly around the robot as if to protect a baby from the wind. Bokhui kept telling them to be careful, both because it was late and so they wouldn't get caught with the robot.

Yeonjae pulled the cart behind her and Eunhye wheeled her wheelchair. They looked like warriors heading side by side into battle.

Bokhui watched until they faded into the distance. She pulled her white coat tight against the cold wind and turned to go back inside. On any other night she would head home to soak in the tub, but she didn't think she could just relax there. She would look through some books and the latest research papers. There had to be a way to improve Today's condition. There had to be a way to at least reduce her pain, even if the filly was going to die in two weeks.

'Doctor?' A familiar voice.

She poked her head back out of the door. 'Oh, hello.'

It was Minju. He was in black sweatpants and a grey hooded sweatshirt, a black cross-body bag slung around his torso. He must be on his way home. Even though they saw each other all the time, the ever-professional Minju sounded happy to see her. Perhaps because they had bumped into each other outside of the stables. 'Are you heading home?'

Bokhui nodded. 'You too?'

'Yes, I'm on my way.'

'Nice seeing you.' Bokhui turned around but then thought of the girls. She called after him: 'Do you have a second to talk?'

Minju nodded, though he looked perplexed.

He sat patiently in the waiting room while Bokhui changed and wrapped things up for the day. Cats, dogs, rabbits and other animals were ensconced in clear cages, either bandaged or hooked up to an IV.

Bokhui checked on each animal. She stroked their heads and scratched their chins. 'Goodnight, I'll be back tomorrow.'

Minju averted his eyes when she turned towards him.

'Would you like to grab a coffee or a beer?' Bokhui asked.

'Well, since it's after work, alcohol is probably better than caffeine.'

'Great. There's a good place nearby.' Bokhui led Minju to a bar she liked.

She had become a vet because of her grades, and because if she was saving a life, she wanted to save an animal rather than a human. She didn't particularly adore animals. She had never even had a pet. The only relevant experience she'd had was a thirty-hour stint at an animal shelter with four friends to fulfil their high school volunteering hours. Looking back, she realized she had sometimes fed stray cats on the way to and from school. Once, she'd snapped a picture of a missing-dog flyer and shared it in the class group chat. Actually, the real reason she didn't have pets was because she had been too afraid. She wasn't sure she could be solely responsible for another living being. She wasn't brave enough to keep an animal in her heart long after its death. When she became a vet, she acknowledged how cowardly she had been. As she met pet parents in her clinic, she realized what it meant to take full responsibility for another life. It was beautiful, awe-inspiring. But she herself wasn't made for it.

Sitting in the bar, Bokhui played with her beer glass, wondering how to begin. She threw out a question. 'Were you the one who gave the girls the robot?'

Minju nodded.

'Isn't it illegal?' She wasn't trying to threaten him. She just wanted to double-check what she knew about the laws around the practice because Minju had acknowledged it so readily.

'Technically yes, but you could consider it a secondary sale.'

'And it's not dangerous?'

Minju laughed incredulously.

Bokhui scowled.

Minju apologized, saying he hadn't meant to laugh at her, but the damage was already done. 'Jockeys are just made to ride horses, so they aren't dangerous in any way. To make them dangerous you'd have to replace the entire software and change their function. That's definitely illegal. They'd arrest you for that.'

'Well, I guess I'm glad to learn it's not dangerous,' Bokhui said. 'Are you aware that the girls are—' she trailed off, wondering if Minju really didn't know.

Minju nodded breezily. Thankfully the gang (calling them a gang seemed the most appropriate term) had talked to Minju before going to see Bokhui. Of course, Minju had tried to stop them. *Are you saying you're going to try to negotiate with the head of racing operations?* he had asked several times, unsure that he had heard them correctly. But the girls nodded eagerly and explained how they would go about executing their plan – it was serious. If things went wrong, Minju might be out of a job. He didn't know if he should cheer them on or try to talk them out of it. What was clear was that he wouldn't be able to stop them. The girls weren't asking Minju for his advice; they were notifying him. The only way for Minju to keep his job was for them to succeed.

'I heard their cousin is a reporter,' Minju said.

Bokhui nodded.

'Apparently that cousin has something on the head of racing operations. So they're going to try to strike a deal with that information.'

'A deal.'

'They're going to demand that he let Today enter the race in exchange for keeping that sensitive information out of the press. I don't know all the details, either. They just let me know that my job could be impacted.'

They were already done talking but Bokhui still had half a beer left. Should she call it a night? But Minju had drained his glass and was scanning the menu. 'I haven't had a drink in a while. Feel free to head out if you're ready to go. I'm just going to get another.'

Bokhui hesitated. 'I'll just finish this.'

Minju ordered another draft beer. Silence stretched between them. It was a weeknight; only two other tables were occupied. The TV was louder than the chatter. They watched the screen without speaking.

Bokhui couldn't stand the awkwardness any longer. 'In school, we used to joke that you should go into mechanical engineering if you wanted to be a vet.'

Thankfully Minju was game to continue the conversation. 'Really? Mechanical engineering?'

'Yes, there's a short story by Ted Chiang where digital entities take the place of pets. What was it called – 'The Lifetime of Software Objects' maybe. It's about AI entities that are outfitted with genomic engines modelled from evolutionary data. Which means these pets don't get sick or die, but they can learn and evolve. Though they do malfunction occasionally.' Bokhui couldn't remember all the details now. Was it the beer? Or because it had been a while? 'Anyway, I read that story a long time ago, but I remember thinking that his vision of the future wasn't too far off. That was around the time when people were talking about industrial humanoid robots being used more widely and how AI programs were catching cybercriminals. And how scientists were growing organs out of a single-cell structure.'

Concern darkened Minju's face.

Bokhui sipped her beer. 'I'm scared that, at some point, we won't be able to save the animals even if we want to.'

Minju waited quietly for her to explain.

'It won't be tomorrow, but it will happen sometime in the future. I think animals are going to give up on this planet. They will have evolved to be incompatible with life here, and they'll be forced to die. I mean, don't you think it's possible they would decide to die if they're shut up in a tiny cage without a ray of sunlight and constantly exploited?' Bokhui laughed sardonically.

Bokhui wished people would be a little more interested in animals threatened with extinction, just as they were in new technologies and the future. But she was mindful of not leading the conversation somewhere too dark.

'I really do think we can avoid the worst-case scenario,' she continued. 'The future has to be better than what we imagine it to be. Instead of taking care of AI pets after all the animals die off, I bet we'll be using AI to commune with animals and look after them when we're not physically there. It could be used to check on their health and tell us what nutrients they need. You know?'

'That's not a bad idea. But it sounds like you might get driven out of business.'

Bokhui and Minju drank their beers.

'I'm still a little scared,' Bokhui confessed. 'That I'll

become the kind of vet who's great at killing an animal so they don't feel pain.' This fear would probably always be present. It would probably stalk her until she quit the job. It might even bother her for a long time after. She thought she would be punished for her part in this system whenever she held animals that had to die because humans couldn't look after them.

'Wait, you just said the future has to be better than we think it's going to be,' Minju protested. 'That means you'll be a vet that *saves* animals.'

Their conversation died down too quickly for them to order another drink.

At the entrance to the bar, Bokhui pushed Minju out of the door as he tried to take out his wallet. She paid for the beers.

Out front, they faced each other.

'Let me know if you can think of any way we can save Today,' Bokhui said. 'I hope I can help, but their plan is outside my area of expertise, so . . . Anyway, thanks in advance for your help.'

Even then, Bokhui didn't understand the full scope of the girls' plan.

A few days later, Eunhye stopped by to tell her that the head of racing operations had authorized Today's entry in the race. Bokhui asked how they had managed to get his signature, and Eunhye just chuckled. All she would say was that they made quite a scene.

Today's remaining life had been extended from two to fourteen days. Bokhui stopped by the stables every other day to give Today IV supplements. On Thursday, she went to the Academy and petitioned once again for the use of nano-endoscopy on animals. She blew up in frustration, asking why they couldn't share this lifesaving technology with animals. The officials reprimanded her but her shouting must have moved the needle, because they said they would review her proposal.

Later that same evening, she met up with Seojin. She was dumbfounded when he filled her in about how the girls managed to get the head of racing operations to sign off on Today. 'Are you okay about it?' she blurted out.

Seojin grimaced as he nodded. 'What can I do? I can always get another exclusive, I guess. I'm telling you, they were treating me like I would be aiding and abetting animal cruelty if I didn't let them use it.'

Bokhui didn't know whether to thank him or tell him he was stupid.

Seojin told her that the girls were training Today late into the evening every day including weekends, as well as during the Chuseok holiday.

Bokhui told Seojin the same thing she had told Eunhye. 'I'm just worried. If Today runs like she used to, she won't even be able to stand upright. I know how much they care about Today so I'm trying not to be too overbearing, but

I still don't understand how they're going to get her to run.'

That was when Seojin shared something absurd.

'They're training her for something else, actually.'

'How do you mean?'

'They're training her to run as slowly as possible.'

EUNHYE

'I'm sorry. You want *what*?' Seojin said again, not comprehending what Eunhye was asking.

'The documents you collected for your investigation,' Eunhye said clearly and slowly. 'About race-fixing at the track.'

Seojin let out a shocked breath and leaned back in his chair. 'How did you know about that? About the race-fixing?'

'Are you serious? You told Dr Bokhui the other night, remember?'

It's just – you know, like, match-fixing. Of course. Eunhye had been right there when he'd mentioned it to Bokhui. Seojin closed his eyes.

When Eunhye had invited him over out of the blue a few days after they first bumped into each other, he'd accepted readily. After his uncle's funeral he had grown apart from that side of the family. Bearing two gift bags laden with fruit and beef, he'd arrived to find his aunt cleaning the patio tables. She hadn't recognized him at first, and a few moments later she'd dropped the rag she was holding, stunned.

Seojin was looking forward to catching up with her, but then Eunhye and Yeonjae had descended on him, insisting that they had to talk to him first because *they* had invited him over. That was how he found himself sitting at the kitchen table. Without even offering him a glass of water, the girls launched into why he should hand over the documents about the race-fixing. They claimed they weren't threatening him, but it sure felt like threats to him.

He let out a slow breath. 'I can't. I don't know what this is all about, but my answer is no.'

'You'll say yes once you know what it's about,' Yeonjae said.

Seojin crossed his arms. 'Fine. Let's hear it.' Even then, he had been certain that he would be unmoved. These were precious documents. He had managed to get his hands on them only after hanging around the racetrack for months on end, talking to racing enthusiasts as they hawked phlegm on the ground. He had document after document revealing how the racetrack officials leaked the bib number of the horse that had the best chance of winning, then, once the high rollers had paid up, fixing the match. These documents were the basis of an exclusive report that would be broadcast within the month. Seojin would sooner die than hand them over.

'Coliiii!' Yeonjae called.

Seojin heard footsteps on the stairs. Tap *pshhh*, tap *pshhh* . . . The strange sounds came closer until they stopped right beside him. He turned to find himself face to face with two glowing holes.

'Hello! I am Coli. I am Today's jockey. I understand you are going to help us save Today?' Coli held out a hand in gratitude.

Seojin stared at the robot.

'You must be the person with the crucial information that will help us save Today.'

Seojin was speechless.

'Thank you so much. You are a hero!'

'We'll owe him for this favour, but he's no hero,' Yeonjae corrected.

Coli looked at Yeonjae, a hand still in the air in an attempt to shake Seojin's. 'But in that movie you were watching yesterday, they called the person who saved everyone a hero.'

'Yeah, but I don't think *he's* quite a hero . . .'

Eyebrows raised, Seojin watched what was unfolding before him.

'We'll blackmail the head of racing operations with your documents. We want a horse – her name is Today – to enter one last race. If he agrees, we'll destroy the documents.

And, really, it doesn't mean that the work you've done is for nothing. We caught them, so they'll stop.'

'Wait, wait,' Seojin said. 'What do you get if this horse enters the race?'

'More time with her. From two days to fourteen.'

Seojin's head ached. What the girls wanted was so simple, so clear, so definite. All they wanted was more time with the horse. But what good would a few more days do? She was still going to die. Seojin wanted to explain how hard he had worked to investigate what was going on at the racetrack, how humiliating it had been. How torturous it had been to coax and pacify and humour all those middle-aged men who were leery of talking. Just thinking about the work he'd put in was practically enough to bring him to tears.

'Can I smoke in your backyard?' he asked. He had vowed to quit smoking three days ago, but here he was, already back at it.

The race-fixing scheme went beyond a simple con. The animals were subjected to brutal physical abuse to deliver the predetermined result. Human jockeys used to be bribed to deliberately lose. Even though the jockeys were now robots, nothing had changed. There were other insidious tactics, like secretly increasing a jockey's weight. As Seojin had a soft spot for animals, he had volunteered to investigate the scheme. He couldn't stand watching horses being abused for human entertainment. He held his face in his hands. He should have known something was up when the girls suddenly invited him over.

When Yeonjae came out to see what he was doing, his cigarette had burned down to a stub. He didn't know where to toss the butt, so he just stuck it in his pocket. 'I was about to head in.'

Yeonjae ignored him. 'She goes to the racetrack every single day. Every. Single. Day. To see this horse, Today.'

'Oh? Okay.'

'Since she was born, Today has loved to run. I don't know all the details, but I think my sister felt reassured by that. Or maybe she felt pure joy.'

Seojin sighed.

'It's just so unfair. That she has to die because she can't run any more.'

'Look, Yeonjae—'

Yeonjae cut him off. 'You're a grown-up. Can't you help us save this horse? Are you really going to be a jerk about it?'

A jerk? It was true. Why was he being a jerk when there was a life on the line? With a groan, Seojin sank to the ground. 'But nothing's going to change even if this horse lives for fourteen days instead of two,' he said. 'You think you'll change her life?'

'Of course we will. There's always a chance. But we can't hope for anything to change if she's not alive.'

Seojin went back inside and shook Coli's hand. His

boss was going to rip him a new one. But hopefully he would understand in the end. After all, it was his boss who had told him that journalism had the potential to save lives.

Coli gripped Seojin's hand. 'Thanks to your decision, Today is going to be happy. And when she is happy, I am happy.'

What a strange robot, Seojin thought.

With Seojin now on their side, Eunhye and Yeonjae next needed to meet with Minju. Strictly speaking, they didn't actually have to convince Minju of anything. They weren't going to give up on their plan even if he didn't approve. They just wanted to give him a heads-up as a measure of their friendship.

When Eunhye and Yeonjae filled Minju in, he looked utterly dazed.

'You were complicit, but we understand,' Eunhye said. 'The system forces you to go along with it. But you do realize you're not completely innocent, right?'

Minju put down the dustpan filled with dung. 'Are you two going to get me fired?'

Eunhye shook her head impatiently. *Did he not listen to a word?* He clearly did *not* understand what was going on. 'You're not a whistle-blower. So why would you get fired?'

'. . . right. Right.'

Eunhye and Yeonjae efficiently tackled the work of persuading Seojin, Minju, and Bokhui like they were completing a quest. Both girls thought they made a solid team, but neither said so out loud.

Coli was the only one who expressed what everyone was thinking. 'We are a good team.'

On the designated day, Eunhye asked Seojin to join them, and Jisu found out what they were doing and wanted to be in on the action. It would be too chaotic for all four of them to go into the small office occupied by the head of racing operations, so they decided that Yeonjae and Jisu would wait outside.

Eunhye led the way down the corridor and knocked on the office door. Seojin let out a deep, shaky breath.

'Come in.'

The head of racing operations was leaning all the way back in his chair, looking at his phone. When Eunhye came through the door, he sat up quickly. 'Who . . . ? What . . . ?' He appeared confused to see a teenager entering his office.

Eunhye rolled herself right up to his desk. She took the authorization form out of her bag and placed it in front of him.

The man squinted at the sheet of paper.

'We've received confirmation from the vet that Today will be able to participate in one last race,' Eunhye announced. 'So if you sign right here, she can do just that.'

The man waved them away without bothering to speak.

Eunhye didn't budge.

He picked up his phone again. When Eunhye still didn't leave, he snapped, 'Stop with this nonsense. Get out.'

Eunhye pushed the form closer to him. 'I don't think it's right to stop her from running when she still can.'

He must have realized that he was dealing with a kid. He forced a smile in an attempt to demonstrate that he was a kind man. An old-fashioned gold tooth flashed in his mouth. 'Look, kid. Horseracing is for adults. Just because a horse can run doesn't mean they can run in a race. If that were true, we would be running an amusement park here. There are a lot of other horses that can race. And she's in a lot of pain. How can a horse like that be in a race? Get it? Okay?' He shoved the form away, and shot Seojin a look: *I don't know who you are, but take this kid and get out now.*

But Seojin took out his business card and placed it on the desk.

The man glanced at the card: *Current Affairs Desk, M Broadcasting Company.* He looked up at Seojin, his gaze a touch more respectful. 'What is this about?'

Seojin dropped his thick stack of documents on the desk with a thud.

The man sat up straight.

'I collected this evidence over the last three months,' Seojin began.

'What . . .'

'These documents are proof that you've been fixing the

races and getting paid by the high rollers. We're planning to air this story as a special.'

The man looked at Seojin, then at Eunhye. This would be a bombshell if it were widely reported in the press, and animal welfare groups would harass him for months on end, too. 'What is this? What are you up to? Are you trying to threaten me?' His voice shot upwards.

Calmly, Eunhye went over her demands. 'If you let Today enter the race, this won't air. Don't you think that's a good deal? If you let one horse compete, it will all go away.'

'What is that horse to you, anyway?' He sounded genuinely perplexed.

Eunhye knew he didn't care that Today would die in two days. 'How long is the sentence for race-fixing again? But I guess you'll have to go to court to fight the charge first. Do you really want to spend your days doing that?'

Scowling, the man signed the form and dragged Seojin's documents across the desk.

Grinning, Eunhye slid the signed form into her bag and then turned back to offer a final piece of advice. 'People always find out if you're up to no good. It's your lucky day that we're the ones who came to see you today. Don't do bad things in the future, Sir.'

BOGYEONG

The day before Chuseok was wet and the temperature dropped precipitously. It was now cold enough
to layer on thick sweaters. Bogyeong could feel the dry
chill in the air when she breathed in. She woke up that
morning to a scratchy throat and a sluggish mind; she
was coming down with a cold. This always happened to
her when the seasons changed. She usually bolted upright
when her alarm rang, but she felt so slow today, her body
uncooperative. She burrowed deeper into the covers. Her
body begged for rest, but she knew she had to take out
the thick winter blankets and beat them, and she would
have to do this before the restaurant opened. She had
only one big group reservation per day during the holiday.
Just yesterday she had worried over how few reservations
there were, but now she was glad for the lighter workload.
Could she even manage that? She felt so dreadful.

She forced herself to sit up. If she let her body dictate her plans, she would end up staying in bed the entire day. A regular had told her that he was selling a robot cleaner at a special price, the hidden salesman in him subtly emerging. She should have bought it from him. *Who doesn't have a robot cleaner these days?* the regular had said, but she had made an excuse, saying she didn't think it could clean as well as a human. The truth was she just didn't want it.

She dragged herself into the living room and turned on the TV. The hosts of the morning show were wearing hanbok to commemorate the beginning of Chuseok. Apparently twenty per cent fewer people were travelling home for the holiday this year. The cameras cut to footage of traffic on the highways. Bogyeong poured herself a cup of warm water and settled on the sofa. The news ticker warned of wildfires and gas explosions in this dry weather. She let out a huge yawn and wiped her falling tears with her sleeve.

The doorbell rang. *Who could be coming by at nine in the morning?* On the first day of the holiday? As Bogyeong was about to haul herself to her feet, Yeonjae galloped down the stairs. She had assumed Yeonjae would still be asleep, but her daughter was dressed and ready. Before she could ask a single question Yeonjae flung open the door. Jisu stood there, holding one gift box of Korean pears and another of premium beef.

'What's all this?' Yeonjae asked.

'Chuseok gifts, obviously. What do you think? Hello, Mrs Kim. These are for you.' Jisu smiled sunnily at Bogyeong and handed the boxes over.

Bogyeong took the gifts, bewildered. She hadn't even washed her face yet. She managed to ask Jisu if she had eaten breakfast, to which Jisu said she had. Yeonjae told Bogyeong that they were headed out.

'Let me peel you some fruit, at least. Where are you going so early in the morning?'

'We'll grab something later.' Yeonjae ran back upstairs.

Jisu stood in the doorway without taking off her shoes, as though she was intending to leave right away. Bogyeong asked her to come in for some fruit again, but Jisu smiled and shook her head.

Yeonjae came down the stairs accompanied by Coli. Eunhye emerged, too, ready to go. *What on earth was happening?* The girls told her they were headed to the race-track and would be back around lunchtime, or maybe later. They left.

Coli, always a step behind, walked leisurely towards the front door, tap *pshhh,* tap *pshhh,* then turned to greet Bogyeong. 'Good morning!'

'What's going on at this hour?'

'We are going to the racetrack for Today's training.'

Why? Bogyeong's curiosity ballooned, but Coli took two steps forward and said something completely off-topic.

'You look different today. Your skin is sallow and you seem tired. I think you should rest at home. I understand that when humans are sick, it is harder on their emotions than on their bodies.'

Something spurted up from inside Bogyeong, but she decided not to examine what that feeling was. From outside Yeonjae called, 'Coliiii!' Coli bowed its green head and told her they would be back, then left slowly through the door. *Pshhh, pshhh.* Coli was the only one who had noticed Bogyeong's condition. Even her own daughters hadn't registered it. She knew Coli had made that determination based on analytical data, but it had been such a long time since she'd heard someone telling her to rest. Although, strictly speaking, it wasn't exactly a person who'd told her to rest.

Bogyeong stood in front of the door, reliving the chaos from just moments before. How wonderful it would be to rest at home, like Coli suggested. She checked the time and rushed to the bathroom.

It had surprised her to discover that Coli was an excellent conversationalist. Bogyeong didn't understand how the robot's conversation system was put together, but she figured it must be in the same vein as a chatbot or AI. Coli was less useful than a smartphone, though. A smartphone provided information and gave her what she wanted based on current trends, but Coli's information was stagnant, without access to constant updates. Learning was possible but wouldn't be checked for objectivity and accuracy. Coli couldn't tell her today's weather or about the latest chart-topper or share real-time traffic information.

But when faced with information it didn't know, Coli could nod and ask questions. It could really converse. Coli couldn't feel sympathy but was made to act as though it did, when sympathy was something even humans struggled with. Only after she'd sat with Coli and had several conversations did she realize what she had really needed all along – a pair of attentively listening ears and a nodding neck. An unexpected being had filled the space left empty for a long time by the man who had promised to listen to her for the rest of her life.

'My name is Coli, you know?' Coli had said once. 'Col-li. Call-me. I believe that sounds similar. You can call for me any time. Call-me.'

'Who taught you that?'

'Did you like that?'

'Not really, but it wasn't bad.'

Call me whenever you need anything. I'll be your personal 119. She remembered that sickly sweet comment from long ago. Whoever programmed Coli's systems had to be an old-fashioned romantic, too. Someone who would say that a pearl lying in the mud was beautiful, someone who dreamed of old-fashioned love stories.

* * *

Bogyeong tossed back some painkillers before heading to the restaurant. She crossed her arms against the unusually cold wind that swirled into her clothes and coughed all the way there. She stopped to look over at the racetrack in the distance. Her daughters were spending a lot of time together these days. It must be related to whatever was happening at the racetrack, but she didn't care as long as it wasn't something bad. When did the two girls first start to grow apart? She knew she must have had something to do with it. Still, she didn't want to feel overly hopeful that they had found a close sisterly relationship. Bogyeong bit her lip, then decisively walked right past the restaurant towards the racetrack. She would check on them and see what they were up to. Then she would head straight back. She was in her work clothes and slippers but she didn't care. She had never been the world's best mother but she should still know what was going on.

Bogyeong had never told her kids that she had appeared in a few short films. It was so long ago, deep in the past. To revisit all that would be to hold on to regret. She wished she were a bit more secure in herself, but she didn't regret meeting the firefighter and falling in love. This version of Bogyeong held a different kind of confidence than the Bogyeong who had tried to be an actress.

Back when Bogyeong had been an actress whose star was rising, directors she had worked with told her to let them know if she ever wanted to act again. She'd avoided their calls with the excuse that she was busy raising her kids. Maybe those directors had tried to hold on to Bogyeong so she wouldn't fall off the radar because they were women, too. That somehow made it even more difficult for her to reach out to them. She would have to be the one to let go. There were so many up-and-coming actresses who had more time and more passion. She vowed to never act in anything again unless it was a role she simply couldn't pass up.

But the firefighter had agreed with the directors. 'You should do whatever you want to do.'

Bogyeong lost the firefighter around the same time she finally folded away her acting dreams for good, and afterwards she never managed to pursue them again. The two incidents appeared unrelated, but as time passed she realized that everything was connected. Life was like ripples on the surface of a lake. Wide, calm ripples crossing one another continuously, the energy coursing into the formation of a wave. Bogyeong often prayed for only waves of good fortune to lap at her shores. What she wished above all else was for her to have a better relationship with her daughters. Each of them was indebted to the other two, which made it all that more difficult to broach the subject. Eunhye was a bruised finger and Yeonjae was a finger with damaged nerves. Both of them had wounds so old that it was hard to remember exactly what had happened, until you glanced at them one day and realized they hadn't healed correctly. Bogyeong couldn't pick off their scabs and put ointment on them. She could only watch as the wounds hardened into scars.

She hovered by the racecourse park's north gate. The gate was open but she wasn't sure if she was allowed to enter. She noticed wheel tracks in the dirt, alongside Coli's footprints. She did spot a CCTV camera pointed at the gate but if she was caught she figured she could explain that she had wandered in by accident.

The grounds were vast, almost as big as an amusement park. She wouldn't have been able to find the track without the signage. Her throat tickled and with each intake of breath, she coughed more. She kept walking until she came across the track, but then she couldn't find the entrance, and went up to some steel bars through which she could see in.

There were her girls. Along with a horse and Coli and the stable manager she had met that one time. Bogyeong stood watching them, ignoring the creeping cold symptoms affecting every part of her body. They were putting on a strange race.

A race that had everyone yelling, 'Slower!' not 'Faster!'

She never did find out what they were doing. She had to return to the restaurant and start work.

Bogyeong rushed around, getting the restaurant ready to open. She felt so unwell that she kept dropping things. She had hired a cook to pitch in during major holidays and weekends. The cook's regular job was at a gimbap place, which was closed at those times. Bogyeong's restaurant wasn't normally that busy, so she preferred the cook just to come whenever she needed an extra pair of hands. The cook wasn't due for another two hours though, so she had to clean and prep a lot of ingredients, and make a batch of fresh kimchi for the day. But her body sank into a chair against her will. She laid her head on the table. Maybe if she rested for five minutes she would feel refreshed. She closed her eyes.

In that brief moment, she had a dream. She was standing in front of their old apartment building, waiting for the firefighter to return. He had been dispatched a long time ago. This had actually happened in real life. Her worry and anxiety had swelled with every minute, growing beside her while she waited. By the time her heap of worry and anxiety had grown to match her height, the firefighter finally came home. He was two hours late. He was holding two boxes of chicken nuggets. He'd had to wrap things up at the scene. He had brought the food in an attempt to make it up to her. Traces of soot smudged his face. Bogyeong tried to rub them off with her palm. When they refused to come off, she tried with some spit.

Why did you buy two boxes? The kids are already sleeping.

The firefighter looked stricken, then said, *One box per person. One for you, one for me.*

Bogyeong sat across the table from him. They ate until they couldn't eat any more.

She wished he would show up in her dream now, the way he had in real life back then. In her dream, she stayed in front of the building, staring down at the dark street. The firefighter didn't appear. Nobody walked towards her down the long, lonely stretch of road, glowing streetlamps dotting the sides. She squatted, keeping her eyes glued on the road.

The heavy reality that she was solely responsible for her two children weighed on Bogyeong, even more than the fact that the firefighter was no longer alive. The weight of reality was such that no emotion leaked out of her. Instead, it stagnated inside her, this water that didn't flow, that couldn't be bailed out. It smelled like mildew. Sorrow sloshed inside her, stale, as she tossed and turned in the middle of the night. Now that her sorrow was starting to rot, she couldn't release it even when she wanted to. She had to keep it tucked inside. Waiting for the day it would finally completely rot and dry out.

Bogyeong could smell that mildewy odour in her dream. Water was all around her. She was now in a reservoir. Not even fish lived there. It was all black; she couldn't begin to guess how deep it might be. An extremely long time later, from the far end of the road, something was approaching. A Darpa. Stalking towards her like a tiger. It held a burned glove in its mouth.

Not you, Bogyeong told the Darpa. *Not you. Tell him to come.*

The Darpa stopped in its tracks and looked at her. Did Darpa eyes always look like that? They were holes, like Coli's.

Aren't you sick and tired of it all?

The Darpa didn't answer.

I said, aren't you sick and tired of it all! I'm sick and tired. Let's just stop already.

Bogyeong had never wondered what exactly she was so sick and tired of, but she was. He was long gone. No matter how much she cried and screamed and made a scene, he would never come back. Was she the one who couldn't let him go? Or was he still wandering around in this realm, unable to rest? She didn't want to forget him but she didn't want to be tied to this spot forever, either. The Darpa laid the glove on the ground and turned around. It walked away but kept looking back at her.

Bye. Be careful, she called out.

When the Darpa vanished into the darkness, she woke up. She remembered laying her head on the table, but when she opened her eyes she saw the ceiling of her bedroom. She sprang out of bed. She didn't have time to wonder how she'd got there; she shoved her arms into her coat, ready to head back to the restaurant.

She pushed open the bedroom door. Coli stood there like a security guard. 'You slept for four hours.'

That was even worse. The big group would be here any minute now.

'Where are you going?' Coli asked.

'To the restaurant,' Bogyeong said as she slipped past Coli.

'Do not worry. Yeonjae, Eunhye, and Jisu took over. The cook who came to work called us, so we walked over from the racetrack. The woman is cooking and Yeonjae is serving. Everything is going smoothly.'

'Still, I should go and . . .' Bogyeong wanted to check with her own eyes.

Coli took her by the shoulders. Or rather delicately placed its hands on her shoulders. That was how gentle Coli's hands were.

'Yeonjae gave me an order that I must stop you from going to the restaurant.'

Bogyeong was stunned into silence.

'She wants you to rest. She said she would get angry if you showed up.'

Bogyeong still couldn't speak.

'I do not want to make Yeonjae angry.'

Bogyeong had been about to shove Coli aside, but her shoulders slumped in defeat. She knew Yeonjae would come and get her if anything major happened at the restaurant. The cook knew the full menu, and Yeonjae could certainly wait tables. But Bogyeong couldn't help feeling anxious.

'Is there a problem?' Coli asked.

A *problem*. Was there a problem? She was anxious, sure, but there was no problem, not really. Bogyeong gave up and went to sit on her bed.

Coli observed Bogyeong's glum expression. 'I understand.'
Bogyeong looked at the robot.

'It is because time does not pass when you sit in your
room, right? I know what that feels like.' Coli looked
around, then pointed to a spot near the door. 'Can I sit
here, if that is okay with you? If it makes you uncomfortable I can sit outside.'

Bogyeong couldn't answer right away. She wasn't
scared of robots. She didn't hate them. But she was still
uncomfortable around them; she wasn't used to them.
The technology she'd encountered while growing up had
been limited to AI in smartphones and other electronic
devices; none embodied a concrete form and moved
about so independently. On the news they talked about
how humanoid robots would become more widespread,
but she didn't think it had anything to do with her. Hadn't
she lived her life thinking that she wasn't part of that great
generation for whom technological development was the
essential thing they lived for? Bogyeong remembered the
old movies about robots attacking humans, and shook her
head. She had talked to Coli so much by now. She must be
on edge because she wasn't feeling well.

'. . . you can stay. Go on, bring in a chair.' If she lay alone
in her room, she might drown in the tears within her.

Coli brought over a kitchen chair and settled right by
the door, hands placed neatly on its knees as it sat tall and
straight.

'Your eyes are too bright,' Bogyeong commented.

Coli's eyes dimmed, now glowing faintly in the dark room like faraway planets. Bogyeong lay in bed and turned to face Coli. She went over what Coli had said. How did this robot know that time didn't pass when you sat in a room by yourself? She couldn't help herself; she asked.

Coli turned its face slightly towards Bogyeong. 'I was given a cement room without any windows. And I sat like this.' Coli pulled its legs up to its chest and wrapped its arms around them. 'It was big enough for me to sit like this. There was another jockey across the way, but it left after a day because it was defective. When that jockey left, time started to go by so slowly. Before I got to that room, I was on a truck for many hours, and there was a window in that truck. When I saw the sun rise in the morning and the world being painted with colours, one hour felt like one minute, but in that other place one minute felt like one hour.'

'You must have been so bored.'

'No, because I do not know what it is to be bored. I just knew that time was passing slowly.' Coli lowered its legs and sat up straight again. 'Yeonjae told me about the theory of time passing at different speeds. She said it is not just that it feels that way but that time really does pass at different speeds. It was real, what I felt when I was racing with Today, like time was folded. It seems that each individual experiences time differently.'

'That might be true.'

'Then that means that humans exist alongside one another but nobody is living in the same time frame.'

Bogyeong stayed quiet.

'In other words they are living in the same time period, but experiencing their own time in their own way, in a way that cannot be shared. Is that right?'

Bogyeong nodded. There was a lump in her throat; she didn't think she could speak normally. Maybe it was because she was unwell.

Coli asked, 'And how are you experiencing time?'

Coli didn't get bored or look elsewhere or repeat the question, even as Bogyeong maintained her silence. Coli waited, like it understood that it shouldn't intrude while Bogyeong was thinking.

For the first time ever, Bogyeong thought about her experience of time. She reviewed her memories, from the earliest she could remember all the way to the present. She took her sweet time. At one point she had believed she was a car zooming at a hundred kilometres an hour, without any safety measures. That she would be disqualified from the race if she lagged behind for even a second. Who knew where the finish line was or what the prize would be? She was in a race she had been automatically entered into the instant she was born. Living her life had felt like that. A single day in her life would speed by, crammed full with a year's worth of events and experiences. She felt anxious if she wasn't doing something. Only if she passed out at the end of the evening in exhaustion did she feel she had spent a productive day.

She thought back over her life. 'Time, for me, is frozen.' *It froze while I was waiting for him, while he was in that burning building. It froze during the span of time I believed he would – must – walk out alive.*

Bogyeong had believed she'd emerged from that place after all these years, but in truth time had been stuck, not ticking forward even one second. She had to be honest with herself: she woke up early every morning and spent all day busy without a break in order to escape that horrible point in time. Time didn't pass quickly or slowly for her. It stood still. Time had unfurled a sail on the water, even though there wasn't the smallest gust of wind.

'Why?' asked Coli.

'I've forgotten how to make time start ticking again.'

Time was stagnant, a puddle. It didn't budge. Even when she thought she was doing fine, that terrible day sucked her back in without mercy.

How did time pass for other grieving people? Were they all frozen, like her? Did time stagnating on Earth exist in a separate realm? What could be done to force all that frozen time to start flowing again?

'I guess you will have to start moving very slowly,' Coli said, turning a little more towards her. 'To go from standing still to running fast, you will need a lot of energy, all at once. I think it would be the same as suppressing longing. Did you not say that only happy moments could push longing down? If you start experiencing tiny joys, very slowly, every day, maybe you will experience the time you are currently living in, and that will thaw the time that has been frozen.'

Tears filled her eyes. She didn't wipe them away. These mildewed tears needed to run down her face. 'Where did you learn to talk like that?'

'I did not learn it. It is similar to when I looked up at the sky and thought of the colour blue-yellow. It is why Yeonjae said I was strange.'

'There is surely no other robot like you.'

'Yeonjae says I was made by mistake. She says I have a chip inside me, the chip that determines who I am, that makes me different from the others.'

Bogyeong listened quietly.

'Yeonjae says mistake is another word for opportunity.'

When had Yeonjae grown into the kind of person who would say something like that? Despite Bogyeong's fears, Yeonjae had grown into a thoughtful person.

'You are looking sleepy now,' Coli observed.

'I *am* tired. I should get some sleep.'

'Should I leave you?'

'You can do whatever you like. I don't mind either way.'

'Doing whatever I like is the hardest thing for me to do.'

Bogyeong smiled and closed her eyes. She didn't mind whether Coli sat there or left, because the robot was very quiet. She fell into a deep, dreamless sleep.

When Bogyeong woke up again, Yeonjae was there instead of Coli. She must have crept in to check on her; when Yeonjae saw she was awake, she jumped like a thief caught in her tracks. Yeonjae then told her that everything had gone fine at the restaurant. It was now closed. Only then did Bogyeong check the time. A little after two in the morning.

'Did you eat?' she asked, and Yeonjae reassured her that the cook had made them noodles.

'I heard Jisu was working, too. Oh, I feel so bad. You should have sent your friend home . . .' she stopped herself mid-sentence. Now was not the time to nag. She studied Yeonjae's placid expression. 'Tell her thank you. Bring her by again. I'll make her something really good.'

Yeonjae brightened a bit. She paused, nodded, and hesitated. She looked like she was waiting for the right time to leave, or like she had something else to say.

Bogyeong went first. 'Coli's really strange.'

'Yeah. Coli *is* really strange.'

'You did a good job fixing it up.'

Yeonjae was quiet.

'You're so talented at robotics. I knew that, of course, but I didn't realize you were this good.'

If she wanted time to flow again, she had to make the current time she was living in tick forward, as Coli had advised. She needed to be happy to suppress her longing. Could she start by untangling the relationships that had begun souring on that terrible day, relationships that had never got a chance to flourish? She had chosen the easiest way to connect with Yeonjae, so easy that she had pushed it aside all this time.

Yeonjae didn't react. She seemed shocked, unable to find an appropriate response.

'I'm sorry, Yeonjae. I should have—'

'It's fine.' Yeonjae cut her off. 'Where is this coming from, anyway?' She scratched her arm, visibly uncomfortable. 'I'm fine, Mom. You don't have to worry about me.'

Bogyeong hadn't given Yeonjae much of her attention when she was small. For that crime she had, at one point, come to the abrupt realization that her daughter was no longer a child. But while that was true, it didn't mean she was fully grown up. All that had happened was that Yeonjae had learned and accepted that she couldn't force the world to act according to her will. Bogyeong had no desire to send Yeonjae into adulthood just yet, to a state in which you were solely responsible for everything and you were forced to swallow grief down.

'How can I not worry?' Bogyeong asked.

'. . . then worry just a little bit.' Yeonjae told her to rest and left.

Bogyeong thought she saw Yeonjae crack a tiny smile. She lay in bed, thinking back to what she'd seen at the race-track. Slowly, slowly. That horse, running ever so slowly, instead of fast. It had to have been the silliest training session in the world.

YEONJAE

'My god, Yeonjae, how are you so slow? Gimme it. I'll do the ones here. Just bring those in.' Jisu snatched the cloth out of Yeonjae's hand and pointed to a pile of dishes.

Yeonjae wished Jisu would go home. But if Jisu hadn't been here they wouldn't have been able to serve all the customers this efficiently, so she shut her mouth and did what Jisu told her.

Jisu had a good head on her shoulders. She was a capable waitress, quick on her feet and attending to customers right away. She was also annoying, which made it harder for Yeonjae to focus. Whenever Yeonjae forgot a wet towel or a cup of water, Jisu tutted condescendingly and took it to the customer herself. Even though Yeonjae had plenty of experience helping her mom out on weekends, Jisu acted as though she were the veteran. Yeonjae couldn't stand it. But there were too many customers for Yeonjae to complain overtly, and so, in her distraction, she kept forgetting things, which meant she had to watch Jisu get haughtier. It was clear Jisu would revel forever in her superiority if Yeonjae didn't take her down a few notches.

Jisu was a straightforward person. Yeonjae had come to that conclusion after being forced to hang out with her for going on three weeks now. Jisu wore her feelings on her sleeve. She often said things that were at odds with what she showed on her face. Yeonjae didn't think Jisu was weird or unlikeable. She found herself staring at Jisu more often, in awe of the expressions on her face that Yeonjae couldn't bring herself to make. An only child, Jisu claimed that it was better not to have siblings because you didn't fight with anyone or get your things stolen, but she peppered Yeonjae with questions that betrayed her curiosity about sibling relationships. How did they share things? Did they wash their faces together? Did it feel like living with a friend?

Jisu claimed she never felt lonely and concluded that she wasn't the type to get lonesome, but Yeonjae thought Jisu was always lonely and just didn't realize it. Lonely and stubborn. These two characteristics merged together to create someone who would resolutely follow Yeonjae home three steps behind her, even when told she wasn't welcome. At a certain point Jisu realized that Yeonjae said no to every question, so she stopped asking if she could come over and just invited herself anyway. Yeonjae argued with Jisu the first few times, telling her she couldn't, but eventually gave up.

Yeonjae couldn't really ban Jisu from coming by, because Jisu had kept her side of their agreement. She had delivered all the parts, without missing a single one. So Yeonjae had to listen patiently while Jisu bragged about her own attention to detail and reliability. Although, at first glance, Jisu had seemed like the kind of girl who cared only about schoolwork, it turned out that she was curious about everything.

'I want to watch you build it,' Jisu had insisted.

'I can't do it when someone's watching me.'

'Then just pretend I'm not here.' Jisu said she needed to be able to explain to her dad what they were doing for the robotics project since she got to skip cram school. She reminded Yeonjae that she hadn't reported the illegal sale of the robot but instead helped her out, which, in her mind, meant they were on the same team. Obviously, that meant she had the right to watch Coli being repaired.

Yeonjae had made up the excuse that she couldn't have anyone watching so that she could get away from Jisu, but when Jisu persisted, she gave up and invited her home.

It was Jisu's belief that one always had to bring something when visiting someone's home, so she brought different gifts of food every day. Sometimes it was an assortment of cookies and other times it was a pack of beverages or a box of fruit. Sometimes she brought burgers or pizza to share. Yeonjae had gained three kilos since she'd started spending time with Jisu. She had always believed she didn't gain weight easily, but the time they spent together seemed to pad out her body.

Jisu sat far away from Yeonjae and didn't make conversation until the repairs for the day were done, keeping her promise that she wouldn't get in the way. But that didn't mean she kept silent, because Coli kept asking Jisu questions.

'Why are you sitting so far away?'

'She told me not to come any closer.'

'Why is that?'

'I don't know. Wanna ask her? I'm not allowed to talk to her.'

Jisu kept making pointed comments like that, but Yeonjae managed to stay calm. She didn't so much as blink as Coli and Jisu talked about her in front of her.

Jisu never left in the middle of the repairs, even if she got so bored that she lay down for a nap. From time to time she nagged Yeonjae, telling her to sit up straight or that she was straining her neck or that she should stretch a little. Yeonjae tried to ignore her, but when Jisu nagged she did force herself to let go of the tension in her body. Her shoulders felt less stiff than usual as a result.

Jisu always got up from her corner by nine, no matter what was going on. She said it wasn't polite to stay later than that at someone else's house. Even when Yeonjae said snarkily, 'It must be exhausting to be you, having to remember all your manners,' she just laughed, telling Yeonjae she needed to learn some manners herself. Yeonjae would carry on working on Coli's legs for a long time after Jisu left, while Coli asked aimless questions.

'Are you and Jisu like Today and me?'

'What does that mean?'

'Are you a team that breathes as one?'

'. . . I guess we're kind of a team.'

'Is Jisu the person you care about most in the world?'

'Nope.'

'I think that is what a team is. Of course, Today cannot express how she feels and I do not have feelings. But if a hundred horses fell into the ocean, I would save Today first. I am sure I would save all the horses in the water eventually, but I would save her before any other horse. That means I care about her.'

'Where did you learn that?'

'I saw it on TV with Bogyeong. They asked who you would save first if people you knew fell in the ocean. The answer was used to rank how important someone was . . . But it is such a strange figure of speech. Why do they believe that you acknowledge your feelings for someone only when you are in a desperate situation? Why not ask who you would give your favourite cake to?'

'Because it's not hard to share something you like. But you don't save someone from a dangerous situation like that unless it's someone special.'

'Why is that?'

'I don't know.'

'Then if ten people fall in the ocean, will Yeonjae save Jisu first?'

'Maybe? If I don't know any of the other people, I guess. But then again I would never go near the ocean with her in the first place.'

'I have not been to the ocean with Today, either.'

Yeonjae often ended up going down a strange rabbit hole while conversing with Coli. That night, before she fell asleep, Yeonjae imagined Jisu tumbling into the ocean. If she didn't know the other nine people, she was sure she would save Jisu first. But if her mom was there, she would save her mom first. If Eunhye was there, she would obviously save Eunhye first, because Eunhye couldn't swim.

But that meant Jisu still came in third.

Was there anyone else who would rank higher than Jisu? Minju? But Minju seemed like the kind of person who would somehow survive, even if he had to resort to doggy paddle. She agonized over Dayeong for a long time until she remembered that Dayeong loved to swim. So it

was decided. Jisu was third. She didn't want to acknowledge that, but it was the truth. She would *never* tell her.
There was no reason to, and she knew Jisu would tease
her about it for the rest of her life. But then she wondered:
where did she rank for Jisu?

That night, Yeonjae told Jisu that she should feel free
to head home whenever, but Jisu stayed until closing and
even helped clean up. She sat down only after the last dish
was in the dishwasher. She rubbed her feet. Yeonjae took
out the cheap ice cream bars they sold as dessert from
the freezer and held out the choices. Jisu picked chocolate. She immediately peeled the wrapper off and took
a big bite. Yeonjae sat next to her and opened the vanilla.

'Oh my god, I'm so tired,' Jisu mumbled through the
ice cream.

'I said you could go home. Why did you stay— Urgh.'
Yeonjae nearly choked when Jisu slapped her, hard, on the
back.

'Is that really all you have to say to me right now?'

Yeonjae was silent.

'Did you hear me? Is that all you have to say?'

Of course Yeonjae knew what to say to Jisu, but it just
wasn't coming out. It wasn't a matter of pride. There
was no reason she couldn't just come out and say it. Was
it that she didn't want to see Jisu acting smug and gloat-
ing, her nose in the air and her shoulders pinned back?

Yeonjae was still struggling to articulate what she felt

when Jisu nodded. 'Okay, got it. You're so grateful that I was here, right? I hear you.' She didn't seem put out.

That would have been sufficient, since Jisu herself had given up on hearing Yeonjae say thank you, but Yeonjae didn't want that moment to pass.

'Thanks.' She immediately took another bite of ice cream.

'*What?*' Jisu lowered the bar from her mouth.

'I shed shank you.'

Jisu grinned and patted Yeonjae's head, hard.

Yeonjae shrugged off her hand and shot her a dirty look.

Jisu was beaming. 'No thanks are necessary between friends!' She laughed loudly, then bit down on her bar.

By the time they finished their ice cream, Jisu's mom had pulled up outside. She didn't get out of the car but called out of the passenger window, 'You must be Yeonjae! Nice to meet you.'

Suddenly shy, Yeonjae bowed without a word. Only then did she realize how incredibly friendly Jisu was, unlike her. Jisu always greeted Yeonjae's mom cheerfully and asked how she was doing.

Jisu hopped in the car and waved out of the window. 'That was a great meeting! Bye!'

What meeting? 'Whaat?'

Jisu gritted her teeth. 'Great. Meeting.'

Only then did Yeonjae remember that Jisu had been lying to her mother. 'Oh, *yeah*. Great meeting.'

Jisu waved out of the window again and Yeonjae stayed rooted to the spot until the car disappeared. She might have stayed out there longer if Eunhye's wheels hadn't caught on the threshold. Yeonjae went over to push the chair forward for her sister.

'I hate it when it does that,' Eunhye said apologetically.

Yeonjae was finally able to lie down around two in the morning. That was when her mom usually went to bed. She and Jisu had hustled to clean up the kitchen but it had still taken them that long. For the first time in her life, Yeonjae realized that her mom got to bed around this time only because she worked hard and with maximum efficiency. Yeonjae couldn't sleep. She tossed and turned, trying to find a comfortable spot. She thought about Jisu. She thought back to the conversation she and her mom had just had. What had made her mom suddenly tell her she was sorry?

She sank deeper into her thoughts. She felt morose. If she was going to lie wide awake like this, she might as well get up and be productive. Yeonjae headed upstairs. Even though she knew Coli didn't feel fear, she always kept a light on in Coli's room. Now she headed straight towards the strip of light visible under the closed door. She opened the door to find Coli looking out of the window.

Coli turned towards her. 'Hello! Why are you not in bed?'

'I can't sleep.' Yeonjae settled next to Coli and pulled the lamp closer. She turned on her school tablet and opened her notebook. Jisu had sourced parts for her, so Yeonjae had to make good on her promise and win them an award. They had been talking about the competition in every spare moment, and had catalogued a long list of ideas in the notebook. They'd narrowed it down to building a Darpa that would make daily life easier. On the tablet, Yeonjae enlarged one of the models she had drawn.

'That looks like the apparatus Eunhye rides on,' Coli commented.

Yeonjae nodded. She swivelled the model this way and that, made it 3D, and imagined the small but significant changes this device would bring forth. She scribbled and drew for a long time, hunched next to Coli.

Coli watched Yeonjae at work, the curve of her head and her rounded back. She glowed when she concentrated. Her body emitted energy, which radiated as light. It was invisible to the human eye, but Coli could detect it. She often radiated light when she worked on Coli's body. When tinkering with Coli's legs, she had glowed, sweating with concentration, and also when studying the plans to see if she had attached a part incorrectly, while shovelling cereal in her mouth. She was radiant now, too.

Coli laid a gentle hand on her back.

'What?' Yeonjae said, but didn't shrug off the hand or sit up straight.

Coli kept a hand on her for a long time, until it could

sense the reverberations in Yeonjae's body. She was vibrating. She was enrobed in happiness. She was alive. She was always alive, of course, but right now she was more alive than ever. What was making Yeonjae's heart pound like this? She wasn't running. She was just mapping out a Darpa on a small screen.

'You are just like Today is when she runs,' Coli observed.

Yeonjae looked over her shoulder at Coli. 'What are you talking about?'

'You are happy. Like Today is when she runs.'

'What would you know about happiness?' Yeonjae said curtly, but she wondered what made Coli think that. She remembered that it had been Coli's idea to enter Today in the race.

'You are happy the moment you feel alive,' Coli said. 'Being alive means you are breathing, and I can feel your breathing through the movement in your body. When that movement is large, that is when you are happy.'

Yeonjae nodded. She turned her attention back to the screen. 'But *you* can't feel anything, Coli.' Happiness had to be the most useless concept if you couldn't feel it yourself.

'I can feel *that*.'

Yeonjae sat up straight. Coli was holding up a forefinger, indicating sincerity. Yeonjae and Jisu had agreed that if they started trading barbed comments, they would hold up a forefinger to indicate that what they were saying was important and not meant to be snarky. Coli was imitating them.

'I cannot breathe but I can feel it indirectly. If you are happy beside me, I become happy, too. If you want me to be happy, you just have to be happy yourself. Is that not great?'

Yeonjae nodded. She didn't say, *That's not the same thing as feeling happiness yourself.* It *was* great. It was pretty cool. 'But what if the person beside you is unhappy?'

'I cannot feel that.'

'Why not?'

'Because I do not try to feel it.'

'Lucky.'

'Do humans feel it when the person beside them is unhappy?'

Yeonjae's screen was asleep by now, but she toyed with her pencil. She nodded slowly.

'Why not just ignore it?' Coli asked.

Yeonjae looked down at her pencil. 'I tried that, but it doesn't work. I was scared that acknowledging it would make me unhappy, too. I know it's terrible, but I tried not to pay attention to that unhappiness. But it just doesn't work.'

'Why not?'

'Just because you don't pay attention to it doesn't mean you can ignore it.'

'Whose unhappiness were you trying to ignore?'

Yeonjae shot the robot a look. 'You can't tell anyone.'

Coli lifted a forefinger. 'I will not tell.'

'My family's.'

'Bogyeong's or Eunhye's?'

'Both.'

'Why is that?' Coli felt Yeonjae's breathing slow way down, the opposite of when she drew plans.

Yeonjae exhaled loudly through her nose. 'You said you want to ignore people's unhappiness, right?'

'Yes, I did.'

'Then you probably don't want to hear what I'm about to say.'

'Why not? You are going to tell me about the unhappiness you ignored.'

'Because it's also the source of my unhappiness.'

Coli did not understand.

'Being tuned in to my family's unhappiness is the same thing as being tuned in to my own. Even though I tried not to think about it.'

She began putting things away. If she stayed any longer, even more secrets would come tumbling out of her. She had talked about it as though it were all in the past, but she was still avoiding it. She didn't know how to stop avoiding it and face her unhappiness straight on. Even though she knew Coli didn't sleep, she said her habitual good night and left the room.

In bed, she stared up at the ceiling, thinking. She had wanted to get to sleep, but then she cursed, spotting the rising sun.

* * *

Two additional people joined training that day – Bokhui and Seojin. Bokhui gave Today an IV supplement in the stables, announcing that it would take about an hour.

'I get infusions, too,' Jisu said breezily. 'When I'm tired or if I feel dizzy, I'll get them on my way to cram school.'

'Why wouldn't you just eat something?' Yeonjae retorted.

'You feel immediately better after an infusion. I get too sleepy if I eat.'

Yeonjae stopped herself from saying anything else. She knew she couldn't begin to understand Jisu's life, and if she opened her mouth Jisu would lecture her, telling her she shouldn't be a sloth.

Yeonjae headed out, while Eunhye stayed with Today in the stall.

Jisu followed Yeonjae. 'Where are you going?'

The trees around the racetrack were about to turn crimson. In the fall, people visited the park in droves to enjoy the foliage, along with the regulars who came for the races. It marked a busy time for the restaurant. The crowds would reach a peak right after Chuseok. And all that work would fall squarely on her mom's shoulders, since Yeonjae had to go to school. Her mom had been unwell lately. Yeonjae couldn't help but worry. This morning, her mom had told her she was all better, though she coughed the entire time she spoke.

Yeonjae sat on a bench. 'How much are those infusions, by the way?'

Jisu told her the name of the clinic she frequented and how much the infusions cost.

Yeonjae had used all her money to buy Coli, so she would have to save up the allowance her mom gave her every month, two hundred thousand won at a time.

Jisu sat next to her and pushed the dirt into a low mound with her shoe. She looked like she had something to say. Finally, she said, 'So, I won't be able to come over on weekdays after the competition next week. My parents think I've been slacking, so I can only come over on weekends. I can't keep skipping cram school.'

'Okay,' Yeonjae said, though it didn't really feel okay. She felt a pang of disappointment and regret. But she also knew Jisu couldn't skip cram school forever.

'*Seriously?*' Jisu looked hurt and angry.

They sat on the bench in silence. Jisu's silence was unusual. Shouldn't Yeonjae say something? But it didn't seem like Jisu was in the mood to talk.

Yeonjae spotted Coli emerging from the stables. Coli walked over to the lawn in front of the stables and sat down. Coli looked up at the sky. Trees rustled whenever the wind blew, the shadows of the leaves dappling Coli's metal exterior. Yeonjae recalled that Coli had fallen off Today while looking up at the sky. A dangerous urge that could get a human rider killed. That didn't make sense, actually. How could Coli even have the desire to look at the sky in the first place?

At first, everyone had opposed Coli's idea of having Today get back on the track. Telling Today to run when she was about to lose her life because she couldn't run any more would be akin to torturing her. But they all eventually gave in to Coli's nonsensical insistence that they had to make her as happy as she had been in the past so that she could return to the past, when she was healthy. Today was happy when she ran. She had been trained from birth to race, and she could only affirm her intrinsic value by running. Coli insisted that Today would be at her happiest, even if it shattered her joints, instead of waiting, locked up, for death.

A few days ago, when Today had emerged after several weeks in the stables, she had nickered with joy and pranced on the track, defying Bokhui's prediction that it would be hard for Today to even stand straight. It was, of course, only a brief moment, followed by Today collapsing in pain, but it was evident that she was joyful. She was not like that when she was in her stall. Coli had been right. Even when it felt like tens of thousands of needles were stabbing her, this horse was happier when in motion.

Today had been trained to gallop at full speed, her vision blinkered. So now, even though she couldn't maintain her previous racing speed any more, she still tried to run at seventy kilometres an hour. At first they struggled to hold her back, to calm her down; she was excited just by being on the track. Even Minju was dragged around, clinging to Today's bridle. Coli was the one who calmed Today down. Stroking the filly's neck, the robot said, 'We can do it.' When the filly heard those words, she magically settled down. They were indeed a team who breathed as one.

Today stood on the track without blinkers. Coli didn't mount her, but instead, held the reins beside her. Even though she was on the track, Today needed to practise *not* running. She had to learn to gambol along at a speed just fast enough to qualify her for the race, a speed that would allow her to be there without going all out, a speed that would not overly tax her joints as she crossed the finish line.

The goal was to have her run at thirty kilometres per hour.

Now, Jisu got up from the bench and flounced into the stables before Yeonjae could stop her. Coli watched her walk away, then went over to Yeonjae.

'The sky is so big and clear, more than any other sky I have seen,' Coli remarked.

'Well, it *is* fall.'

'But why does the sky get so big and clear in the fall?'

Yeonjae tried to remember what she had learned in science class. 'It just is.'

Coli turned to sit on the bench but momentarily lost balance, tilting to one side. The robot grabbed the bench and managed not to fall to the ground.

'What was that?' Yeonjae asked, surprised.

Coli sat on the bench. 'I am not sure. This has been happening recently.'

Starting about four days ago, Coli's lower body had become harder to control. Coli was sometimes unable to maintain its balance and would suddenly bump into something. It repeatedly had to sit down after standing up. From time to time, its movements were abruptly curtailed. It wasn't severe enough to affect function and it only happened now and then. Coli had determined these were minor defects that did not pose real problems, and kept repeating that things were fine, even as it readily turned to show its back to Yeonjae. She pressed a button to pop open the back panel, but she didn't immediately spot any problems. Everything was working as it should.

'If you do not see anything that needs fixing, you do not need to fix it,' Coli said, staring straight ahead. Coli noticed Jisu just inside the stables, hovering by the doors, glancing over at them.

'Maybe I need to take you apart and put you back together.'

'Please refrain from saying such terrifying things.'

'What are you talking about? It's not terrifying.' Yeonjae closed the cover with a click. Coli was right. It didn't look like anything required immediate repair. Later, when she had more time, she would take Coli apart and put the robot back together.

Coli turned to sit properly, looking out at the greenery. 'Everything looks so fresh, does it not? The sky is blue and the leaves are green.'

'All the leaves will turn red in a few weeks.'

Coli turned to look at Yeonjae. If Coli actually had expressions, Yeonjae would characterize this one as disbelief. 'Why?'

'. . . Because it's fall. That always happens in the fall.' Yeonjae didn't feel like going into it.

But this time Coli did not let it go. Why did leaves that were green turn red in the fall? Coli had been created in March and did not understand the changes in the natural world that took place in September. If Coli had not met Yeonjae, it would never have been able to see the magic of leaves turning red. Coli would have been dragged off one early morning on to a subcontractor's truck, dumped out at an industrial park, and disassembled.

'It's just what happens,' Yeonjae said without any further explanation.

'Why is this what happens?'

'Do you really need a reason for everything?' Yeonjae grew irritated.

'Yes, because there is a reason for everything in the world.'

'Where did you hear that?'

'I did not hear it. I know it. I know this to be true. The reason I exist is to be a jockey, and there is a reason for a human giving orders. Nothing in this world exists without a reason.'

Yeonjae opened and closed her mouth, searching for a rebuttal. This robot knew too much for Yeonjae's limited ability to explain the world. Then again, Coli had been programmed with all the knowledge that humans had been steadily accumulating over centuries, so its knowledge would obviously be superior to any one human's. Yeonjae brushed her hair back. She had just wanted to sit here without thinking about anything, but talking to Coli had given her a lot to ponder. Yeonjae pushed her hair back again. 'No, you're wrong. There isn't always a reason for something. Humans just make up reasons after the fact. So if you want to talk about what comes first, a reason is definitely not it.'

'But I am not wrong . . .'

'Anyone can be wrong. Being alive means you're constantly wrong.' Yeonjae felt this to be a clean, neat answer.

'This is the second time,' Coli said.

'Huh?'

'This is the second time I was told I am alive. You are the second person to tell me that.'

Yeonjae didn't say anything.

'That makes me happy,' Coli said. Coli had no expression when saying that, just as it did not have a mouth to say it with. Coli just had two holes facing Yeonjae and a sensor that detected sound and glowed whenever it spoke. There was nothing that showed that Coli was happy, but Yeonjae believed the robot. Coli was genuinely happy right now.

'So you did not have a reason for taking me home?'

It was nice that a humanoid robot could learn so quickly.

'Right. There was no reason.'

'Thank you. I like you for no reason, too.'

Yeonjae was grinning at Coli's unexpected confession when Jisu came back. She still looked sullen. 'Minju's looking for you.' Jisu turned on her heel and went straight back to the stables.

'I think you need to talk to Jisu right away,' Coli said.

On any normal day, Jisu would have said everything she wanted to say, pointing out exactly what about Yeonjae was not up to her standards, but today she didn't say a word despite her obvious anger. Yeonjae headed towards the stables, vowing to talk to Jisu very soon.

Minju was looking at a screen in the stables. He pulled up the racing regulations, which had changed two years ago. He underlined a sentence with the highlighter function. *At least one bet is required for a horse to enter a race.*

Yeonjae looked at Minju, waiting for an explanation. Though, to be fair, she didn't need one to understand what that meant. What Yeonjae really wanted from Minju was a solution. Like crypto or the lottery, horseracing had the potential to transform a life, all through probabilities. At least one person had to bet on a horse before the animal could set foot on the track. In other words, no idiot would bet on a gravely injured horse, a horse that hadn't even entered a race for a few weeks. Bluntly speaking, there was a 0.001 per cent chance that someone would place a bet on Today, who had been sidelined for nearly a month. Yeonjae and Eunhye were under eighteen, and Minju and Dayeong were staff and therefore not allowed to place bets. That left only Bokhui and Seojin. Could they really ask them for anything more at this point?

'How much would someone have to bet?'

'There's no minimum, but it would be effective only with a pretty big amount,' Minju explained. 'You can't tell which horse will be at the starting gates even on the day, because it's all done by computer. The algorithm adds up the total bets, participants, history of wins, period of inactivity, things like that, and ranks all the eligible horses. Which means Today's not a shoo-in even if Bokhui and Seojin make bets. Today would have been categorized as ineligible since she hasn't run in a while. You get better odds if someone who's made a bet before does it, not someone doing it for the first time. Basically the algorithm gives weight to a gambler's gut instinct.'

'So it has to be someone who's placed a bet before?'

'Yeah. Ideally if we got just one person who has made a bet for at least twelve weeks straight to bet on Today, we'd be able to get her on the board in last place. But I don't know why someone like that would bet on Today . . .'

'I know why.'

'What?'

A face had suddenly popped up in Yeonjae's head.

Yeonjae poured hot water into her cup of instant ramen. She weighed down the flap with her wooden chopsticks and went back to the table.

'How about some kimchi, too?' Her former boss brought cabbage kimchi from the refrigerated section and sat across from Yeonjae.

His Betty had accumulated a collection of nicks and scratches since the last time Yeonjae was at the convenience store.

Her former boss noticed Yeonjae looking at the robot. 'Boys always get in my Betty's face. They use her to practise their kicks, can you believe it? You can't imagine how many times I've had to call for repairs. I've sunk so much money into those repairs.'

'But I guess it's still cheaper than a human?' Yeonjae crossed her arms and looked pointedly at him. Was he really complaining to her?

Chastened, he murmured, 'I mean, I'm just saying . . .'

Yeonjae split her chopsticks and peeled back the flap of her cup. She swished the perfectly cooked noodles and grabbed a big mouthful to blow on them.

It was a quiet holiday, without any customers. Her former boss had long ago cut ties with his family and was, as expected, alone. He was happy to see Yeonjae. He had beamed at her and welcomed her solicitously.

'How about some fruit?' he suggested, as though he were about to set up a holiday feast with what he sold in the convenience store.

Yeonjae shook her head, slurping noodles.

Her former boss hadn't forgotten his promise that he would give her free ramen any time she stopped by. But Yeonjae wanted something much more than ramen.

As Minju explained how things worked at the racetrack, her former boss's face had flashed in Yeonjae's mind. Every Saturday she had been forced to endure him bragging about how fast his horse had been the previous week.

Yeonjae gulped down cold water.

'Want some ice cream?' her former boss asked.

Yeonjae cut straight to the chase. 'How about you make a bet on a horse?'

'Huh?'

'I know the perfect horse for you.'

'Wha— what?'

'She'll one hundred per cent come in last,' Yeonjae said. 'But you need to bet on her anyway.'

'You want me to bet on a horse that will one hundred per cent come in last?'

'Yes.'

'Me?'

'Yes.' *God, how many times was he going to ask the same thing?*

'Why?'

Yeonjae parroted back what he had told her just a few weeks ago. 'It's important to keep challenging yourself and trying new things, isn't it?'

His head dropped. 'Oh, yeah. Right.'

Yeonjae felt oddly liberated.

He looked up and asked her what exactly was going on. It didn't seem that Yeonjae was just pulling a fast one on him. She had never asked him for a thing in the entire time he had known her. And like Yeonjae reminded him, he was always sinking money into horseracing, which had given him about a forty per cent rate of return. He figured he could afford to lose a bit of money for Yeonjae if there were a good reason for it.

She launched into the story of Today and her sister, and the robot jockey that only wanted Today to be happy. Even as she spoke she felt she was summarizing a maudlin tearjerker of a TV drama, so she avoided his eyes, but then she heard sniffling. Her former boss was crying. His eyes began to pool; he pulled a napkin out of its holder on the table to wipe the tears.

Yeonjae was dumbfounded. 'You don't need to make an ass of yourself.'

'You can't call a grown-up an ass.' He blew his nose loudly, then nodded. He promised to place a bet.

It wasn't an insignificant amount, so before she left she stopped to double-check that he really would. She did feel a little guilty, as though she were forcing him to do this. He went on about how it wasn't that much money, but then, remembering how he was always penny-pinching around Yeonjae, quickly backtracked. 'Well, what I mean is, it's not that big a deal if I think about how much I've already sunk into that place, kiddo.'

'You can't blame me later, okay? You can't make me pay you back or anything like that.'

'Hey, come on. You're really treating me like I'm some kind of lowlife.' He grabbed a granola bar from the display by the register and tossed it to her.

She managed to catch it with both hands. Why was he being so showily generous? She didn't mind his kindness, though.

'Look,' he said. 'If someone's asking for help, it's not right to pretend you can't hear them.'

Yeonjae was quiet.

'It's a grown-up's duty to help when a kid asks, and . . .'

Yeonjae cut him off and waved. 'See you next week. Bye.' She had to stop him from pontificating in the most cringey way. He was watching way too many Japanese dramas. He took away all kinds of strange notions from those shows, acting like he was the cool young proprietor of a snack bar in Manhattan or something. She didn't mind, but she did wonder how he would ever meet anyone if he kept acting like a blowhard. In any case, her former boss's surprising generosity helped remove a layer of the resentment she'd harboured towards him.

When Yeonjae returned to the racetrack, the training session was long over. Jisu had gone home. Yeonjae texted her, asking when she had left, only to receive a chilly response: *Earlier*. Jisu must be pissed off.

Coli chastised her. 'How can you understand each other if you do not talk? Can humans read each other's true feelings?'

But she couldn't utter words she so rarely used in her life. Even asking why someone was mad was impossible for her. The holiday went by while she kept tapping out and retapping a single sentence. She helped out at the restaurant every day, as her mom was still under the weather. In addition to the usual big groups, families brought grandparents to feast on samgyetang. Yeonjae didn't really have time to be on her phone, but she checked it every chance she got to see if Jisu had texted. But the holiday came to an end without a peep from her.

So it was on the last night of the holiday that Yeonjae sent a text: *See you tomorrow*. That felt completely unrelated to the fundamental issue at hand. Jisu didn't respond. Yeonjae felt that something had shifted in their relationship. She had never wanted to be in this position. She started sighing copiously. She started wondering about human nature. She checked her phone again. Jisu had left her on 'delivered'. She couldn't keep waiting like this. But she failed to immediately land on a solution.

At school, Yeonjae told Jisu that she had found someone to place a wager on Today. But Jisu seemed aloof. Everything Yeonjae said was met with a lack of enthusiasm. Jisu didn't come over during breaks to yammer on about the competition. She finally did come over at lunchtime, and silently led Yeonjae to a bench in the yard. Yeonjae could have broken the silence by making normal conversation, like *How was your holiday?* or *Is everything okay?* She knew that, but still she couldn't bring herself to say anything.

They finished discussing the competition and Jisu turned off her tablet. 'Okay, so I'll memorize the presentation, and you just prepare for any questions we might get. We're set, right?'

The only possible answer here was *yeah*. But Yeonjae hesitated. If she agreed that they were set, Jisu would go straight back to class without looking back, even though they still had twenty minutes before the bell.

Jisu put her trash in a plastic bag as she waited for Yeonjae's answer; she had brought them both buns and milk for lunch. Yeonjae quickly dropped hers in the bag. 'Thanks.'

Jisu just nodded.

How can you understand each other if you do not talk?

Yeonjae reached out to grab Jisu, who had stood up to leave. 'Are you mad at me?'

Jisu's brows furrowed.

'I'm not being difficult. I'm just asking. Because I should if you're mad.'

'You should what?'

'Apologize.'

Jisu studied Yeonjae before letting out a huge sigh. She sat back down. Jisu knew Yeonjae was trying her best, knew she was the kind of person who would wonder about something all by herself and then give up without ever asking. That was why Jisu was trying not to open the floodgates on how she felt. She hadn't brought it up because her feelings had been hurt, and she was sure Yeonjae wouldn't change even if she told her.

Jisu was mad for a single reason, but it wasn't a simple one.

'You don't think we're as close as I think we are,' she said.

It was true. Yeonjae wasn't sure if she was as close to Jisu as Jisu seemed to think. She also didn't know what Jisu thought of her. This was a problem that couldn't be solved by numerical values. Jisu had tried to understand Yeonjae to get along with her, but Yeonjae hadn't done the same for Jisu.

Yeonjae had never sought to be understood. In her mind, wanting to be understood was selfish. Everyone had their own hurt feelings and baggage that they tried to shove away. Everyone faced situations they were power-less over. Yeonjae had to stop everything, no matter where she was or who she was with, and head straight home whenever Eunhye needed help. Her friends only knew that she had an older sister. When they asked why she had to drop everything and go home, she just said that her sister needed her. Her friends heard her but didn't under-stand. At some point it had become too much. When that line was crossed, people would invariably remark on her self-centredness. *This keeps happening. You keep ditching us. What the hell?*

Because she gave up on being understood, she gave up on understanding others, too. Yeonjae never asked anyone why they did something. She just figured, *I guess that's what happens when you do that*, and let it go. It required too much thinking to figure out if the other person was doing something because they liked you or because they didn't. Everything got easier once you gave up on the expectation of being understood. You never got hurt when there were no expectations. Yeonjae's world had been peaceful until Jisu came barging in; still and quiet, without a single wisp of a breeze.

Then, Jisu had blown into her life like a gale. She'd flung open Yeonjae's sail. Who knew there were people like Jisu in the world? Yeonjae hadn't been a fan ini-tially but she had warmed to her. She found it funny how Jisu snapped at her out of the blue, unable to keep that temper in check. She had begun feeling much less annoyed by her. Sometimes it felt like a given that Jisu would be by her side. But when Jisu mentioned she would be coming around less often, Yeonjae figured it was out of her hands, even inevitable; Jisu couldn't keep skipping cram school. That was why she had said 'Okay', but Jisu had erupted. Now she was telling Yeonjae that she was mad because Yeonjae hadn't been put out by the news.

'I know this is just how you react to everything,' Jisu said, her voice wobbly but her eyes blazing with anger. 'I knew you were obsessed with robots but I didn't realize you were emotionally like one, too. Coli is more human than you.'

Was she just being mean now? Yeonjae forced herself to keep listening.

Jisu let out a sigh. 'You should have said, *That sucks*. Not, *Okay*. If you thought it sucked, I mean. If you didn't feel that, of course I can't do anything about that, but I thought . . .'

Yeonjae jumped in. 'It *does* suck.'

Jisu fell silent.

'Of course it sucks. But I can't tell you to quit cram school just because I think it sucks.'

'But you're still supposed to say it sucks! Then I would come hang out whenever I could. God, why do I have to

spell out every little thing? I know you're clueless, but still.'
Jisu still sounded mad but her expression had softened.

'It sucks,' Yeonjae said again. She hadn't said that in a
long time. That phrase was tinged with sorrow. In fact,
as she uttered the words, a feeling of sadness and disappointment broke loose emotions she hadn't felt in a while.
She was on the verge of tears. If she cried now, Jisu would
tease her mercilessly for the rest of her life.

When she got home, Yeonjae decided, she would tell
Coli that humans had no way of knowing what someone
else was feeling without talking about it; everyone just
assumed they knew what others felt.

They walked back to class, Jisu chattering about everything they hadn't talked about in the last few days, and
Yeonjae listened, nodding vigorously in case Jisu thought
she wasn't. Jisu had a sharp tongue but she never exaggerated or lied. They made a good team. Yeonjae preferred
when people spoke frankly so she wouldn't have to rumin-
ate on her own and come to strange conclusions.

'I get it. I really do,' Jisu said. 'My mom said that people
who have more going on at home end up retreating from
others. They become numb. They go into their shells so
they don't get hurt. So I get why you are the way you are.
Which is why you should try to understand me, too.'

'How?'

'I have no patience, and I do things on the spur of the
moment. People say I'm rude. You know all that, though.

My mom says people will talk shit about me if I'm an ass-hole. I tell her I learned all this from her, so why should I talk nicely just so people say nice things about me? Right? My mom says I need to because I'm a girl. Oh, did I tell you? I told her about your mom and she's so excited. She used to watch that movie all the time. What if we hung out with our moms sometime? My mom would *die*.'

Yeonjae was certain that she wouldn't have run off during the relay race years ago if she had invited her mom, her sister, Jisu, and Coli to watch. She would have finished. She would have come in first. You didn't have to be under-stood by everyone in the whole world. You just needed to be understood by the people you wanted to understand yourself.

After school, Yeonjae helped herself to some fermented kimchi stew at the restaurant and filled her mom in. That Jisu's mother had spent her twenties watching Bogyeong's film, and that the four of them should get together.

'What? What did she say?' her mom kept asking. It wasn't that she didn't understand; she just couldn't believe that Yeonjae was suggesting something like this.

Yeonjae shovelled a huge spoonful of rice in her mouth, giving her mom a beat to get used to the idea.

Her mom checked her calendar app. 'What does Jisu's mother do? Does she have time on a weekday?'

'I want to see it, too.'

'Okay, you want to . . . hm? See what?'

'*Your film.*'

Her mom choked on her stew and began coughing.

A simple search showed that they could purchase the thirty-minute film in HD, despite her mom worrying that they wouldn't be able to find it. Yeonjae streamed the movie on the wall in Coli's room. The title and the names of the director and the leads appeared slowly. The name *Kim Bogyeong* felt at once familiar and alien. Yeonjae hugged her knees to her chest, as though she were about to watch a horror movie. Coli hugged its knees to its chest, too. Thanks to Coli, Yeonjae didn't feel alone. Coli wasn't warm, like a living organism, but Coli always made her feel comforted.

'I told you I didn't have a reason for bringing you here, but that's not true,' she told Coli. Having recently fully understood that no one could know what you were thinking unless you talked to them, Yeonjae wanted to tell Coli the whole truth. 'I felt sorry for you when I saw you lying there in that pile of hay. You were destroyed, but you told me the sky was beautiful. I wanted to see if I could fix you up. You would be scrapped if I left you there. I felt empathy, I guess. I would do it again. This whole time I thought I didn't like robotics. And I realized that I do like it while I was working on you. You may not respond. That is an order.'

Coli obeyed, but for the first time ever felt an urge to go against a direct order. Did that urge bubble up from somewhere inside? Something must have been dislodged.

Coli waited for that urge to subside, unable to interrupt Yeonjae, who was immersed in the film.

Jisu held out a herbal pill that people took to calm their nerves. Yeonjae just stared at it. Jisu unwrapped it and shoved it in Yeonjae's mouth. The bittersweet musty taste spread in her mouth.

In the rear-view mirror, Jisu's mother glanced at the girls. 'You two nervous?'

'Nope,' Yeonjae said.

A huge banner announcing the competition hung over the entrance to the university auditorium. The crowd was packed shoulder to shoulder, especially with college admission hinging on this competition – truly an enormous number of participants for the middle of a weekday. Jisu's mother was about to get out of the car but Jisu closed the driver's door, telling her she didn't have to come along.

'Let's go.' Jisu sounded like a solemn warrior heading on to the battlefield.

Earlier that day, when Yeonjae was about to leave, Eunhye asked what they had prepared for the competition. Yeonjae told her she didn't have time to explain and rushed out, but then ran back in. 'Eonni, what you want most of all is to be free, right?'

'I'm already free.'

Yeonjae grinned and ran back out.

The students entered the auditorium, five teams at a time. Five professors and three technical engineers sat in the front row. Yeonjae and Jisu were scheduled to go fourth. They sat and watched the other presentations. The proposed projects were as diverse as they were imaginative, from a drone that could fly in a stiff breeze, even in natural disasters like typhoons, to a physical diagnostic AI device that could be installed in public spaces, to a next-generation Darpa that could enhance the performance of existing Darpas. Students cited as inspiration the research materials they had come across during their overseas travels or study-abroad programmes. Their ideas would improve the world. Yeonjae reviewed their deck. She wanted to make sure there were no typos, but she was also worried that her idea paled in comparison to the others. She stared down at her plans. They were too simple.

Jisu squeezed her hand. *You have the best idea.* Jisu conveyed this without saying a word, then thumped her on the back as a reminder to sit up straight.

Now it was Yeonjae and Jisu's turn. Yeonjae stood at the back of the stage, displaying the PowerPoint slides as Jisu presented. Jisu was speaking clearly so that everyone could hear her. The judges listened intently to Yeonjae's idea of a 'soft-wheelchair'.

The 'soft-wheelchair' would operate similarly to the Octobot, a soft robot that Harvard researchers developed back in 2016. The wheels, made from composite silicone, would be much thinner and more resilient than regular wheels; a flexible artificial muscle would be inserted into the wheel. It would retain a circular shape normally, but when it encountered a barrier, like stairs, it would use pneumatic pressure to change shape so it could fit around the obstacle. And the artificial muscle, reacting to a conducive polymer, would turn the new shape solid, enabling you to climb the stairs easily. With this technology you would even be able to climb a mountainous terrain pocked with boulders and stones.

Jisu had absolute faith in Yeonjae's idea. Eventually Yeonjae started sneaking looks at the judges. She felt proud whenever they nodded their heads. Jisu successfully completed her fifteen-minute presentation, and one judge even clapped. Jisu looked back at Yeonjae and smiled, and Yeonjae managed to contort her frozen features to approximate a smile, too. Jisu valiantly answered any questions. Then, a professor looked at Yeonjae, who was still standing at the back of the stage. 'How did you come up with this idea? Yes, you. I'd like to hear from you.'

Jisu held the mic out to Yeonjae, who tottered up to her. Yeonjae wouldn't be able to tell the panel that she was inspired by various educational experiences that broadened her knowledge base, like the others. Yeonjae hadn't yet had the chance to go out into the world. The judges would be disappointed by her answer. For Yeonjae, home was still her entire world. Yeonjae let out a slow breath to calm her nerves.

'It's so that nobody has to be lonely.' Yeonjae paused and shot Jisu a look, but Jisu didn't look alarmed. She must not sound insane. She gathered up a little more courage. 'Someone I know has to make more preparations than anyone else, just to leave the house. But she can't just leave when she's ready. She ends up not going out a lot of the time. Not because she doesn't want to. It's because it's too hard. She can't go to a lot of places without someone else's help. Some people say you should just get surgery, but that can be too costly for a lot of people. She doesn't necessarily want two legs, anyway. Legs are just shapes and forms. What she really wants is to be free. She wants to be free to go wherever she wants. You don't need a lot of money to be free. What you need are really well-made wheels, wheels that can go up and over anything. If our society can't get rid of stairs, then we just need to make wheels that can go up the stairs. That's why technology should be advanced, isn't it? To help strong people get even stronger.'

Yeonjae took a breath and got to her conclusion. 'The time has come to reinvent the wheel, which was the most significant invention in the history of humanity. The wheel took ancient people to very far places faster, and I believe it could do that for people living in our world today.'

'Can I ask who this person is, this person who needs

to prepare at such length before going out?' asked the professor.

'It's my sister.'

The professor smiled. 'Thank you for your presentation.'

Once they were offstage, Jisu pulled Yeonjae in for a hug. Yeonjae tried to shove her away, but Jisu didn't let go. Yeonjae gave in and stood quietly between Jisu's arms.

In that moment Yeonjae couldn't know that, in a few days, they would learn they had passed the prelims, or that they would go on to present again in the final round, ultimately winning second place overall. She didn't know that their idea would be selected for a science technology project or that, exactly five years later, she would present Eunhye with the wheelchair she had invented for her.

Before she got to experience all of those triumphs, Yeonjae had to face a wrenching loss.

COLI

'Does the wind always feel nice and cool?' Coli asked Minju.

Oh, that feels nice and cool, Minju had said to himself, stretching in the autumn breeze. He looked down at Coli. He was about to say yes, but then changed his mind. He crouched on the ground and invited Coli to sit, too. Coli mimicked Minju's bent legs to simulate crouching and settled next to him.

'It can feel nice and cool or warm or freezing or damp.'

'Why is it all different?'

'Wind is created by the movement of air. So it depends on what the air feels like. In the winter, the air is cold, so the wind is cold, and in the summer, the air is hot, so the wind feels hot.'

'And why does the wind blow?'

'Because the air keeps moving. There's this thing called

air pressure. It's a mass of air that moves from the highest point to the lowest. Constantly. And that's how it circulates on Earth.'

Coli stretched a hand towards the sky, but could not sense the movement of air. Coli could tell the air was moving, though, as Minju's hair was dancing and the leaves were fluttering. The way Today's mane flowed like water. The only difference was that the wind blew on its own while Today created hers.

As Yeonjae had predicted, a few leaves were starting to turn red. There were so many fascinating changes but Coli could not understand the reasons behind them. Coli remembered Yeonjae saying that not everything had a reason. It would take a very long time to figure out every single reason for why something happened. Maybe some robots had all that knowledge, but that information had not been inputted into Coli.

'They're all running late today, aren't they?' Minju asked.

'Yes. They said they were going to have a celebratory lunch. They received good news last night.'

The previous night, Yeonjae and Jisu had spent the whole evening staring anxiously at their phones. Eunhye had let Coli know that the girls should be left alone and that Coli should not ask what was going on; they were expecting the announcement of which teams would move on to the next round at eight o'clock. As soon as the clock struck eight they both stared in unison at their phones. Jisu started to scream. She dived into a hug with Yeonjae. Jisu said she would buy Yeonjae anything she wanted to eat, but she ended up going home because it was already late, promising to return the next day.

Even though Yeonjae had betrayed only a quiet smile, Coli could tell how thrilled she was from the way she quivered inside. She did not scream or dance but she was just as happy as Jisu. Coli, as always, detected slight changes in Yeonjae's emotions that none of the others caught.

'You were very happy, were you not?' Coli asked later that night, before Yeonjae left the first-floor room.

Yeonjae did not bother hiding her grin. 'Why are you even asking? You know the answer already.'

Coli and Yeonjae had another secret, which was that she watched her mom's film every spare moment she had. Even on her umpteenth rewatch, Yeonjae focused on each scene and every line as though she were seeing it for the very first time.

'Do you like it that much?' asked Coli.

Yeonjae shook her head. 'It's not my kind of film.'

'Then why do you watch it so much?'

'Because it's fascinating.'

'What is?'

'What my mom was like before she had me.'

'Bogyeong now is the same Bogyeong as back then,' Coli remarked.

Yeonjae watched the film five more times, then spoke.

'Yeah, you're right. She's the same person now as she was back then.'

After that she still watched the film three more times. After the first time, Coli had memorized the location of every object that appeared onscreen, but Yeonjae discovered something new with every viewing. Humans could look at the same thing but see something different every time. Coli thought humans were really quite peculiar: time flowed differently for each person even when they shared the same space; they remembered different things even when they looked at the same thing; and they did not know how others felt unless they talked to each other about it. Sometimes they said one thing but meant another. They seemed intent on using all their energy to constantly hide their true feelings.

Even so, from time to time, humans understood what others were feeling even if they did not talk about it, and faced in the same direction even as they looked at different things. Their experience of time sometimes aligned even when they were apart. It was confusing, complicated stuff. But it seemed like it could be fun, too. If only Coli had feelings, life itself would have felt like a series of fun quizzes.

Minju lay in the grass with his arms behind his head. Coli could not mimic him very well, so just watched as Minju closed his eyes and relaxed.

'How do you feel about the race tomorrow?' Minju asked.

'Fine.'

'Yeah, I guess that makes sense. Weirdly, I expected you to say you're nervous.'

'Did you want me to say I am nervous?'

'It's been a long time since you've ridden, that's all. Everyone gets nervous when they do something they haven't done in a while.'

'You always treat me like a human,' Coli said gratefully. Minju laughed.

'But I do not want to be a human. I am happy when you treat me like a human because that means you consider me to be someone real. I want to be a machine that is beside humans for a long time.'

'Why?'

'Because I am a machine.'

After Minju it was Yeonjae. After Yeonjae it was Bogyeong. And then it was Eunhye and Jisu. They all treated Coli like a living being. Coli categorized them as unusual humans. Only humans must have the ability to love something that was not alive. Coli remembered Bogyeong's story of how she had cried when she sold the car she and the firefighter had bought as newlyweds; Coli could understand just how much she had loved that car.

Bogyeong said she would close the restaurant tomorrow to watch the race – it would be the first time the restaurant had closed on a Sunday. Only now had she come to the conclusion that it would be okay to close for a day, that they would not starve if she took a day off. She wanted to watch the jockey Yeonjae had repaired in action. Bogyeong had sneaked into Coli's room late at night, after Yeonjae had gone to bed, to tell Coli that she refused to miss anything else Yeonjae did. She vowed to work hard to prevent the gulf between her and her daughter from widening. Coli was not sure why she was making it that promise, but listened carefully and nodded. 'I am rooting for you.'

'Does that feel comfortable?' Coli asked Minju now.

'Of course. I'm lying down.'

Coli laid its body on the grass like Minju. Coli bent its arms behind its head, mimicking Minju. Coli could not tell if that was what being comfortable was, but the sky was front and centre when in this position. The way the sky had looked when Coli had been on the haystack.

Back then, Coli had known humans would come to cart it away, just like F-16. Coli had known it would never return, just like F-16. But then, a girl had arrived. Woo Yeonjae, a girl so slight that she did not seem strong enough to pick Coli up. Yeonjae bought Coli with eight hundred thousand won, all the money she had. That was the moment things took a turn for Coli, as humans liked to say. It was the beginning of Coli's second act in life. That is, if what Coli experienced could be called life.

Coli was taken to a quiet house that somehow felt lonely. Three people lived in the house but only one person at a time made noise, in designated time slots. They lived together but were trapped in their own personal timelines that did not intersect. Coli knew that their silence would not continue for long. Noise would seep into the others' lives through the cracks that had slowly started to form. It would begin aligning their separate timelines, making it so that time would not rush past too quickly.

'Will Today die after the race?'

Minju was awake, but he did not answer.

Coli had come to realize that a human's silence tended to mean *yes*. So that meant Today would die, after one last hurrah. Unless yet another miracle happened, one that would lead to a second act for Today.

Today had improved significantly, but Bokhui said sternly that this was just temporary. She reminded every-one that Today would never return to her former state. If the filly ran faster than thirty kilometres per hour, she risked collapsing on the spot. According to Bokhui, Today appeared to be better only because of the IV supplements and painkillers. But Coli believed that Eunhye was the real reason for Today's recuperation. Perhaps Eunhye had made Today feel better by visiting her every day, whisper-ing encouragement, giving her apples and carrots and almonds. Just the way Yeonjae had made Coli better. Only happiness could suppress pain. Coli recalled how Eunhye had rejoiced when Today was able to stand on her own legs again.

'Eunhye will be very sad if Today dies,' Coli said.

'She will be. But she'll be okay.' Minju yawned.

'How can you be so sure?'

'Because she will be. I just know that to be true.'

'But that might freeze time.'

Minju glanced at Coli, not understanding, then closed his eyes again.

Coli had many more questions to ask. But Coli did not want to be the one to chase away Minju's relaxed expression. Coli remained worried about Eunhye. But Bogyeong would be there for her. And Bogyeong knew how to get frozen time to tick forward again.

Coli looked back up at the sky. Once, Yeonjae had said that her eyes teared up when she looked up at the sky because it was so bright, but Coli never generated tears no matter how long it looked up at the sky. Yeonjae had told Coli that even if you did not tear up you could still describe the bright sky as dazzling, especially if it was the most beautiful sky you had ever seen. Coli wished it had a mechanism to produce tears. Then, tomorrow, after the race, Coli could shed tears, while hugging Today and congratulating her.

Minju was not sleeping after all. 'Time keeps passing as long as you're not dead. Even if it stops for a moment it's not a problem.'

Coli did not respond.

'In fact, maybe it's not a bad thing for time to stop for a

moment. If you speed through life you miss things. Someone famous said that.'

Coli nodded.

Minju fell silent. He had fallen asleep.

Today had undergone special training to stop her from running flat out on the track. Though she had been trained to run as fast as she could since birth, she now had to lope along very slowly so she would not get hurt. Whenever Today tried to speed up, Minju, Yeonjae, and Eunhye had waved their hands on the sidelines, coaxing her to go slow. *Slowly, slowly, relax, take a deep breath, take a look at the sky, take a look around you, feel how Coli is moving on your back . . .*

So she had practised slowing down. You had to be the fastest horse to come in first, but a slow horse would not be ejected in the middle of a race. It was not against the rules to run at a leisurely pace.

We all need practice slowing down.

Coli would never learn that the press would pick up Today's story after the race, making her famous. Or that the treatment of racehorses would be scrutinized anew, or that a petition to save Today's life would circulate, or that Today would move to Jeju Island and live on vast meadows, looking up at the sky whenever she wanted to. Coli would never learn any of that. But Coli was happy in the moment. It was as if Coli already knew what the future held.

This is where the second act of Coli's life ends. Now we must return to the beginning – and the end – of the story.

Back to that moment when Coli is falling.

I wonder what you thought about my story. What did you think about my short 'life'? Did you feel the reverberations, too? Did you feel the vibrations going through me? They made me think I was breathing even though I cannot. I want to hear your answer but I do not have the time. I do not have any more time left.

They sit together in the grandstand, all the people who filled my life. Before the race, I saw Yeonjae alone. She grabbed me in a hug so tight that we were physically pressed together. She leaned her forehead against my chest and said as though casting a spell, 'You can do it.'

I was not sure if she was talking to herself or to me, so I stayed quiet. I relaxed my arms around her, I let go of her hand clinging to mine, and we said goodbye by the haystack in the stables where we first met. If I had known that would be the last time I ever saw her, I would have told her how glad I was to have met her. But I do not have the ability to see into the future, so I just watched as she walked away from me.

I went over to Today. She was waiting for me, saddled up, wearing her hood with her number on it. Like always.

I grabbed her bridle and stroked her neck and spoke to her, just like Yeonjae had to me.

We can do it.

We are on the track. Today, the former champion facing euthanasia. Me, in the saddle. I stroke her mane. I hear the roar of the crowd. I find my humans among them and wave. We get ready, and I hold Today's reins tight. Numbers appear on the gigantic screens above, counting down from ten. It is a beautiful day. As the numbers count down, the screens open slowly, letting the breeze in. I know that because I see Today's mane rustle. I recite the numbers as they count down.

Three, two, one.

Unlike the other horses, Today begins very slowly.

The other horses streak forward. Today takes her first leisurely step. Her breathing is a little laboured. Maybe her joints are aching.

You do not have to run if it hurts too much, I remind her. *You are already on the track. That is more than enough.*

Giving up when something is too hard is a valid option, too. Though it takes a lot of effort for a living being to voluntarily give something up.

I hear jeers from the stands. The crowd is unhappy that a slow horse is on the track. Does Today understand what they are yelling? A beer can clangs down in front of her. She is unbothered. But then, more cans start raining down. They make an announcement: people are requested to refrain from throwing things on to the track. The crowd is angry. The mood is unusually chaotic. I hear curses instead of cheers.

It is all right. Do not pay any attention to them. You do not need to listen to what they are saying. You are in your own lane. Just follow your own path. At your own speed.

This lane is reserved for Today and Today only. The jeers from the crowd do not matter. I keep telling Today the same thing over and over so that she pays them no mind.

Do not pay any attention to them. That noise is nothing. You do not need to listen to it. You do not have to listen to what everyone else is saying. This is your life.

I catch Yeonjae's angry voice and Jisu swearing in the stands. It is a phrase so crude that I cannot bring myself to repeat it. But they do not need to get so angry. Because I can tell that Today is happy. She is vibrating with every step. Just like the very first time we raced together.

You are happy! I whisper to Today. *You were able to go back to the past.*

If I had been satisfied with that, if I had just ignored Today's desire to run faster, my life would not have ended there. But happiness suppresses pain. In this one moment, she could run like she used to. This is our mistake, something we did not foresee. An opportunity, to borrow Yeonjae's words. But now, my body, made partly of aluminium, is heavy, much too heavy for Today to manage as she runs. Today cannot reach her top speed with me on her back. Her joints would be ruined once and for all.

That is why I do what I do next.

I let go of the reins.

I know Minju will be mad.

I hug Today around the neck. I feel her happiness as vibrations, as ringing, as trembling.

Do you want to go faster?

Today answers by speeding up. When I fell the first time, only my lower body was destroyed, but Yeonjae did not add a hydraulic motor when she rebuilt me. There is no way for me to absorb any impact, so this time round, the most critical mechanisms inside my body will be destroyed. Very little of me will survive this fall, and, even if my hard drive can be repaired, I will not be revived as *me*.

I am not afraid.

I do not have regrets.

I think about my reason for existence: to save this horse and to make her happy.

Today's heart is pounding. This horse that nobody thought could ever run again is revelling in her second shot at life, and that is being conveyed to me through her heartbeat. *Faster. Faster.* Today wishes to run faster even if it means her legs will cave in. She wishes to revel in the freedom that running brings her.

That is when I fall off Today.

My second fall.

I spend the world's longest three seconds suspended in the air. It is taking much, much longer than when I sat alone in the jockeys' quarters. During this very long time I can look back at my days in full.

This is the end for me. I am being shattered into pieces, from my buttocks to my upper body, but I do not feel anything resembling pain.

I just see the clear blue sky above.

I knew a thousand words when I first came into this world. I also know the names of a few people who cannot be described fully with a mere thousand words, names that contain more meaning and are more expansive than a thousand words. If I had more words in my vocabulary, would I describe these dear people in a specific way in my final moments? Do I know any words containing the right proportion of longing, warmth, and sorrow?

I lived a short life formed only by one thousand words, but from the time I looked out of the window of the truck, reciting all the words I knew, to now, each of the thousand words I know felt vast, like the sky. Discouragement, hardship, sadness – all the words you know as well as I do, each and every one of them – are a thousand blues.

I look up at the sky one last time. It is blue-blue and dazzling.

AUTHOR'S NOTE

My shoes tend to wear out quickly. Apparently it's because I walk fast. When someone told me that, I wanted to ask, *How does walking fast make your shoes wear out quickly?* but I let it go. I do walk fast and my shoes do wear out quickly. Perhaps it's fine to lump those two facts together.

Much of the time I found myself feeling busy but lethargic. And much of the time I couldn't bring myself to take a break, afraid of becoming swept up by emotions. Even now, as I write this author's note, I can't imagine ever taking a break. Probably because it would make me feel like I'm lagging behind. Maybe that's why I sometimes feel that my life is too busy, too packed. Everyone is living overwhelming lives. Everyone is busy, at least in my corner of the world.

For the Korea Sci-Fi Literature Award, I was planning to

submit a different novel, a space opera with a much larger scope. Although I only had the last chunk left to write, the characters I created for that novel began feeling fake. I couldn't keep working on it. For a while I didn't bother opening my laptop because it was such a struggle to write a single word. That was mid-September. *I'm writing fiction, which isn't real life, so why does everything feel so fake?* I worried while I kept working both as a tutor and as a barista. One day, the sole of my shoe fell off as I was rushing to make it to work on time, agonizing over the failure of my novel. That was the only reason I stopped. I noticed then that I was out of breath. I thought I had been walking, but I'd actually been running the entire time. It occurred to me that my feet were rooted too firmly in reality for me to imagine a story set in space. I don't mean that all sci-fi is completely removed from reality. It's just that I was completely removed from my own novel.

My novel *A Broken Bridge* was published in 2019, so I was still eligible for the Korea Sci-Fi Literature Award, which was only open to writers who had been published less than two years ago. I thought it might be my last opportunity. And because the 2020 Korea Sci-Fi Literature Award was cancelled because of COVID-19, it did turn out to be my last chance. I wondered what I should submit for my last chance at an award to which I'd always wanted to apply. I wanted to write a really great sci-fi novel, but I couldn't. I didn't think I could write a really great sci-fi novel yet. So I figured I should write something I could do really well.

At the very bottom of my notes app is this sentence:

We all need practice slowing down.

I don't remember when I wrote that down, but I found myself studying it. I thought about how fast the world was changing, about the people we aren't able to hold on to, and the natural world. And I wrote *A Thousand Blues*.

After writing this novel, I've been practising slowing down. So that my hurrying feet do not step on an ant walking by.

Born in 1993, **Cheon Seon-ran** is a beloved author of the 'MZ Generation' (Millennials and Gen Z) of South Korea. A graduate from the department of creative writing in Anyang Arts High School, she holds a master's degree in creative writing from Dankook University. She often dreams of living in a world where humans become the minority in a world of flora and fauna and what the end of the world might look like, and what is happening elsewhere in the universe. One day, she decided to pen her thoughts in this novel. *A Thousand Blues* won the 4th Korea Sci-Fi Literature Award. She is the author of several novels and short-story collections.

Chi-Young Kim's translation work from Korean into English includes the Man Asian Literary Prize-winning *Please Look After Mom* by Kyung-sook Shin, in addition to works by Gu Byeong-mo, Kyung Ran Jo, Ae-ran Kim, among others. Her translation of *Whale* by Cheon Myeong-kwan was shortlisted for the 2023 International Booker Prize.